Praise for Dan Shamble, Zombie P.I.

"*A dead detective, a wimpy vampire, and other interesting characters from the supernatural side of the street make* Death Warmed Over *an unpredictable walk on the weird side. Prepare to be entertained.*"

—Charlaine Harris

"*Sharp and funny; this zombie detective rocks!*"

—Patricia Briggs

"*A darkly funny, wonderfully original detective tale.*"

—Kelley Armstrong

"*Master storyteller Kevin J. Anderson's* Death Warmed Over *is wickedly funny, deviously twisted and enormously satisfying. This is a big juicy bite of zombie goodness. Two decaying thumbs up!*"

—Jonathan Maberry

"*Kevin J. Anderson's* Death Warmed Over *and his Dan Shamble, Zombie P.I. novels are truly pure reading enjoyment— funny, intriguing—and written in a voice that charms the reader from the first page and onward. Smart, savvy—fresh, incredibly clever! I love these books!*"

—Heather Graham

"*A good detective doesn't let a little thing like being murdered slow him down, and I got a kick out of Shamble trying to solve a series of oddball cases, including his own. He's the kind of zombie you want to root for, and his cases are good lighthearted fun.*"

—Larry Correia

"Kevin J. Anderson shambles into Urban Fantasy with his usual relentless imagination, and a unique blend of hardboiled detective who's refreshing, if not exactly fresh."

—Vicki Pettersson

"Death Warmed Over *is just plain good fun. I enjoyed every minute it took me to read it.*"

—Glen Cook

"The Dan Shamble books are great fun."

—Simon R. Green

"Down these mean streets a man must lurch.... With his Big Sleep interrupted, Chambeaux the zombie private eye goes back to sleuthing, in Death Warmed Over, Kevin J. Anderson's wry and inventive take on the Noir paradigm. The bad guys are werewolves, the clients are already deceased, and the readers are in for a funny, action-packed adventure, following that dead man walking ..."

—Sharyn McCrumb

"A zombie sleuth prowls the mean streets as he works a half-dozen seriously weird cases ... Like Alexander McCall Smith's Mma Precious Ramotswe, the sleuths really do settle most of their cases, and they provide a lot of laughs along the way."

—Kirkus Reviews

"Anderson's world-building skills shine through in his latest series, Dan Shamble, Zombie P.I. Readers looking for a mix of humor, romance, and good old-fashioned detective work will be delighted by this offering."

—Romantic Times (four stars)

Dan Shamble, Zombie P.I.

TASTES LIKE CHICKEN

Dan Shamble, Zombie P.I.

TASTES LIKE CHICKEN

New York Times *Bestselling Author*

Kevin J. Anderson

WordFire Press
Colorado Springs, Colorado

ISBN: 978-1-61475-634-7

Cover painting by Jeff Herndon

Cover design by Janet McDonald

Edited by Rebecca Moesta

Kevin J. Anderson, Art Director

Book Design by RuneWright, LLC
www.RuneWright.com

Published by
WordFire Press, an imprint of
WordFire, LLC
PO Box 1840
Monument CO 80132

Kevin J. Anderson & Rebecca Moesta, Publishers

WordFire Press Hardcover Edition December 2017
Printed in the USA

Join the Kevin J. Anderson Readers Group and
get free books, sneak previews, updates on new projects, and other
giveaways.
Sign up for free at wordfire.com

Contents

Tastes Like Chicken

DEDICATION

To Bradley Joseph Francis Birzer and Dedra Birzer, for their generosity in granting me access to such a wonderful mountain retreat, where I can find time to hide from my deadlines and actually write novels like *Tastes Like Chicken* for the sheer love of it.

CHAPTER ONE

ome monsters are friendly. You learn that while working as a private investigator in the Unnatural Quarter, where you never know what size, shape, species, or temperament your clients might come in.

Some monsters want to live their daily lives without undue hassles, just like anybody else.

Some monsters even eat cookies and are adored by children nationwide.

But some monsters eat people. They're vicious, violent things that deserve to be called *monsters*.

The demon Obadeus fit into that last category, without question. And McGoo—Officer Toby McGoohan, beat cop in the Quarter and my best human friend—had tracked Obadeus down before he could murder again. I was along for backup, moral support, and, if necessary, a diversion.

Serial killers are bad enough, but a *bloodthirsty demon* serial killer, now that's not a good thing at all. Obadeus's death toll now stood at nineteen, and since demons can be a little OCD about round numbers, we knew he would strike again just to make it an even twenty.

Fortunately for us, although not for his numerous victims, a monster with so much enthusiasm for killing isn't very good at covering his tracks. Some supernatural psychologist or monster profiler might speculate that Obadeus wanted to be caught, deep down inside. I had a different theory: he was just too lazy to clean up his messes.

We had tracked the demon down to his lair, which Obadeus called his "man cave." The place reeked. The walls were decorated with dripping blood and flayed skin or pelts from his victims, both human and unnatural. I didn't envy the crime-scene cleanup team, or the landlord who would have to make the place ready to rent again, after McGoo and I took care of this creep. At least Obadeus wouldn't get his cleaning deposit back, so there was some justice in the world.

The big demon bolted from his blood-soaked lair just as we arrived—which was a lucky break, because McGoo and I didn't exactly know how to arrest a serial-killer demon from the Fifth Pit of Hell. I had no idea where the pits of hell fell, on a scale of one to ten, but pit number five must be a nasty place if it had spawned something like this.

Obadeus was ugly, with a capital U-G-L-Y. He had a leathery hide with knobs, warts, scales, and leprous patches, a face full of spikes and tendrils, triangular pointed ears, and a jaw that extended all the way to the back of his head filled with enough fangs to keep an orthodontist in business for life.

"Ick," McGoo observed. "He makes vampire bats look cute."

Whether Obadeus was insulted, or enraged, or just shy, he spread his thorny wings and lurched toward the door of his lair, where the two of us happened to be standing. Letting out a roar that sounded like a cow caught in a barbed-wire fence, Obadeus charged past, knocking both of us aside like bowling pins, and smashed out the door. He ran off into the streets.

"We must be scarier than I thought," I said as the demon fled. "He could have torn us limb from limb and sipped our entrails through a straw."

"Law enforcement carries great weight." McGoo drew his Police Special revolver, and I pulled my .38, which I considered to be just as special, even though it didn't have the word "Special" in its name. We set off after Obadeus in hot pursuit.

It was the dead of night in the Quarter, which meant the streets were busier than at any time of day. Though the monster's great wings got in the way as he bounded out among the pedestrians, they also generated a tailwind for him as he flapped them, giving him a boost as he ran.

"Make way!" I shouted. "Killer demon on the loose!"

Werewolves, vampires, and witches scattered. Obadeus charged along, batting them aside.

I put on a burst of speed, which isn't always easy for a zombie. McGoo fired his revolver in the air. "Halt! In the name of the law."

Apparently Obadeus didn't respect the law as much as McGoo hoped. He kept running.

"You missed," I said.

McGoo pointed his revolver ahead and shot straight at the demon's back. The bullet ricocheted off the pellet-hard skin and chipped the bricks on a nearby building. "Not much difference even when I don't miss."

We sprinted past the closed-down Recompose Spa, which had formerly been the closed-down Zombie Bathhouse. Though the doors were barred and the windows dark, a pair of gaunt gray-skinned zombies stood outside the entrance, bare chested and wearing only white towels around their waists. They stared at the locked door, their faces slack and expressionless. They'd probably been there for days waiting for the place to reopen.

With such blotchy and decaying skin, the zombies were long past an easy restorative treatment. Though I was running after a hellish demon covered with the blood of nineteen victims, I had to frown at my fellow undead. Though they were waiting at the spa, they clearly hadn't taken care of their own corpses. I'm a well-preserved zombie myself, and it doesn't come easy. I take pride in my human-like appearance, even though my flesh-colored skin needs a touchup now and then. Some people even consider me handsome, at least in dim lighting.

I placed one hand on my fedora, so it wouldn't blow off as I ran. Wind whistled through the bullet hole in my forehead. One of these days I was going to get it filled in again, but not now.

As Obadeus stormed past the bathhouse and spa, the waiting zombies stood in his way. With a sweep of his massively muscled arm, he smacked one of them in the head—which not only cleared

3

the sidewalk for Obadeus, it relieved the zombie of his head. Detached, it rolled and bounced in the gutter, still making breathy, offended noises. The other zombie watched his companion collapse in two different directions, then turned back to the door, as if still expecting the spa to reopen at any moment.

"That's twenty!" Obadeus crowed in triumph.

"Doesn't count," I replied. "He's still alive and kicking … sort of."

"Darn!" the demon grumbled. Despite his vicious crimes, Obadeus apparently didn't like to use harsh language.

We kept running, but the monster was pulling ahead.

"Hey Shamble, I have an idea," McGoo wheezed. His freckled face was flushed. "Get ahead of him and let him bite you—the arm or shoulder will do well enough. While he's distracted, I'll put handcuffs on him."

"I've got a better idea," I told him, without wheezing. I wasn't out of breath because I didn't need to breathe, strictly speaking. "Let's not listen to any of your suggestions."

An old man was sitting on a bench reaching into a bag full of dead flies, which he tossed toward a flock of bats that swooped around, nabbing the treats out of the air. Obadeus roared, and the old man fell off the back of the bench. The bats scattered.

An animated skeleton pushing a grocery cart out of a small market tried to clatter out of the way, but the demon maliciously snatched him by the rib cage, hooking a long claw beneath his sternum and swinging him around before smashing the skeleton into the brick wall, shattering him into a pile of bones. I wasn't sure if that counted as victim number twenty. With the undead, it can be difficult to determine the exact point at which a murder is committed.

Obadeus roared and kept running.

McGoo fired his revolver again—I think he just liked the sound—and we continued our pursuit.

O O O

A killer demon running amuck didn't cause as much panic as you might expect. The Unnatural Quarter is full of strange creatures, some warm and fuzzy, others scary and fuzzy. Obadeus was arguably on the hideous end of the spectrum, but when the world is full of monsters right out of legends and superstition, most people aren't too judgmental.

Several years ago, when the reality-bending event called the Big Uneasy changed all the rules, humans had reeled in shock to see the return of vampires, werewolves, ghosts, succubi, banshees, even elves and fairies.

Not everyone viewed this change with a sense of wonder.

Eventually, most of the monsters gathered in the Quarter, where they could be themselves and not feed upon humans. Statistically speaking, unnaturals were much like anyone else: decent, law-abiding citizens with a few bad apples among them. When I was still alive and ambitious, I had set up shop as a private investigator, realizing that even vampires, werewolves, and mummies still got divorced, faced blackmail, needed to recover missing items, and so on. The usual caseload for a P.I.

My partner at Chambeaux & Deyer Investigations, Robin Deyer, is a young firebrand, a bleeding-heart human attorney who wants to see justice for unnaturals. Officer McGoohan, after too many politically incorrect jokes in his old precinct, found himself transferred to walk the beat in the Quarter.

Like any disadvantaged ethnic group, the unnaturals faced prejudice from outside humans and had to work hard to maintain a good image. In order to temper their predatory tendencies, Monster Chow Industries mass produced tasty food for all types of unnaturals. Their major factory on the edge of the Quarter delivered enough synthetic flavored protein, at reasonable prices, to keep the monsters from eating people. And not being eaten kept the rest of the people happy. The world should have been full of peace and harmony.

But some monsters—like Obadeus—were feral, primal throwbacks. They *liked* killing people. They were a menace to society. As Obadeus's horrific murder spree continued, panic spread even outside the Quarter.

An old werewolf was found entirely skinned, his pelt taken as a trophy. A vampire piano player who had never harmed anyone, except occasionally making bad choices in his song selections, was found decapitated, his mouth filled with garlic pesto. Five humans were gutted, their organs displayed in full Jack-the-Ripper glory. Witches were impaled with their broomsticks. An amphibious creature was locked inside a solar tanning bed until she had dried into jerky.

It was horrible. All of law enforcement was desperate to catch the killer.

And we had found him.

O   O   O

As we kept running, McGoo fired a shot from his other revolver, the police *extra*-special, which was loaded with silver bullets. At least those rounds made divots on Obadeus's scaly hide. But such minor wounds only annoyed the demon more, and he was already very annoyed. Snarling, he flapped his bat-like wings and leaped up to grab a fire escape ladder, but the ugly demon was so massive that his weight ripped the fire escape stairs from the brick wall. The entire structure came clattering down around him like the bars of a cage. Obadeus ripped the bars free and lurched to his feet just as McGoo and I caught up with him.

Flustered, the burly demon ducked into a wide, shadow-filled alley, from which we heard squawking and clucking and saw a flash of white feathers. A panicked wild chicken flapped its wings furiously as it tried to lift off the ground. At the end of the alley I saw a rickety pile of coops with the doors open, chicken wire strung across the opening. A dozen more birds strutted around squawking.

Feral chickens, the worst kind.

But even though rampant feral chickens have become an increasing problem in the Quarter, this wasn't the problem that concerned me at the moment.

Obadeus snarled at them, and the chickens scattered back into the garbage-strewn shadows.

Finding himself cornered in a dead-end alley, the demon from the Fifth Pit of Hell turned, hunched down, and spread his bulging arms. He extended his claws, and thrust up his wings. Obadeus snarled at us with a face full of fangs exuding bad breath.

Caught up in the desperate chase, McGoo and I charged into the alley shoulder to shoulder. Each of us had our guns drawn, knowing they were totally ineffective. The bloodthirsty demon was trapped, and he knew it.

We had him exactly where we wanted him.

"Uh-oh," McGoo said.

"Now what do we do?" I asked.

CHAPTER TWO

Each time Sheyenne appears, she brightens my day—and right now my day certainly needed brightening. As McGoo and I stood facing the murderous creature from the Fifth Pit of Hell, not to mention the flock of feral chickens, my ghost girlfriend appeared beside us in the alley.

She has beautiful blue eyes, long blond hair, curves in all the right places, and a sparkling personality that shines through her translucent form. Sheyenne is a former medical student and a smoking-hot lounge singer. She and I had a fling, just one night back when I was still alive. Then she was poisoned to death and I was shot in the back of the head. So much for the relationship we had planned. It happens.

Fortunately—if anything about the situation could be called fortunate—the Big Uneasy changed the rules. Sheyenne came back as a ghost, and I rose from the grave as a zombie. Back from the dead and back on the case. Once I solved Sheyenne's murder and my own, Chambeaux & Deyer Investigations continued with our regular clientele. Business wasn't exactly thriving, but it wasn't dead-on-arrival either. Even as a ghost, Sheyenne served as our office manager, receptionist, and all around "best foot forward." She opened the mail, did the filing, monitored the budget, chased past-due invoices, and managed the complicated paperwork so Robin and I could focus on our cases.

I wasn't sure why she would show up while McGoo and I were facing off against Obadeus. Seeing Sheyenne, the demon gave a lascivious, hungry growl. At first I was angry that this ugly thing was lusting after my girlfriend, until I realized he saw her as prey. That was worse.

I stepped in front of her protectively. "Sheyenne, what are you doing here? Can't you see there's trouble?"

"I know." She drifted closer. "And you could use some help, Beaux."

McGoo and I kept our guns pointed at the demon, who was beginning to realize that our weapons posed no threat to him … and neither did we.

Sheyenne wavered in front of me. "Remember, this came in the mail from that new spell subscription service? I figured you could use it." She held a piece of paper printed with big, bold letters.

FREE SAMPLE!
ALTERRO'S SPELLS 'N SUCH

"It's a *demon-shattering* spell, Beaux."

"It's junk mail, Spooky!" I did recall Sheyenne showing me the flyer and asking if we wanted to subscribe, and I'd brushed her off with something like, "When in the world will we ever need a demon-shattering spell?"

Now Sheyenne flapped the flyer in front of me until I was forced to take it.

"It's your only chance," she said.

O O O

Now that Chambeaux & Deyer Investigations had grudgingly joined the UQ Chamber of Commerce, we got more mail solicitations, flyers, catalogs, and free samples than I could imagine using. On the day the Spells 'N Such flyer arrived, I remember Sheyenne diligently sorting through the mail. She used her poltergeist powers to tear open the envelopes, unfold the letters, and separate the bills from the disappointingly few checks from clients.

The main thing that caught my attention was a charity flyer, a plea from the AAA, Agricultural Avian Activists, led by an earnest do-gooder werewolf (and quite possibly their only member) named Maynard Kleck. Maynard was distraught over the plight of feral chickens in the Quarter. "Flocks of them have no homes, and they just need a place to roost."

I had seen chickens running loose in the streets, and I knew most of them came from a well-meaning resident who simply wanted to bring more birds to the gloomy Quarter and had turned them loose to multiply. Chickens knew how to multiply, and now they ran through the city leaving feathers and droppings in unwanted places. They had effectively become the Quarter's new pigeons.

Sheyenne had skimmed the solicitation, then showed it to me. "Do you think we should contribute something?"

Robin came out of her office, her big brown eyes showing deep concern. The mere mention of a creature in need usually drew her attention. "It sounds like a terrible plight. Maybe we should do what we can to help Mr. Kleck and his organization?" She gave a sympathetic cluck. "Those poor chickens!"

"You know what McGoo would say," I replied. "The best way to get rid of unwanted chickens is to eat them. Then everybody's happy, except for the chickens."

Sheyenne showed me the next item in the junk mail, the flyer from Spells 'N Such, a new by-mail subscription spell service, much like those recipe-of-the-week clubs that sound so good when you first sign up, but the recipes keep coming and keep coming and you never actually use any of them ... especially when you're a zombie and don't do much cooking. Then you can never get off the mailing list.

I frowned at the arcane symbols and the "quick and easy phonetic pronunciation" beneath them. "If Alterro's going to give a free sample, why doesn't he send something people can use? A demon-shattering spell! When would that ever come in handy?"

It seemed funny at the time.

O O O

I snatched the paper from Sheyenne. McGoo and I advanced down the alley, trying to look intimidating. We hoped that Obadeus didn't come to his senses anytime soon. The bloodthirsty demon must have assumed we possessed some kind of superpowers, otherwise why would we have been so foolish as to come after him in the first place? But the demon from the Fifth Pit of Hell had no idea just how foolish we really were.

I slipped the .38 inside the pocket of my stitched-up sport jacket and decided to rely on the spell after all. Could I really trust some hokey mumbo-jumbo that arrived via bulk-rate mail?

With a revolver in each hand, McGoo matched me step for step. As we came closer, Obadeus flared his gargoyle-like wings, facing us. The chickens squawked and scuttled around. One pecked at the demon's scaled foot.

Sheyenne flitted in. "I'll stall him, Beaux. Read the spell!" She swooped toward the demon, who slashed at the air, ripping his claws through her shimmering translucent form. Sheyenne flickered and drifted away laughing, taunting. Of course he couldn't harm a ghost—but he could piss *me* off.

I started reading the spell, ignoring the helpful tips on how to get the most out of my trial subscription to Spells 'N Such. The words were like a child's jump-rope chant, cutesy and rhyming, and I felt ridiculous. I knew we shouldn't bank on this, but I continued to utter the silly sounds.

McGoo lunged forward to block the demon's outstretched claw as he tried to snatch the spell paper from my hands. Obadeus struck him hard, knocking my best human friend against the alley wall with enough force to stun him.

That was the last straw. I meant to finish the spell, whether it worked or not. Obadeus would probably tear me limb from limb, after which my personal taxidermy specialist, Miss Lujean Eccles, would have to spend hours stitching me back together like an undead Humpty Dumpty.

I completed the spell, pronouncing the words according to the helpful phonetics. I was surprised to feel the paper tingle in my fingers, which are normally numb and don't usually detect things of a tingly nature. The air started to glow and sparkle.

The astonished demon recoiled, his face folding back in a grimace, his fanged mouth dropping open in disgust. He writhed and cringed like someone who had unexpectedly stepped in a large, fresh dog turd.

Sheyenne flitted next to me. "It's working!"

Searing silver and blue threads appeared in the air, slicing down like piano wires. First one, then four more, then a dozen, all wrapping around the burly demon. Obadeus struggled as the silver filament cut into him, burning and smoking through his armored flesh. His roars and growls changed to wails as the silver lines intensified.

The chickens clucked and scattered, running around in circles even though no one had cut their heads off.

The sound of chimes rang in the alley, drowning out the sounds of the scampering chickens and the howling monster. With a mighty flash and a whoosh of released power, the demon-shattering spell did exactly what its name implied.

Obadeus let out a final roar, and then splintered into glowing, gem-like blobs.

I shielded my eyes.

Sheyenne cried, "Oh, pretty!"

Sparkling pieces of shattered demon sprayed everywhere like reflective bits from a disco mirror ball, and the panicked chickens squawked as they flapped their wings and finally fled the alley.

McGoo picked himself up, shook his head, and retrieved his blue patrolman's cap, which had fallen to the ground. "Huh. No more demon … and no more chickens. Sounds good to me."

"Case closed." I had a big grin on my stiff face.

Sheyenne said, "Not until all the paperwork is complete."

CHAPTER THREE

After shattering a monstrous serial-killer demon, I looked forward to resting in peace back at the office. Forget about the horrific Obadeus; the worst part of the ordeal had been all that running! My street shoes weren't designed for jogging and my stitched-up sports jacket wasn't made to be an exercise shirt. My stiff, heavily embalmed body was going to be sore. And McGoo wasn't a model of physical fitness either.

Sheyenne reached the offices ahead of me. Ghosts move faster since they can go directly through walls, take diagonal shortcuts through city blocks, and even walk right through inconveniently placed people.

She smiled up at me from the reception desk, sparkling and translucent as usual. "I'm already typing up the incident."

"Better you than me, Spooky." I gave her an aspirational kiss on the cheek. I hate typing; rigor mortis and nimble fingers do not go hand-in-hand.

"The Quarter was on edge because of Obadeus, and now he's gone, thanks to you." She batted her eyelashes at me. "At the next Chamber of Commerce meeting, they'll probably give you a key to the city."

"The city isn't locked," I said. "But if the publicity helps us get new clients, I won't complain." I hung my fedora on the hat rack and shrugged out of my rumpled sport jacket. I was going to sit back and relax at my desk, shuffle through old files, and mull over incomplete cases, hoping they might solve themselves, although they usually don't.

Robin emerged from the conference room holding her magical legal pad. "I'm glad you got that monster off the streets, Dan. You and Officer McGoohan have made the Quarter safe for all citizens, living or dead." She smiled, looking justified and proud. I like to make Robin proud. She's a good kid.

Even though our caseload ebbs and flows like a toilet that occasionally backs up and then drains, I love being a private investigator. It's the core of what I do, the beating heart in a man whose heart doesn't beat anymore. Despite being a zombie, I'm never going to turn into one of those homeless decaying wrecks who moans and complains about brains all day long.

Robin gestured to the conference room door. "Can you step in for a minute? I'm meeting with a client, and we could use your advice."

Robin is young and beautiful in an I-don't-even-realize-I'm-pretty sort of way, with coffee-colored skin, big brown eyes, and a contemplative expression that lets you see the wheels turning in her mind. She wants to achieve justice for the downtrodden unnaturals after the Big Uneasy.

"New intake? What's the case?" I braced myself.

"New client, old friend," she said.

Inside the room, a young man with round owlish glasses and a bleached goatee sat in a chair, looking uncomfortable. I had seen Fletcher Knowles plenty of times when he was alive and bartending at the Basilisk Nightclub. I almost didn't recognize him now as a ghost.

"I'm surprised to see you here, Fletcher," I said. I felt a sudden slimy chill. "Are tentacle beasts still harassing the nightclub?"

"No, the sewers have been quiet recently. This is about something else." He sighed quietly. "I'm surprised to be here myself. I thought the afterlife was supposed to be peaceful, but even as a ghost I'm still having problems. Being an unnatural leaves me with certain legal disadvantages."

Fletcher Knowles was one of the original co-founders and partners in the wildly successful Talbot & Knowles blood bars, which were springing up on every corner in the Unnatural Quarter. Originally, Fletcher had sold black-market blood, infringing on Talbot's legitimate business, but they had combined forces into a juggernaut chain of high-end blood drinks. Still, Fletcher's real love was his nightclub—Basilisk: A Place Without Mirrors. He'd been a relatively inactive partner in the blood bars, but now that he was dead, Fletcher had more time on his hands.

"Sorry to hear you're having trouble," I said. "Robin can help."

Fletcher was a good enough sort when he'd been alive, but he and I had history, both good and bad. Sheyenne had worked in his nightclub as a singer to put herself through medical school. I'd met her there when I was a human P.I., and she stole my heart (not literally—these days you have to be careful with your metaphors). Basilisk was also the place where she'd been poisoned and behind which I, myself, had been shot in an alley while looking into— among other things—Fletcher's black-market blood business.

Still, you have to look on the bright side. I had met my true love at his nightclub, after all, and that made up for a lot of bad things.

Oh, and not long ago, Fletcher was murdered by a writhing mass of slimy tentacles that emerged from the sewers behind the club, so I guess karma evens out.

Now he was a client.

Robin sat down, resting her yellow legal pad on the table. The No.2 pencil lifted itself and magically started taking notes. The legal pad and pencil had been a gift from the actual manifestation of Santa Claus, one of our clients, who had hired us to find his stolen naughty-and-nice list.

"Fletcher's been forced out by the new landlord of the Basilisk. The nightclub deed he signed was written by an old-school lawyer who used outdated contract law. Fletcher lost ownership of the club upon his death. Even though he's still mentally active and certainly capable, he's no longer part of management. The new owners don't want him involved, thinking it would add confusion."

"They're probably right," Fletcher said. "They seem very confused."

"Isn't there some legal wrangling you can do?" I asked. Robin was a veritable rodeo star when it came to legal wrangling.

"I'm afraid his involvement with Basilisk is off the table, unless they decide to hire him back as a bartender," Robin said. "However, as you know, Mr. Knowles is also the co-founder of a very successful chain of blood bars. He was a Board member emeritus, and now he'd like to be a more active partner."

"I want to keep myself busy," Fletcher said.

Always the perfect receptionist, Sheyenne flitted in carrying a cup of green tea for Robin and a cup of old coffee for me. She hadn't even bothered to heat it, because she knew I wouldn't drink any; holding the coffee cup was just an affectation that helped me to feel normal.

Seeing Robin's determined expression, I asked, "So what's the problem?"

"They're cutting me out of the blood bars, too," Fletcher said. "Harry Talbot, that bastard. He was my best friend. We were partners. We used to go fishing together as boys. But now ..."

"Fletcher wasn't closely involved in the joint company," Robin explained. "In the interim, the Board of Directors managed to install new members in secret, a hostile takeover. They had enough votes to remove Fletcher, and he's no longer allowed to participate in running the Talbot & Knowles blood bars."

"It's only a matter of time before they take my name off the signs," Fletcher groaned, sounding bitter. "They'll just be the *Talbot And* blood bars."

"This could be a long, ugly, and convoluted fight," I pointed out.

"This is unjust, and we'll fight it to the end!" Robin vowed, as she usually does.

"I've decided to pursue endless legal action as a hobby in my retirement," Fletcher explained. "It'll be more satisfying than buying an RV and driving around the country. It was my company, my dream. Look at how the blood bars have blossomed since the Big Uneasy! I want to sit in on the meetings, take part in the decisions, make my opinion heard." His spectral face looked forlornly at the table. "I just want to do something."

"If you really want to sit in on the meetings, there's a way," Sheyenne said. She had that quirky mischievous smile. "You're not used to this yet, Fletcher, but I've been a ghost longer than you. There are certain advantages to being incorporeal. You can just slip in, poke your head through the wall, and eavesdrop on the meetings. How are they going to stop you?"

Fletcher shook his head. "It's against the rules. They passed a corporate resolution that forbids my presence or participation, specifically by name. Harry's got a vendetta against me. Or somebody on the Board does."

Robin nodded solemnly as the magic pencil continued to scribble furious notes on the yellow legal pad. "I'm afraid corporate minutes are binding against ghosts."

"Harry and I had become best friends," Fletcher moaned. "We brainstormed the new company, painted the sign for the first store in his garage, rode our bicycles to the blood banks to get our first samples."

"Did he come to your funeral?" I asked.

Fletcher paused to consider. "I don't think so. I was only partly present."

"That might have been your first clue that something was wrong," Sheyenne said.

"Please help me," he said. "This is all I have left."

I nodded. "Robin will file every form that's ever been invented."

"At least the appropriate ones," Robin corrected.

I stood. "And I'll have a look around to see what I can find out."

CHAPTER FOUR

Even when I was alive, I never acquired a taste for the "caramel macchiato, extra foam, more-expensive-than-a-car" fancy drinks at upscale coffee houses, and as a zombie it certainly didn't matter to me. Old bitter coffee hit my tired taste buds just fine, and I wasn't going to waste money on a brain-matter latte if I couldn't enjoy it. McGoo was the only one who had a fondness for sissy drinks, particularly a cinnamon latte.

I knew, of course, that vampires were just as picky and discriminating with their gourmet blood drinks. I thought they were overcompensating. Since Fletcher Knowles was now one of our clients, I had to at least respect the popularity and booming business of the Talbot & Knowles blood bars. Since humans in the outside world were extremely nervous about monsters, especially hungry ones, they were happy to see vampires enjoying fancy blood frappés and plasmaccinos. Blood bars were popping up on every corner like toadstools in a shady graveyard.

The dirty dealings that ousted Fletcher from the Board had occurred behind closed doors at the corporate headquarters downtown, but I wanted to see the blood bar customers in their native element. Several days later, after I had taken care of some loose ends at the office, I decided to go to the nearest Talbot & Knowles blood bar, a thriving café that occupied the shell of an old gas station. The distinctive crimson awnings provided deep shade for day-owl vampires who liked to sit with their laptops and pretend they were writing a script.

To use the proper vernacular, I just wanted to case the joint, but when I arrived, I found more excitement than I expected.

Tensions were riding high after the violent serial killings by the demon from the Fifth Pit of Hell. Humans had good reason to be nervous about unnaturals.

The blood bars were supposed to show that outsiders didn't need to fear vampires anymore, just like the widespread distribution of Monster Chow products satisfied the appetites of the rest of the unnaturals. All the blood drinks served by Talbot & Knowles baristas were certified organic, voluntarily donated or purchased, some even synthetically produced. A vampire satisfied with a fresh arterial espresso wasn't likely to attack some bicyclist out on a late-night ride.

Now, though, vampire protesters were lined up with angry signs and black parasols to shade them from the sun.

"Lower prices on blood!" someone shouted.

"A Cadillac blood plan is great for those who can afford it, but what about common vampires? We need blood, too!"

"Mmmmm, delicious blood!"

The vampires were getting restless—not surprising since at this time of day they should have been home resting in their coffins. Trying to enjoy their drinks while ignoring the hubbub of protesters, several upscale vampire customers sat under the blood-red awnings. One earnest young vampire with a full head of brown hair and long sideburns busily typed on his laptop, paying little attention to the disturbance. He must have been in the middle of writing a good scene.

I shambled up, calling no attention to myself so I could watch the protests from the fringe. I approached one busty lady-of-the-night vampire who wore a clingy black formal gown that revealed cleavage that should have been classified as a national monument. Her long black hair had a single white streak down the left side, and her fingers were covered with enough diamond rings to open up her own jewelry store if she divested her fingers.

"Even if you can't afford fancy blood drinks, basic blood is widely available, isn't it?" I asked her. "Why the complaints?"

Her lips turned down in a frown, exposing her delicate pointy fangs. "What would you know about it? You're an entirely different sort of undead." She sniffed, looking at my forehead. "I'd get that hole in your head plugged up before more of your brains leak out."

"It's more of a problem when the rain leaks *in.*"

Eventually, she deigned to answer my question. "Basic blood tastes like crap. We'd all be happier vamps if we didn't have to feel guilty when we treat ourselves to a specialty drink."

"Is that what you hope to accomplish by protesting here? That corporate headquarters will lower prices franchise-wide?" I doubted the new hostile-takeover Board of Directors would be eager to do that.

"Oh, dear no! That's an impossible dream. We just want them to issue coupons."

The young blood barista came out, wiping his hands on his red apron. He looked nervously at the protesters. "Why don't you go protest somewhere else? This is harming our business."

"Exactly the point, moron," said a potbellied vampire in a plaid shirt. He wore a trucker cap with an extra-wide bill that shaded most of his face from the sun. His enormous bushy beard made him look as if he hadn't shaved since the Hatfields and the McCoys were friends. "I ain't interested in your hemo faggot concoctions!" The redneck vamp was with two similarly dressed men, probably brothers or cousins … maybe both.

The young writer under the crimson awning finished a paragraph and looked up from his laptop. He scowled at the protesters, annoyed that they had interrupted his concentration. Flagrantly, he picked up his tall glass of iced blood with a froth of cream, slipped the straw between his two fangs, and slurped loudly.

The bearded vampire shouted, "Forget those damned artificial drinks. We like the natural stuff, fresh from the source!" His two brothers/cousins nodded, waggling the bills of their caps up and down. In unison they scratched their beards, and cockroaches tumbled out onto the sidewalk, as if even the insects couldn't stand the facial hair environment.

"You mean drink from … people?" gasped a shrill, gray-haired vampire woman who looked like someone's undead grandma.

"That's right. I'm Ernie. You might've heard of us—we're from Suck Dynasty."

"Don't be so barbaric," said the erudite, busty lady-of-the-night next to me. "We're civilized creatures now. If we're going to live in harmony in this world, we're supposed to drink blood out of containers."

"That's right, little lady," barked Ernie. "And containers that hold blood are called *humans*." His two brothers/cousins chortled.

Even the protesters began to get angry with one another, waving their signs as well as holding them up for shade. The mood was getting ugly.

The vamp writer with his laptop lounged back, arrogantly watching them. He made a point of taking a long slow sip through his straw as he drained the blood from his chilled glass with a satisfied sigh. "Ahhh, nothing like a perfect blood drink made exactly the way I like. There's a special piquant flavor, a fizz in the back of the mouth." He twirled his straw, rattling the ice cubes before he slurped the last bit of moisture in the bottom. "This is the best I've ever had. You should all go try one." He was egging the protesters on, provoking them.

I stepped forward before this got out of hand. "Let's calm down. No need to get their blood boiling."

Several vamps in the crowd looked up at the crimson awnings and muttered, considering the idea. "Maybe we should try one. I'm thirsty."

"It'll make ..." said the vamp writer, as he heaved a ponderous breath, "... you feel ..." His voice deepened. He began to shudder. "Full of energy!" His voice was like a growl pressed into words. His shoulders stiffened, and he clacked his fangs together. His eyes burned with a reddish glow. "*Destructive energy!*"

He curled his hands into claws, scraping the surface of the tabletop, then he leaped up, knocking the metal chair backward. With a wild roar, the vamp writer snatched his laptop and hurled it into the crowd where it smashed into the Suck Dynasty rednecks.

I cringed, hoping he'd saved his draft file to the cloud before smashing the laptop.

With an even louder roar, he grabbed the table and spun around to smash the plate glass sun-treated window in front of the blood bar. Protesters screamed and backed away. The vamp writer's fangs elongated into sharp tusks two inches long, and his features grew more hideous. He thrashed around, slashing the air with his claws.

"Whoa, you may want to consider switching to decaf!" I said.

The berserk vampire launched himself at the crowd. He slashed at the grandma vampire, and she squealed, scrambling for her wire-rimmed glasses before they were stepped on.

The brave and rowdy Suck Dynasty vamps weren't very brave when they saw someone actually fighting back. They tripped over one another as they retreated through the crowd.

Doing my civic duty, I tried to block the crazed man before he could attack the curvaceous lady-of-the-night vampire, but he bowled me over and knocked me to the ground.

The buxom vampiress backed away, but the raving monster's claws caught the front of her dress, tearing the fabric and exposing cleavage that went nearly down to her navel. The rampaging vamp paused in shock, ogling her large breasts.

In detective school I was taught never to ignore the cleavage gambit. "Everybody, pile on! We can overpower him."

The protesters closed in. Some of them battering the berserk vampire with their signs. Since I was on top of the wild man, I received half of the blows.

"Dogpile!" called another vamp, and he dove on top of me to help hold the struggling man down. I felt like an undead sandwich. More and more threw themselves on top of the squirming mound.

Beneath me and a dozen other heavy bodies, the rampaging vamp thrashed and squirmed, then finally went limp like a deflated tire. I heard wailing sirens in the distance and tried to hold out. Finally, he lay still, and I groaned to my fellow tacklers. "You can unpile now."

Slowly, the weight of the helpful vampire protesters diminished. The young vamp writer lay unconscious on the sidewalk, as if whatever supercharged him had burned itself out. I retrieved my fedora and saw to my dismay that it had been stomped flat.

I couldn't understand what had happened. Sitting under the crimson awning, the vampire writer had seemed so calm, so sedate. What could have driven him into such a frenzy?

I reassembled myself as best I could, and watched as the ambulance pulled up. The EMTs, the emergency mortician techs, strapped the victim down on a gurney and hauled him away.

As the crowd started to disperse, McGoo arrived, late as usual. When he asked me what had happened, I said, "I'll tell you the whole story in the Goblin Tavern. And you're buying."

Chapter Five

Cops and detectives have their own special watering holes, the darker and dingier the better. Ostensibly, they are strategic places where they can pick up intel and talk with confidential sources or undercover informants. In reality, ours was just a place where we liked to drink.

The Goblin Tavern was a fixture in the Unnatural Quarter, a friendly pub where unnaturals of all species, as well as curious and brave human visitors, could hang out, surrounded by a comforting pall of ancient cigarette smoke infused with the sour smell of spilled beer.

Francine, the hard-bitten human bartender, was tougher than most of the monsters who gave her trouble—and very few of them gave her trouble more than once. Francine had been divorced several times and would have been divorced more often, if she hadn't run out of candidates. She had a salty disposition, a cigarette-ravaged voice, and a weathered face that needed more makeup than she could afford.

Previously, Francine had worked in any number of biker bars in seedy districts, and the Unnatural Quarter was just another job. She had worked at this tavern long enough that she practically owned it. I think she had a room in back, but I couldn't recall ever seeing her leave the premises. Unnaturals being what they were, both nocturnal and diurnal, the Goblin Tavern never closed.

Francine apparently slept very little, which would account for her haggard looks and grouchy disposition.

But she was our bartender, and when McGoo and I entered, she lit up like a ray of moonshine. "Hello, boys. Haven't seen you in ages—not since last week. Or was it yesterday?"

"We were busy, Francine." McGoo sidled up to his usual bar stool, and Francine quickly tossed him a rag before he could plant himself.

"Mind the seat! We had a slime family in here for dinner, and they took up that side of the bar. You know how their kids leak all over the place."

McGoo swiped the smooth wooden seat, then tossed the now-sticky rag onto my stool, which had up until then been clean. I pinched the cloth with two fingers and draped it over the bar so Francine could disinfect it, burn it, or reuse it—her choice.

"We were hunting down a serial-killer demon, and we got him!" I said, feeling a flush of pride. "The streets are now safe for monsters of all kinds."

"Saw it on the news." She picked up the TV remote, clicking it on to see if our exploits were being broadcast at that exact moment, like on a typical cop show. She cracked her knuckles and stepped closer. "The first round's on me—and you should have the good beer, not that swill you usually drink, Shamble."

"It's Chambeaux," I said, without much enthusiasm. Francine knew my name, but everyone got it wrong on purpose. "The good stuff's not necessary for my zombie palate. I can't taste it anyway."

"He's right, Francine," McGoo said, settling onto his now-dry barstool. "Give me two of the good ones, and I'll buy a cheap beer for him." He was good at negotiating, and accounting.

Francine yanked the tap like a hangman's lever on a gallows, pouring our beers.

I shifted in my seat and gave McGoo the full, strange details about the vampire writer who had gone berserk at the blood bar. "When I got there, I was more worried about the protesters turning violent. The young vamp was sitting quietly with his laptop and his iced blood drink. He seemed like a snob, one of those wannabe writers who works on his great American movie script without ever finishing it."

"Better than the Necronomicon study groups," McGoo grumbled. "They take up all the tables and argue over chapter and verse, as if they had a personal relationship with the Mad Arab himself."

I sipped my beer, then wiped foam from my gray lips. It tasted warm and bitter, pretty much like everything tasted. I couldn't tell if the bartender had given me the microbrew or not. "Delicious, Francine. Noticeably different from the old beer, thanks." I turned back to McGoo. "There was a trio of vampire brothers, or cousins, who called themselves the Suck Dynasty. They advocated attacking humans to drink fresh from the source."

McGoo let out an angry sigh. "Yeah, I know those boys. They usually don't cause trouble except when they play country-and-western music too loud. It makes the neighborhood werewolves howl."

"I'm more worried about the sentiment, in case it spreads," I said. "This long after the Big Uneasy, the world was just starting to settle down, but now with the Obadeus murders, and these hicks openly pushing to prey upon non-volunteer humans ..."

As if on cue, the TV news inhuman-interest story about do-it-yourself mummification kits for friends and family ended, and a public-service announcement came on the bar television. "These are trying times," said a man's soft and gentle voice, "and we are *trying*. Believe me, at Monster Chow Industries we are trying!"

His voice was molasses sweet like everyone's favorite uncle, the one with the perfect haircut, the V-neck argyle sweater, the penny loafers. That exact man appeared on the TV screen, smiling. "My name is Cyrus Redfarb, the newly appointed spokesman for the Monster Chow line of textured flesh substitutes and palatable, humanely-sourced blood alternatives. You'll be seeing a lot of me in the coming weeks." He sat down in an overstuffed leather chair next to a crackling fireplace. He crossed one slender leg over the other, revealing his argyle socks. His movements were just a little awkward and jerky, as if he had practiced too much.

"I'm coming to you from the Monster Chow studios in our lovely factory with this important message. Unnaturals must blend in with society, and our company gives them the means to do that." He laced his fingers together, holding one knee. "This new world of ours is full of wonders as well as fears. We all have to get along. I want to be your friend. Monster Chow Industries wants to be your friend."

"I'm getting diabetes from all that sugar," McGoo muttered.

The primary Monster Chow factory had opened up not long after the Big Uneasy. It was a powerful statement, showing that unnaturals were willing to put aside their predatory ways, that they would accept substitutes for the real thing, that humans didn't need to fear.

Redfarb's bright blue eyes were intense. "There's no such thing as predator and prey. Right now, we're all just *people*—of whatever color, belief system, or flavor, natural or unnatural. Wolves and rabbits can live together in peace, so long as there's enough Monster Chow to go around. Your grocery stores and eating establishments will soon feature an expanded line of our products, not just Werewolf Chow and Ghoul Chow, but also Mummy Chow, Witch Chow, Gargoyle Chow, and Zombie Chow. Even Vampire Chow packaged in flavorful single-serving shakes. All with delicious new recipes." When he smiled, his shoulders twitched oddly, as if all the parts of his body weren't connected properly.

Redfarb unfolded himself from the overstuffed chair and stood in front of the fireplace. He walked over to a silver tea set and poured himself a cup, then took a dainty sip and looked back toward the camera. "I just started my position, and I have a lot of work to do. Because we want to calm everyone's fears in light of certain violent incidents, I will usher in a new era of transparency for Monster Chow Industries.

"Our factory has never been a tourist attraction, but as of today, we will give unprecedented access, tours to any groups who want to see the humane and innovative ways our chow brands are created. I myself will make numerous public appearances to help spread the word."

He set his teacup down and folded his hands together before leaning very close to the camera. His bright blue eyes seemed glassy. "Monsters don't have to eat people. Our chow brands taste just like human! We believe that if you just try one of the numerous free samples we will distribute throughout the Quarter, you'll agree that it's better than ever with our new secret ingredients. And happy monsters make for happy humans. One world, a big friendly neighborhood. Thank you, and have a very nice day, or night—your preference."

"That certainly didn't whet my appetite," McGoo said.

"I wasn't hungry to start with." I drank more of my beer.

McGoo savored his second expensive microbrew, and we had a moment of quiet in which neither of us needed to say anything. Then my cell phone rang, Sheyenne calling from the office.

McGoo's phone rang at the same time, and both of us answered, leaning in opposite directions so we could talk. Sheyenne said, "Beaux, I just got an odd call, some woman insisting that you go down to the Hellhound bus station and meet the 10:13 arrival. She sounded angry and hysterical, and she told me to tell you, and I quote, 'She's your problem now.'"

"Who's my problem? I have enough problems. I didn't order any more."

"She said her name was Rhonda," Sheyenne said. "Wasn't Rhonda the name of your ...?"

I suddenly felt deader inside. "I'm on it, Spooky." I hung up and looked over at McGoo as he ended his own call. His face was so white his freckles stood out like blackheads.

"It was Rhonda," he said. "She says I have to go to the bus station."

Of all the terrifying and unpleasant things I'd encountered in the Unnatural Quarter, including the bloodthirsty demon we had just shattered several nights before, nothing is quite as frightening as a call from an ex-wife.

CHAPTER SIX

Awkward.

I could feel it, and I saw McGoo fidgeting, too. The mere mention of Rhonda was enough to set our teeth on edge, as if we had signed up for a couple's root canal. As we made our way from the tavern to the Hellhound bus station, we had trouble making conversation.

McGoo told another one of his stupid jokes, hoping to lighten our mood. "Hey, Shamble, you know why the skeleton didn't ask a girl to prom?" He paused a beat. "He didn't have the guts!" It was no funnier than the jokes usually were, and my obligatory laugh had a nervous tinge.

I finally said, "Any idea what this is about, McGoo? Sheyenne didn't give me much information."

"You know Rhonda," McGoo said.

Yes, I did. We both did. Intimately—and the thought made me shudder.

"Rhonda's never been good at saying what she really means," McGoo continued. "She wasn't much of a conversationalist in the best of times."

McGoo's ex-wife suffered from a severe case of avoiding direct answers to direct questions. When you asked her where she wanted to go out to dinner, she'd give a rambling and oblique reply that mentioned politics in Venice or Rome, from which you were supposed to infer that her answer was "Italian food." McGoo had put up with Rhonda for three years, although my torrid little affair with her afterward lasted only a couple of weeks; I guess I'm a fast learner.

McGoo didn't look at me as we kept walking toward the station. "She just told me the bus number, said I had to be there. No other details."

"'She's your problem now,'" I quoted to him. "That could mean a lot of things." But McGoo and I both had a pretty good idea what was up, even though we didn't admit it.

Arriving at the Hellhound bus station, we looked at the boards and saw that the 10:13 bus was fifteen minutes late. "Great, let's drag this out even longer."

The Hellhound bus line was a new service established for unnaturals with special travel needs, blackened windows for sunlight-sensitive travelers and widened seats to accommodate ogres, oversized demons, and other creatures with unnaturally large buttocks, special seat backs with wingspace for gargoyles and other flying things.

On one of the benches inside the bus station, a skeleton sat motionless next to a battered old suitcase. He seemed to have missed his bus … maybe ten years ago. I couldn't tell from the look in his eye sockets whether he was awake or asleep.

Up at the ticket counter a mummy was arguing over the extra baggage charge to bring his sarcophagus along, pointing to reduced rates for vampire coffins and complaining about discrimination. Nearby, a vending machine sold packets of the various kinds of NEW! IMPROVED! Monster Chow.

One entire rack of paperbacks contained volumes of the "Dan Shamble" adventures released by Howard Phillips Publishing. The cover artist hadn't come close to matching my likeness, and the stories sounded overblown and improbable, with titles like *Slimy Underbelly* and *Hair Raising*. But unnaturals seemed to enjoy reading them on long cross-country bus rides; I just hoped they didn't get motion sickness.

A gargoyle family with two miniature kids walked into the main gallery, where one of the small winged tykes strained rambunctiously against a leash around his neck, trying to fly away. The tether slipped out of his mother's hand, and the gargoyle kid flapped up toward the arched ceiling. With a sigh of impatience, the father flew up with his much larger wings to seize the child and bring him back to earth.

McGoo and I found a bench and sat down with a sigh. "This should be interesting," I said in resignation.

"Yeah, *interesting* is my favorite thing these days," McGoo said. We fidgeted for several minutes.

Awkward ...

McGoo and I had been young and stupid. We'd both dated and eventually married women with the same name. Rhonda. Mine was a blonde, McGoo's was a brunette. We expected to take the world by storm. The four of us did a lot of things together, double dating, best friends, but just as our careers spiraled away from our imaginary goals, so did our marriages. The sweet, beautiful, and sexy Rhondas rapidly turned into henpecking and shrewish Rhondas ... though they would probably describe the situation in different terms; McGoo and I hadn't turned out to be knights in shining armor either.

My Rhonda and I split up around the same time McGoo and his Rhonda split up. Maybe it was because we liked to do everything together.

In one of those "the grass is always greener" moments, I came to a bourbon-induced epiphany, back when I was human and back when I could enjoy a good bourbon. The problem hadn't necessarily been *Rhonda*, I decided—it was just that I had married the *wrong* Rhonda.

The four of us had done so many things together, and I suddenly realized all the times that McGoo's Rhonda—the dark-haired one, just so we don't get them confused—must have been flirting with me, coming on to me. Since she'd broken up with her husband and was "lonely" (which I didn't realize meant "desperate and needy"), we had a wild fling. Enjoyable, sweaty, heavy-breathing good times. My future seemed bright ... for about two weeks, then I came to my senses.

I confessed to McGoo, and he did his duty by saying "I told you so." Except for the fact that he, too, briefly got back together with his Rhonda ... until he realized what "lonely" truly meant in her mind.

While I'd been off in my fling with dark-haired Rhonda, I was isolated and paid very little attention to my friend, or even what my own estranged wife was doing. To this day, I suspect McGoo had his own little thing with her, but every time I tried to raise the question he got all funny and avoided answering by telling more stupid jokes. I didn't press him, primarily because I didn't want to hear any more jokes.

Now at the bus station, McGoo broke the silence. "What do you think she's like?"

"Who, Rhonda? And which Rhonda?"

"No, the little girl. Rhonda said she's ten years old." He paused. "You know that's who's on the bus."

I sighed. "The kid's been raised alone all these years by Rhonda. What do you think she's like?"

"You just answered my question, Shamble."

Shortly after our mutual breakup with our mutual, and even exchangeable, Rhondas, the Big Uneasy occurred. The return of all the monsters caused plenty of turmoil. Since neither of us wanted anything to do with our Rhondas, we hadn't kept up with their lives, didn't keep them on our Christmas card lists.

Not long ago when we were working the case of the sewer slumlord Ah'Chulhu, McGoo had received a call from out of the blue—Rhonda seeking child support. He hadn't even known there *was* a child, much less one with a balance due. McGoo had offered to pay his ex if she came down to the Quarter, but Rhonda never responded. We assumed it was a hoax.

Apparently not.

"But why would she call me, too?" I asked.

"Moral support," McGoo said. "That means it must be bad."

"A few nights ago we were running through the streets after a serial-killer demon. Tonight we're just meeting a little girl at a bus station. That's got to be an improvement, right?"

He frowned. "Remember, we're talking about Rhonda."

Two zombie teenagers rattled the Monster Chow vending machine in an attempt to score a free packet, but when an item finally dropped into the bin it was only Harpy Chow, and the zombie teens were not interested.

The questions kept bothering me. "And why would Rhonda put your daughter on a Hellhound bus? That makes no sense."

McGoo shrugged as if to demonstrate that he had long since stopped trying to make sense out of Rhonda. "Maybe it was the most direct route to the Unnatural Quarter? Don't think about it too much."

Finally the black luxury-liner coach rolled into the station, letting out a hiss of air brakes as loud as a Medusa on a bad day. With a hollow rattle, the skeleton sitting on the nearby bench leaped to his feet, showing more excitement than I expected from a pile of bones. The bus door opened to reveal the driver, a goblin hunched over a wheel that was wider than his shoulders. He wore a snappy-looking gray bus driver cap and gray jacket that matched his gray skin.

Passengers began to file off the bus, the usual assortment of vampires, werewolves, zombies, ghosts, and ghouls, as well as a terrified-looking old human couple who must have boarded at the wrong bus stop.

Nervous, McGoo and I stood together a few steps back from the open door watching the unnaturals disembark, not sure what to expect. We recognized the kid as soon as she stepped off the bus.

"That's her!" McGoo said, his voice cracking. I couldn't deny it.

She was a ten-year-old waifish girl with light brown hair done up in pigtails that stuck out like mouse ears on either side of her head. She was cute, I'll grant her that, with large eyes, an elfin face, a pink sweater, and a pleated plaid skirt. I couldn't see any hint of McGoo's features on her face, which was a good thing.

She was also a vampire.

Pinned to the front of the girl's fuzzy pink sweater was a laminated index card on which Rhonda had written, "I'm supposed to meet Toby McGoohan and Dan Chambeaux. Don't mess with me!"

I lifted my stiff arm and waved at her, because it seemed the appropriate thing to do. McGoo stood like a statue, and I elbowed him until he waved as well.

The girl saw us and came forward. She wore a pink backpack that apparently contained most of her worldly possessions, and carried a small suitcase that held the rest. "She said you'd meet me here." She seemed angry, maybe at us, maybe at her mother, maybe at the world.

"And we're here!" I said in a bright voice, wanting to make her feel at home. "Welcome to the Unnatural Quarter."

"You're ... Rhonda's daughter," McGoo said stupidly.

The girl sniffed. "She said she was going to call my father to come get me." She looked from McGoo to me. "I'm supposed to stay with you, now that I'm a vampire."

Her comment took us both aback, for more reasons than one.

McGoo and I looked at each other and swallowed in unison. He spoke to the girl. "You're supposed to stay with us? But we don't ... I can't ..."

"You know how good Rhonda was at planning ahead, McGoo," I pointed out.

"I don't even know your name," he said, bending down to be closer to the girl's height.

"It's Alvina, so now you know. That means I can stay here." She plucked at the index card pinned to her sweater and grimaced. "Can you take this thing off me? I hate it. It makes me look like a little kid."

"Why couldn't you take it off yourself?" I asked.

"Mom used a silver safety pin, on purpose, and I can't touch it. This sucks." She made an angry grumbling noise. "Another stupid disadvantage of being a stupid vampire."

"I know plenty of smart vampires," I said as I fumbled with the safety pin to remove the offending index card, but my fingers were too stiff and clumsy. McGoo helped, and his hands were shaking too; eventually, we removed the badge.

"Thanks, that's better." She sighed. "I'm not angry at you. It was *her.*"

"You're a vampire," McGoo said. Not his wittiest comment.

"I know," said Alvina. "Does that mean you don't like me? I couldn't help it. I cracked my head open in a stupid skateboarding accident. I lost a lot of blood. Mom said the regular clinics were too expensive, and the cheap one accidentally used contaminated blood for my transfusion. So here I am, a ten-year-old vampire. Just great." She sighed again, even louder than the first time. "She says I belong in the Unnatural Quarter with all the other little monsters, and the big ones too." She set down her suitcase and unslung her backpack. "This sucks. I hope you have a place for me to stay. I brought all my dolls." She looked expectantly from me to McGoo, then back at me again.

"So," asked the cute little girl, "which one of you is my father?"

CHAPTER SEVEN

t that moment, in a miraculous rescue, Robin called to remind me that we had an important meeting related to Fletcher's case, an opportunity to get first-hand information on the violent blood bar incident I had witnessed earlier that day.

Though McGoo was clearly out of his depth, he offered to take Alvina down to precinct headquarters with him, where she could settle in for a while.

"A real police station!" Alvina said. "Can I arrest criminals? Can I help you interrogate them? Can I play with handcuffs? This doesn't suck at all!"

McGoo forced a bright, awkward smile. "You can do anything you want, little girl." No doubt, that's what he thought absentee dads were supposed to say. He muttered quietly to me, "We're going to have to figure this out, Shamble."

Even though he was originally the one marked for child support, that didn't prove anything; it just meant Rhonda could more easily pin it on her ex-husband. Eventually, we'd need to talk to Rhonda, too, and that was an experience neither of us looked forward to.

I said awkward goodbyes to McGoo and the vampire kid and left the bus station as the gargoyle family and the solitary skeleton stowed their luggage and boarded the coach. A mummy hurried out of the restroom, racing to get on board before the bus departed. He was in such a rush that he didn't notice a long and embarrassing bandage trailing behind him like a strip of toilet paper.

I made my way to the UQ Medical Center, which catered to various sorts of unnaturals, particularly those that didn't have supernatural healing skills. The vampire writer who had gone berserk after drinking his iced blood at the protest rally was being treated here. We wanted to find some answers.

I found Robin and Fletcher in the lobby. She had been sorting through papers in her briefcase, while her yellow legal pad and magical pencil dutifully took notes on the matter as they waited for me. Fletcher's ghost was nervous, pacing back and forth like a young father in a maternity ward. He was so distracted he walked right through the furniture without noticing.

Robin looked up at me, while her pencil kept writing. "The patient's being held in the security ward, Dan. I got special permission for us to speak with him about his reaction to the blood drink. No charges have been filed yet. Many of the protesters don't want to admit they were there." She frowned, and somehow that made her beautiful face look more determined. "Even the Suck Dynasty brothers won't have anything to do with this, and they usually want publicity."

I remembered how Ernie and his brothers/cousins had reacted when the vamp writer went on his rampage. "Of course not. They ran like a proverbial flock of feral chickens as soon as our guy threatened them."

"We need to learn why he went nuts after drinking product from one of my blood bars," Fletcher said with a groan. "What if our supply's been contaminated? What if there's a health scandal?"

"I thought they weren't your blood bars anymore. Isn't that the whole reason you hired us?" I said.

"Harry and I started that company from scratch, after you helped us resolve our differences. I still have pride of ownership, even if I don't have legal ownership."

"We're working on that," Robin said. "After the incident this afternoon, the Talbot & Knowles corporate headquarters vehemently denies all responsibility."

"Harry Talbot was never like that before," Fletcher said. "Now, he's just so ... so corporate."

"Corporate people often are," I said.

Robin was all business. "Maybe this incident doesn't have anything to do with artisanal blood drinks. Let's go talk with the victim. His name is Travis Spade, and he's being tended by the hospital's most renowned witch doctor."

Robin went to the receptionist, a darling sparkly-winged fairy who sat in a tall booster seat behind the desk, who gave us the room number for Travis Spade. We rode the elevator up to the sixth floor, checked in at the desk, and were directed down the hall to where the patient was being confined, treated, and tested.

We found Travis Spade sprawled in his hospital coffin bed, hooked up to numerous medical machines and monitors. The vampire looked very different from the cocky aspiring author who had taunted protesters at the blood bar. He was gaunt and weak, particularly for a vampire. He seemed jittery as he lay back, unable to sleep. At least his eyes had reverted to normal from the blazing scarlet gaze, and his fangs were no longer tusks, but perfectly average pointy teeth.

The footboard and side walls of the hospital coffin bed were raised, and generic soil had been spread on the sheets to provide comfortable, homey confinement. The TV in the corner of the room was tuned to a channel that only showed reruns of daytime women's talk shows.

When we entered, Travis twitched, as if to flee, but his wrist had been handcuffed to a rail on the side of the bed—a precaution in case he went berserk again. "Who are you? My lawyers?"

"I'm a lawyer," Robin admitted. "And we'd like to ask you a few questions about your drinking habits."

I stepped close to the coffin bed, wondering if Travis would remember me as the one who had tackled him. "I was there when the ... incident happened. In fact, I helped to subdue you. You were very strong."

"Sorry about that. I don't understand what happened. I was just sitting under the awning, enjoying my second grande iced blood, and working on my screenplay, but those noisy protesters made it hard to concentrate on my dialogue."

I thought of the buxom lady-of-the-night and her over-abundance of cleavage. "Yes, they were a little distracting."

"Do you remember which specific blood drink you had?" Fletcher asked. "I'm one of the cofounders of the Talbot & Knowles blood bars."

Travis Spade's eyes narrowed in suspicion. "You're going to trick me into signing a release and promise not to sue? What if I was poisoned?"

"Let me clarify. We don't represent the blood bars," Robin said. "Mr. Knowles is a client of ours on an entirely different matter, but we are concerned about the cause of your misfortune."

"It was misfortune for a lot of people," I said. "But it did break up the protest."

"All I had was a light, arterial, cold-pressed iced blood drink," he said. "With a dollop of soy milk."

"Do you remember which blood type?" Fletcher asked.

"O negative I think, though it's a little bitter to my tastes. They had run out of the B negative and didn't want to brew more at that time of day."

Fletcher looked at us and explained, "During slow hours, we only keep the best-selling items fresh and available."

Travis rattled his handcuff again and looked disappointed. "The witch doctor took blood samples to have her Igors run a thorough chemical analysis. We'll know more when we get the results. It might just have been low blood-sugar levels. Sometimes that makes me a little edgy."

"And did you add sugar to the blood? Real sugar?" I asked. "Or did you use an artificial sweetener?"

Travis mumbled, embarrassed, "Artificial sweetener."

"That might be the key," Robin said. "Those chemicals are dangerous. Something triggered that extreme reaction."

"At least it was only temporary," Travis said. "I'm fine now."

I tried a different approach. "You had a laptop. What were you working on?"

He brightened, obviously more interested in talking about his creative work. "My screenplay is a profound drama about the human condition and the inhuman condition, and the differences between the two. I've been on both sides of the issue, so I feel I have something to say. I'm sure it'll win awards and be critically acclaimed."

I nodded solemnly, knowing that awards and critical acclaim are often the kiss of death for sales. Sitting up in his coffin bed, he grew more enthusiastic. "In the first scene, we open with a full moon and a howling wolf, which, according to tropes, would make the audience assume the film is a romantic comedy. But then the camera shifts and—"

Fortunately, this all-too-detailed description was interrupted when the witch doctor entered the room. She had tangled black hair, a pointed black hat, and a full black dress over which she had pulled a white physician's smock. Her long, hooked nose displayed a prominent wart, as did her protruding chin. Her nametag read ZONDA NEFARIOUS, WD.

I'd had many dealings with witches in the Quarter, particularly Mavis and Alma Wannovich, the sisters who published the "Dan Shamble, Zombie P.I." fictionalized cases. In exchange, the Wannovichs performed a monthly maintenance spell to keep me intact and freshen me up. Once, they had even invited me to a meeting of the Pointy Hat society for all the witches in the Quarter.

Zonda Nefarious, however, was not the ladies club sort of witch. She was an actual doctor, and a well-respected one. "Ah, Mr. Spade, are these your next-of-kin? We've run the blood tests. Tsk-tsk." She looked down at her clipboard, then glanced at the three of us. "Would you like your guests to leave the room? It's private medical information."

"No, I want to find out what it is," he said. "I want them all to find out so they can clear my name. It wasn't my fault. I'm not responsible for my actions."

"Again, I'm not your attorney," Robin said.

"But you're *an* attorney," said Travis, "and that's the best I have right now."

Fletcher's ghost drifted closer to the doctor to try to peek at her clipboard. "Was it something in the blood? Bad blood means bad publicity."

Zonda pressed the clipboard against her ample breasts to protect the patient's privacy. "Bad blood means a lot of things, and we have indeed found some irregularities. Do you use any recreational drugs, Mr. Spade?"

"No!" he said indignantly. "My vampire metabolism burns it up too fast. I usually just drink Monster Chow vampire shakes. Some of the new flavors are really good, especially the raspberry, but I do go to the Talbot & Knowles blood bar every afternoon. It's part of my process."

Zonda Nefarious scribbled something else on her clipboard.

"And he used artificial sweetener," I said.

"Artificial sweetener? Tsk-tsk." The witch doctor gave her patient a scolding look. "You need to tell me these things! They could be relevant."

"What results did the analysis yield?" Robin held her yellow legal pad, and the pencil poised itself to write.

"We did find chemical irregularities, something strange in Mr. Spade's blood that triggered his reaction. Some kind of super stimulant that burned off quickly."

"But where did it come from?" Fletcher sounded desperate. "Was it the Talbot & Knowles specialty blood drink?"

"I can't tell. The blood barista had already cleaned and sterilized Mr. Spade's glass before the police could take it as evidence."

"Our blood baristas are very well trained in efficiency and customer service," said Fletcher.

"None of the other blood samples in the store showed any irregularities, so the source may have been something else altogether. We'll keep you here for observation, Mr. Spade," the witch doctor said. "My Igors want to run another set of tests in the lab."

Robin handed over her card. "We're also privately investigating this matter. We'd like to be kept in the loop."

"I'll get to the bottom of it," said Zonda. "This could be a public health matter."

From his hospital coffin bed, Travis said, "It's already delayed the completion of my script, so it does affect everyone, culturally speaking."

Chapter Eight

The next day Robin joined me for lunch at the Ghoul's Diner, which proved just how much she appreciated my company. Even though the sign in the diner's flyspecked window prominently announced YES, WE SERVE HUMANS!, nobody quite knew what that meant.

The menu didn't have a lot to offer normal people with normal digestive systems. Strictly speaking, the menu didn't have much to offer unnaturals either, because the food tasted so terrible, but many monsters don't have acute taste buds and they eat whatever putrefying mass is put in front of them. They came to the diner out of habit, for the camaraderie. Certainly not the service.

"I'll have the peanut butter and jelly sandwich, please," Robin said to Esther the waitress, a metallic-plumed, pinch-faced, and bitter-as-grapefruit-extract-with-lemon harpy.

"What?" Esther squawked as if Robin had accused her of a crime. "No one orders a peanut butter and jelly sandwich!"

"I do," Robin said calmly. "It appears to be the safest thing on the menu."

"What?" Esther shrieked again. "Are you insulting our restaurant?"

"No, I am ordering a peanut butter and jelly sandwich." Robin had spent enough time in courtrooms with bombastic opposing counsel and unruly witnesses that she was not easily ruffled. "With a dill pickle, please. What are you having, Dan?"

"I'll have the special," I said, not wanting to provoke Esther's ire. I didn't know what the special was, but I knew it wasn't going to be special. I also knew how easy it was to offend the harpy waitress, who chewed gum and cracked bubbles like small-caliber gunfire.

"Coffee with that?" Esther said.

"Yes, please. And in a clean cup."

"No special requests!"

"I'll have green tea," Robin said.

"What? Nobody orders green tea."

"I just did," Robin said, then opened her briefcase to remove her yellow legal pad to review the notes her pencil had scribed for her.

Seated in the booth, I waved at Albert Gould back in the kitchen, where he mixed up orders and ponderously loaded plates with whatever seemed handy. Albert is a dreary, stinky, decomposing ghoul who doesn't know anything other than being a short-order cook at his diner. He does a brisk business for breakfast and lunch, which means the Ghoul's Diner is open 24 hours, since unnaturals eat breakfast and lunch at all different times.

Robin tapped her pencil on the paper. "I've tried to acquire the Board meeting notes from Talbot & Knowles, but since they're privately held, the records are unavailable. They aren't required to provide anything about the hostile takeover. Harry Talbot refuses to return phone calls, and I think that upsets Fletcher even more than being ousted from the company."

"Do you think he has a case?" I rested my elbow on the flecked tabletop, hoping the speckles were a pattern, rather than maggot droppings.

"I'll make one. I'm putting together a very strong legal challenge. Fletcher co-founded that company, and even though he's dead, he's still perfectly competent. Worst case, the new Board will need to pay him off substantially."

"Wouldn't he rather go back to working at the Basilisk Nightclub? He seemed happy there."

Robin responded with a bright but hard smile. "A large enough payoff would let him open an *entire chain* of Basilisk Nightclubs, without interference from troublesome landlords ..."

Esther returned to our booth where she set down a plate with a peanut butter and jelly sandwich on white bread, sliced into two uneven pieces at an angle that was definitely not diagonal. The sandwich had been placed right on top of the juicy dill pickle. "PB&J," said the waitress as if it offended her.

Next, she dropped a cup and saucer on the table with a hard rattle. The cup held a tea bag and tepid water with green algae floating on top. "Green tea."

Then Esther placed a grayish bubbling mass on a blue plate in front of me. "Today's special." I watched the amorphous meal roil, saw a bubble rise up in the middle, then pop like a fart. "Enjoy," she said, and it sounded like a threat.

"Excuse me, Esther. You forgot my coffee."

"Didn't forget it, hon. Just didn't bring it."

The door opened with a jingle and McGoo, in his blue beat cop uniform, walked in with the cute ten-year-old vampire girl at his side. He looked a little harried, and Alvina seemed unsettled. I waved, and they made their way over to our booth, walking past a round table where the Necromancer's Club was having a business meeting. At an adjacent two-top, an Egyptian mummy and an Aztec mummy, apparently on a date, shared a milkshake with two straws to rehydrate themselves.

"Hey, Shamble," McGoo said as he slid into the seat next to Robin, while Alvina sat politely beside me. "What's a zombie's favorite breakfast cereal?"

"I prefer pancakes," I said, but I didn't manage to derail him.

"Raisin brain!"

I gave Alvina an apologetic look. "McGoo, you shouldn't be talking like that in front of the kid. You'll ruin her expectations of humor for life."

"I'm not a little kid." Alvina sounded defensive. "I'm ten, and I just started puberty. Becoming a vampire made it worse, and I'm going to stay this way. This sucks."

Robin's brow furrowed. "I remember my teenage years. It was a nightmare."

"Some unnaturals actually enjoy nightmares." I was trying to sound reassuring, but I failed.

Esther came back to the booth, gave the newcomers an accusatory glare. "Now what?"

"I'll have what he's having, please," McGoo said offhandedly, then took a look at my plate of gray goop and changed his mind. "No, I'll have what *she's* having."

"We don't serve peanut butter and jelly sandwiches," Esther said.

"Yes you do, it's right there."

"We're all out," Esther said.

McGoo didn't back down. "Then make some more."

The harpy waitress huffed.

Alvina said brightly, "Do you have Monster Chow?"

Suddenly the conversation in the diner stopped, as if a gunslinger had walked through the doors of a saloon in one of those old cowboy movies. "We're a diner, young lady. We make fresh home-cooked food, not that packaged stuff."

Behind the counter Albert wiped his hands on a rag, then tossed the rag into a soup pot before he marched out.

"I like Monster Chow," Alvina said. "Do you have any breakfast cereal? That'll do."

"You're eating breakfast cereal for lunch?" I asked.

"Your mother lets you do that?" McGoo added.

"I like how it turns the milk bright red," Alvina said.

After a long, tense glower, Esther admitted, "I might have one box of Unlucky Charms in the back." She strode off with a flair of her razor-sharp plumage.

Albert Gould shuffled around the corner and stood in front of the table. His face sagged and his skin turned various shades of green, purple, and yellow. "Monster Chow is gonna put me out of business. Take a look at this lunch crowd. It's half what it usually is."

I realized he was right. "It'll pass, Albert. People still need to eat, and they come here to socialize."

Albert made a slow turn to look at his clientele. "Would you want to socialize with any of these?"

"I see what you mean," McGoo said.

"With all the new brands of Monster Chow, the flavor options and the pricing ..." When Albert shook his head, grayish stuff dripped from his tangled hair and splattered on the table, on the floor, and in my food. Robin managed to hold up a napkin to shield her peanut butter and jelly sandwich. "People would rather have convenient packaged lunches. They don't respect good cooking anymore."

I looked at the gray eldritch horror on my blue plate. "I guess they don't."

Albert shuffled back behind the counter, where he took dirty dishes from the tub and scraped the leavings into a stew pot for the beginnings of tomorrow's Today's Special.

I leaned closer to Alvina. "How was your first night in the Quarter?"

Alvina shrugged. "His place is a dump."

"What were you expecting?" I asked.

Blushing, McGoo spread his hands. "I wasn't ready for this. I would have cleaned up."

"I've been to your apartment, McGoo. It doesn't look better even when it's clean." I turned to Alvina. "But my place isn't much of an improvement. It's dusty as a morgue."

"Actually, morgues aren't dusty," Robin said. "They're very clean, once the blood and other fluids are cleaned up."

"I'll have to make changes and find a place for her to sleep, if she's going to stay with me off and on," I said, then looked closely at Alvina. "If you'd like that."

"Yes, she would," McGoo said, quickly adding, "but not all the time."

"At home with my mom I always slept on the couch," Alvina said. "I was pretty much raising myself."

Knowing Rhonda, that might have been a blessing for the girl.

"I tried calling her mother," McGoo said. "No answer. Voicemail greeting said that she's dropped off the face of the Earth."

"That's preferable to actually speaking with her," I said.

Robin frowned and looked at McGoo. "And you didn't know you had a daughter until Rhonda asked for child support?"

Alvina chirped, "Actually, I don't even know which one is my father." She looked from McGoo to me, pointing fingers. "She says I'm their problem now."

Awkward.

"The timing was … questionable," I said. "It could be either of us."

"Can't you get a blood test?" Robin asked, then caught herself. "Ah, I've had cases like this before. After conversion to a vampire, DNA tests are no longer reliable."

"She does look a lot like me," McGoo said.

"No she doesn't." I leaned over to nudge the girl. "Don't worry about what he says, honey. He wasn't trying to be mean to you."

"Is it better if she looks like you, Shamble?" McGoo sounded offended.

"I think so," I said.

Alvina gave me a look of blunt honesty that only a child can manage. "You need to fix that hole in your forehead."

"I've been meaning to get around to it."

"If she's going to stay with us in the Quarter, then Rhonda can't ask either of us for child support," McGoo said.

The girl was making the best of the situation, and she didn't seem upset about the uncertainty. "It'll be fun here. Lots of other vampires, people with shared interests." Alvina grinned. "Want to know what I've been doing? I write a blog, and I have a very active social media presence. I've built up a following. People really like to read my stuff."

"She sounds awfully smart," McGoo said.

I agreed. "More evidence that she's my daughter, not yours."

Robin took a delicate bite of her sandwich just as Esther brought the two other meals. For McGoo, she had actually put the dill pickle in the middle of the peanut butter and the jelly. He didn't mind, just picked it up and took a bite. The harpy set a cardboard box of Unlucky Charms Monster Chow in front of Alvina, who dumped it in a bowl and added milk. Sure enough, the liquid turned bright red like arterial blood. Grinning, the kid picked up her spoon and began wolfing down the meal.

"We want what's best for Alvina," Robin said. "I propose that we all help out. Since nobody knows who the real father is, Dan and Officer McGoohan will take turns, and Sheyenne and I will help out."

I brightened. "It'll be one big melded nontraditional family."

"That'll work," McGoo said. "I'd be asking for your help with babysitting and daycare all the time anyway."

"I don't need babysitting and daycare," Alvina huffed, then took a long slurp of her red milk from the cereal bowl.

"But you still need to clean up your apartment, McGoo," I said. "You too, Shamble."

I wondered how long Rhonda intended to leave her daughter with us. As a vampire, Alvina would remain a little girl for a very long time, always stuck in puberty.

Esther finally brought a mug and set it in front of me, but I saw that she had given me another glop of green tea instead of the coffee I had ordered.

"Don't forget to tip," she said, then flounced away.

CHAPTER NINE

Being a partial parent was going to change my life—a lot. It might be as much of a transition as when I came back from the dead.

Though Alvina was reticent to talk about it, I had the distinct impression that she and Rhonda hadn't gotten along, but I don't think it was the kid's fault. I thought she was rather pleasant.

That evening, McGoo brought her over to my apartment. My turn. Sheyenne and Alvina worked together to make up the sofa with a blanket and pillow so the girl had a place to sleep. Usually when I needed to rest, I would just stand in a corner without moving for a while, but that wouldn't do for a kid. Sheyenne had spent the afternoon working with me, dusting and straightening up. I was actually surprised at how bright the place looked when it was clean.

We were going to have a nice quiet family evening, getting to know one another, maybe playing a game or two, but our fun, homey plans changed dramatically when McGoo's radio squawked. "Robbery in progreth! A blood-delivery vehicle ith being hijacked!"

The police dispatcher was a banshee with a lisp. Sometimes when she grew excited, she would scream too loudly and blow out the radio systems across the entire precinct. On the other hand, she could ride along in a patrol car and serve as a fully functional siren. Now, she was calling any officers in the vicinity to respond.

"That address is only a block away, Shamble," McGoo said. "Backup won't get there in time."

"I'm your backup," I said, ready to race out the door. Then we both stuttered to a halt and turned to Sheyenne in embarrassment. "Uh, can you watch Alvina while we—?"

"Of course, Beaux. We'll be just fine. Go stop the bad guys."

Alvina waved goodbye to us and said, "Be careful, Daddies." I felt a lump in my throat.

We bolted out into the street and heard the sounds of gunfire not far away. Unnaturals out for a nighttime stroll were running the opposite direction, wisely fleeing the shootout. Not being nearly as wise, McGoo and I ran directly toward the gunfire.

At an intersection of two alleys that were narrow enough to hinder vehicular traffic, we spotted a large armored truck with *Bubba's Bloodmobile* painted on the side. *Fresh from the artery, perfect for all occasions.* The armored blood truck was painted a rich crimson, with sparkles and stripes to make it look a little like an ice cream truck. Opposite from us, a long, black hearse had pulled up to block the intersection of the alleys. It was a deluxe model that had seen better years. A dumpy, heavyset woman with permed gray-brown hair under a pillbox hat and a matronly black dress stood with four young men, all of them taking cover by the hearse. They were all shooting pistols or rifles at the bloodmobile as if trying to win a stuffed alligator at a carnival game.

Bubba's Bloodmobile had two flat tires, and I noticed a spike strip studded with long rusty nails on the road just outside of the alley. This had been a trap. Gangsters had ambushed the truck.

Even with all the distraction of the constant gunfire, I recognized the woman from her mug shots. "It's Ma Hemoglobin and her boys," I groaned.

She'd given us trouble before. This wasn't going to be easy.

A human security guard in a rent-a-cop uniform was hunched over the steering wheel of the armored blood truck, apparently unconscious, or maybe just pretending. In the Unnatural Quarter, rent-a-cops and nighttime security guards have a high mortality rate, and they know to lie low in any dangerous circumstance.

His big-muscled copilot was a burly golem who had lurched out of the bloodmobile door, ready to defend the cargo, but oddly he wasn't moving either. He seemed petrified in place. Bullet holes had peppered his soft clay, causing no real harm, but his body had an unusual, high-gloss sheen. I suddenly understood. "They varnished him!" That was one way to petrify a golem.

"He's gonna need hours in a turpentine bath to recover from this," McGoo said in angry disgust. "Those bastards!"

Ma Hemoglobin heard his comment even over the continuing gunfire, and she responded with clear annoyance. "They're not bastards. These are my legitimate sons! Six boys from seven husbands."

I didn't try to do the math, but only four of her sons were with her now; they were all she had left. "You're short two boys, Ma," I called, knowing the comment would rankle her.

In my previous encounter with Ma Hemoglobin, two of her human sons—Huey and Louis—tried to ambush me on a long-haul trucking route, and that little adventure didn't have a happy ending for them ... But Ma Hemoglobin still had four spares: two human sons and two vampires. They were all dressed in similar flannel shirts and stained jeans, but they had dissimilar features that suggested a number of different fathers.

Crouching for cover, I drew my .38 and McGoo pulled both of his revolvers. We started firing immediately, doubling the sounds of gunfire, enough that we would surely draw noise complaints from any neighbors who were trying to sleep.

"You'll never catch us alive!" Ma Hemoglobin bellowed.

We approached, taking shelter among parked cars. The back doors of the bloodmobile were open, facing away from us. One of the vamp sons emerged, carrying an armful of blood bags, but I wondered why they weren't doing a fire-brigade to empty out the whole armored vehicle if they were really trying to steal the cargo. Ma Hemoglobin's gang weren't very competent hijackers.

The security guard remained hunched over the steering wheel, though I saw his eyes open, dart around, and quickly close again as he pretended to be unconscious. I couldn't tell what Ma and the boys were actually shooting at, because the gunfire kept going long after the driver had been knocked out and the golem petrified.

Though bossy and unattractive, Ma Hemoglobin wasn't stupid, unlike all or at least several of her sons. Her real last name was Hamanubin, but once she'd gotten involved in black-market blood supplies in the Unnatural Quarter, the nickname stuck. Shortly after the Big Uneasy, she started stealing blood from refreshment stands and hospital blood banks, selling it to vampires in back alleys. By opening up their widespread blood bars, Fletcher Knowles and Harry Talbot had removed the necessity for the black-market red stuff, and the Hemoglobin gang had grown more desperate.

Ma Hemoglobin should have been locked in prison for life. McGoo and I had arranged to whisk one of the key witnesses into the witness-protection program, but thanks to the usual red tape, her trial date wasn't even set yet. Ma had been released on bail to go about her daily activities—which unfortunately included armed robbery.

After the vamp sons retreated to their getaway hearse with an armful of blood sacks, Ma shouted, "Too much gunfire, boys. We can't stand the heat. Dewey, throw the blood in the back of the hearse. Ben and Len, cover us from the rear window." She flashed a grin. "Charlton, you ride up front with me, dear."

Bullet starbursts ruined the black exterior of the hearse as well as the jaunty crimson walls of Bubba's Bloodmobile. As McGoo and I kept shooting, the Hemoglobin gang piled pell-mell into the hearse. Ma sat behind the wheel and, after ensuring her boys all had their seatbelts buckled, gunned the engine and roared down the narrow alley. The side mirrors scraped sparks on the brick walls as the hearse disappeared into the night.

McGoo and I could barely squeeze our way around the broken-down bloodmobile, and I almost stepped on one of the rusty nails from the spike strip. I gasped, then let out a sigh of relief at the close call, since stepping on a rusty nail can be a very dangerous thing.

As soon as Ma Hemoglobin and her gang had escaped, the rent-a-cop regained consciousness with remarkable speed. He let out an exaggerated groan and sat up. According to the front of his shirt, his name was Bill. I might have seen him before, but most security guards are named Bill, so I could easily get them confused.

"We saved most of the cargo," I said, sure he would be relieved. "Ma Hemoglobin got only a handful of packets."

Bill said, "After our tires blew out and I lost consciousness, they broke into the back of the truck. I don't know what they were doing all that time, but that's when the gunfire started. Not sure what they were shooting at, though. I was unconscious and Urg was petrified. Four of those boys jumped him with spray cans of shellac."

"If you were unconscious, how did you see all that?" I asked.

Bill blushed. "I, um, was drifting in and out."

McGoo rapped on the hardened finish of the golem's skin. "His name is Urg?"

"We think so. He's not very articulate."

The golem's eyes flicked back and forth, and he was a quivering mass straining to break free. McGoo considered and shook his head. "It's high-gloss finish instead of satin. That'll be more difficult to dissolve."

"Bubba's has a good health plan," Bill said. "We'll be okay."

Five minutes after they would have been helpful, four squad cars rolled up, lights flashing. As the UQPD cops boiled out of the vehicles, I clapped a hand on McGoo's shoulder and took my leave. "I've got to get out of here as quickly as possible."

McGoo blinked. "Why? The danger's over now."

"I don't want to fill out any paperwork. I'd rather spend time with Alvina."

Chapter Ten

Thanks to Sheyenne running our office in such a professional manner, I was now a respectable businessman—at least that's what she had said when she insisted that I join the Unnatural Quarter's Chamber of Commerce. Worse, she expected me to attend their meetings.

It seemed a waste of time better spent pondering cases, but even Robin weighed in on the matter. "It'll help make connections for us, Dan. These days, it's all about networking. At the Chamber luncheons you'll meet business owners, store managers, restaurateurs, insurance agents, accountants, car salespeople, and all kinds of entrepreneurs. Who knows when one of them might run into a personal disaster or have legal difficulties?"

"We can always hope," I said. "Why don't you go, Robin? It's a luncheon, and you enjoy food more than I do."

"Too much work to do," she replied, which somehow suggested that I did not. "Besides, your name's first on the door. Chambeaux & Deyer Investigations."

"The price of fame," I said with a sigh.

Sheyenne hovered in front of me, sparkling and beautiful. "Don't you want to have lunch with me, Beaux? I'll go along." That was an argument I couldn't refute, so I agreed.

The Chamber of Commerce met in the banquet room of a local supper club, a place often used for wedding or funeral receptions, as well as tightly scheduled and alternating luncheons for the Rotarians, the Oddfellows, the Optimists, the Lions Club, the Mad Scientists Club, the Pointy Hat Society, and many other respected civic organizations. Some businesspeople were so intent on networking that they joined all the clubs, made all the connections, but never had time to run their businesses.

When Sheyenne and I entered the banquet room, many Chamber members were already exchanging business cards, talking over one another as they described "how I can help *you* succeed."

Most of them had joined a new connection-sharing service designed for unnatural businesspeople called ChainedIn. Sheyenne had signed us up, too, but it hadn't yet spawned any business. Some people came to the meetings for the food, others for the conversation; some actually listened to the weekly guest speaker, who was occasionally (though not often) interesting. I attended out of a sense of obligation.

"Dan Shamble!" cried a high-pitched and grating voice. "Good to see you here. Would you like to join my network?" A simian-looking creature in a pinstriped suit that hung loosely on his small angular form scuttled over to me. I recognized Edgar Allan the troll, a real-estate agent who specialized in selling and subletting plots in the Greenlawn Cemetery.

He extended his hand like a magician preparing a card trick. "Here, have my new business card. Have several. You can share them."

"I already have plenty of your old business cards," I said.

"Not this one. It's got my ChainedIn connection on it."

I took the cards because it was easier than *not* taking them. Edgar Allan was persistent and motivated, always pestering us to let him find us new offices, even though Chambeaux & Deyer Investigations had been in our same old building for nearly ten years. Our offices weren't anything special, but it was home.

"How's the real estate business, since the sewer slumlord Ah'Chulhu was sent back to the Nether Dimension?" Sheyenne asked.

"Doing well, doing well," Edgar Allan said, pocketing his extra business cards. "There's always a need for good properties. I'd love to show you some new commercial space. You won't be disappointed."

"I disappoint easily," I warned him.

Sensing he wasn't making headway, the troll spotted a withered old female mummy accompanied by a vivacious werewolf vixen and a buxom slinky vampire with porcelain skin and altogether too much red lipstick. Edgar Allan immediately forgot about us. He grinned at the desiccated woman. "Neffi! Can I follow up on our conversations? I have a new property that would be perfect for expanding the Full Moon Brothel." Neffi, the ancient Egyptian mummy madame, was a shrewd businesswoman who had survived in the Unnatural Quarter through sheer toughness and obstinacy.

I said hi to Neffi, then also greeted the manager of the All Day/All Nite Fitness Center, several pawn shop owners, and Albert Gould from the Ghoul's Diner. I shuddered to think that he might be catering the banquet luncheons.

Sheyenne nudged me with an intangible tingle. "See, Beaux—many of these are clients of yours."

"And I got their business long before we joined the Chamber of Commerce," I pointed out.

As the meeting came to order, I took an empty seat next to an earnest after-life insurance agent in a plaid jacket and an off-putting friendly manner. "I'm fully covered," I explained quickly. "Thanks anyway."

When the supper club's waiters and waitresses served the luncheon, we were surprised to receive only packets of various kinds of NEW! IMPROVED! Monster Chow. The Chamber president, a gregarious hunchback who almost certainly had a successful political career ahead of him, stood up as we all looked dubiously at the packaged and brightly labeled meals offered to us. Sheyenne's plate was empty; apparently, the company hadn't yet figured out how to make Ghost Chow. The package on my plate said Zombie Chow, "Now with more brains!"

The hunchback grinned, lifted up a gavel, and pounded on the banquet room table in front of him. "Your attention, please! I'm sure you've noticed something different for our luncheon today. I'd like to thank Monster Chow Industries for providing our meal.

Since these are free samples, the cost isn't taken out of our budget, so we'll have more money in the treasury for our Fourth of July Parade Fund!"

A smattering of applause went around the table.

"Today we have a very special guest speaker, talking about something that affects everyone in the Quarter, unnaturals and naturals alike. Please give a warm welcome to Mr. Cyrus Redfarb, the new spokesman for Monster Chow Industries."

We all turned to look, curious. Applauding, the other Chamber members faced the back door of the banquet room where Cyrus Redfarb emerged in his V-neck argyle sweater, polyester slacks, and signature loafers. The man's eyes were a startling shade of green, which was odd because they had looked so blue on the TV commercial. A syrupy smile covered his face, and his neat brown hair was perfectly arranged. His movements again seemed awkward. I wondered if he was nervous appearing before our little group. Some monsters in the audience actually whooped and whistled.

"Welcome Chamber members. I'm so glad to be your neighbor." His voice was soft and smooth like black velvet, the kind with gaudy pictures of Elvis painted on it. "Our Monster Chow factory has always been important to the Quarter and important to unnaturals, because it reassures humans that we don't have to eat them."

"But they taste so good," grumbled a ghoul who sat across from Albert. He poked skeptically at his package of Ghoul Chow.

"And so does our product," said Redfarb. "Our new and improved recipes received high marks from our test subjects. This is a new day for Monster Chow Industries, a great expansion, but we have to start with baby steps. Kindness begins at home, and that's why I've come here to give you these samples. The Monster Chow produced under the previous management was nutritious, but a little bland. There's only so much anyone can do with basic texturized protein substitutes. But now that I am the new spokesman, I've brought aboard true culinary wizards, sorceresses of savory, divas of desserts."

I could tell it was a practiced routine, though his shoulders twitched occasionally, as if he were having a muscle spasm. Cyrus

Redfarb had been cycling through the civic organization luncheons, taking his message about new Monster Chow all across the Quarter. "In the outside world, humans fear unnaturals, and we have to assuage that fear. We need to be nice to one another. Monster Chow helps accomplish that. When the news is full of stories like that terrible, nasty, and misunderstood demon Obadeus"—Redfarb clucked his tongue like a school teacher scolding a student—"it undoes so much of the progress we've made since the Big Uneasy. Naturals and unnaturals can be good neighbors. If everyone eats Monster Chow, then humans can sleep well at night."

"I sleep during the day," one vampire accountant mentioned.

Sheyenne leaned closer to me. "It is a nice sentiment. I do wish all the unnaturals and naturals would get along."

"Then we'd hardly have any clients," I said. "At least now we have job security."

I had seen outspoken fringe groups of unnaturals who wanted to go back to the past, when humans were rightly scared of monsters. Some unnaturals didn't want peace and harmony, mostly the surly ones who couldn't make friends anyway. I suspected that the murderous Obadeus wasn't really an anomaly but a symptom of a larger problem of growing anger among low-information unnaturals.

One news crew had interviewed the Suck Dynasty vampire brothers/cousins. "See these fangs," said Ernie, the big bearded leader, using a discolored fingernail to tap a discolored tooth. "They weren't made for drinking shakes out of a package." His yellowed fangs weren't made for being shown on TV either.

I said in a low voice, "Given the alternative, I agree with you, Spooky. Even if monsters stopped being monsters, Chambeaux & Deyer would still have enough divorces, bad business dealings, and lost-and-found items to keep us busy. Let's hope for peace and harmony."

Redfarb continued his speech, extolling the community service work his company was doing. He was bending over backward to reestablish good will throughout the quarter.

"As of this week, we are opening up the Monster Chow factory to public tours, which will include free samples in our tasting room afterward. I encourage you all to sign up and stop by for a visit."

"We just might have to do that," I whispered to Sheyenne.

"Like for a date?" She brightened, literally and figuratively.

As an incentive to buy our loyalty, Redfarb brought out a small box and distributed plastic keychains around the table. "These are Monster Chow keychains. Collector's items—only 20,000 made, each one individually numbered. It's my special gift to you, because in my eyes every one of you is special."

The keychains were flat plastic tchotchkes with the Monster Chow logo on the front and a textured design printed on the back, along with a serial number. As the freebie box went around the banquet room table, the vampire accountant who had spoken up earlier pocketed two and passed the rest on. Edgar Allan admired them, holding one up in his thin, gray fingers. "Oooh, individually numbered!"

I scrutinized one of the keychains, then moved to put it back in the box. "I don't need a new keychain."

Sheyenne stopped me. "That's not polite, Beaux. We can throw it away later."

I slipped it into my jacket pocket. Sheyenne always has excellent business sense.

CHAPTER ELEVEN

obin spent the afternoon poring over paperwork for the Talbot & Knowles hostile-takeover case, trying to find a loophole, or a noose, that Fletcher's ghost could fit through. I decided to help by leaving her alone.

A tall, hairy Bigfoot strode through the office door, ducking low to avoid banging his head on the lintel. When we didn't notice the enormous figure at first, he loudly jingled a box for donations. "Help the chickens?"

The big furry creature with big furry feet had been hired by Maynard Kleck of the Agricultural Avian Activists, AAA, to raise money for the construction of more community coops to house the Quarter's feral chicken population.

"How'd you get talked into that job?" I asked the shaggy beast. It was hard to look him in the eye; he always seemed to be just out of focus.

"Normally, my friends and I collect for the Bigfoot/Yeti Visibility Society, but we also freelance."

"The Bigfoot/Yeti Visibility Society? Are there many Bigfoots out there?"

"It's a very large organization," he said in a deep growly voice. "And we prefer *Bigfeet* as the plural." The furry shelf of his brows hooded over as he narrowed his yellow eyes. "I've been to your

Kevin J. Anderson

office three times in the past month, Mr. Chambeaux. Didn't you notice? Don't you remember?"

I honestly didn't, and the Bigfoot seemed dismayed. "We get a lot of solicitors," I said. "Umm, did we give you a donation?" I looked to Sheyenne, and she rustled through the records at her desk.

The Bigfoot let out a long, deep-throated sigh. "We're down-trodden, unseen members of society...."

To assuage my guilt, I put a dollar into his collection bucket, thereby acknowledging that the feral chickens were indeed a problem. The Bigfoot shuffled out of the office, and I soon forgot about him.

Alvina was spending the day with us until we eventually came up with a longer-term solution than just taking turns between my apartment and McGoo's. For now, the kid was still settling in. She seemed remarkably resilient and good natured. In Alvina's previous life, her mother had been gone half the time, and as a matter of survival, she had learned how to feed herself, making macaroni and cheese, tuna sandwiches, or breakfast cereal. Now that Alvina was a vampire, the simple, higher-carb options weren't palatable any more. At least she was fond of Unlucky Charms cereal, which had all the protein and plasma a young, growing vampire might need. It said so right on the box.

I was relieved the kid could take care of herself, because even though we were glad to have fresh young blood in the offices, none of us knew what to do with a needy child. Alvina occupied herself just fine, though. She happily set up her lavender laptop at the far end of the conference room table while Robin worked at sorting papers and digging out folders from bankers' boxes.

Sheyenne followed me in as I carried another box for Robin. The kid sat quietly with the adjustable chair cranked to its max height. Looking at her, I wished I'd known her before the skateboard accident and the botched blood transfusion. What had Alvina been like as a normal little girl?

I didn't want her to think of me as a deadbeat dad. Watching her intent expression as she worked on her laptop, I blurted out, "Alvina, you know that McGoo and I didn't abandon you, right? Your mom honestly never told us you existed."

68

The girl looked up at me with round eyes that belonged on a really kitschy painting. "She barely noticed that I existed, and I was *living* with her." Alvina sighed. "It sucks to be invisible."

"The Bigfeet and yetis would agree with you," I said.

Sheyenne's expression filled with warm understanding. She drifted closer to the vampire girl. "Alvina's an interesting name. I don't think I've ever heard it before."

"Mom was hoping I'd be a boy. She named me after a character from those chipmunk movies. I was a chubby, cute baby."

I remembered how much Rhonda loved the chipmunk movies.

"You're still cute," Sheyenne said, but Alvina didn't take it as a compliment. Instead she hunched closer to the screen of her laptop, and her fingers scurried over the keys.

Interested in what my daughter, or potential daughter, was doing, I said, "I can show you how to find cute kitten videos. There's a really good one with two calico kittens playing with a giant spider."

"Those videos are for kids," Alvina said, a little defensive. "I'm doing work, building my fan base, expanding my social media reach."

"Social media outreach? You mean like …" I fumbled for the correct cool and modern terms. "Like a MySpace page?"

Alvina gave me a withering look that expressed her embarrassment that I was one of her fathers. "I write a personal-interest blog, and I'm getting more and more hits every day. It's just part of my social media platform. I have a profile on all the popular services, and I cross post. I'm working on metadata and search-engine optimization to attract more views, and I hope to monetize it through sponsors and online ads."

"I knew you were smart," I said, more convinced than ever that she was my daughter, not McGoo's. "Do you have a ChainedIn profile?"

Again, she gave me that look. "Of course I do. Everybody has one."

If I didn't have such pallid skin, I would have blushed.

Troubled, Robin looked up from sorting papers in the boxes. "Honey, it's dangerous for a little girl to be so active online. There are some bad people out there who do terrible things to children. Pedophiles and child molesters."

"The real monsters," I muttered. "You also have to watch out for internet trolls, and here in the Quarter you have to watch out for real trolls."

"Don't worry." Alvina continued staring at her screen while tapping rapidly on the keys. "I have a completely different online identity and a fake avatar named Alvin. My profile says I'm a fourteen-year-old boy. It's my secret identity, and sometimes he seems even more real than I am."

"Your mother must be so proud," I said.

"My mother never reads my blog."

"I'll read it. What's your blog called? What's it about?"

"I Was a Teenage Vampire," she said. "I'm only ten, but it's really not much of a stretch since I somehow got yanked into puberty. Somebody needs to speak for all the vamps caught in the transformation during puberty, and I sure understand the problems they face."

"Yeah, a lot of people use skateboards." I agreed, thinking of her tragic accident.

"And there are a lot of bad blood transfusions," Robin added.

Alvina was glad to talk about her blog. "When I turned, I was preserved in the body of a ten-year-old girl forever, because vampires don't age."

"Some parents wish their daughters would never grow up," Sheyenne said. "It makes them feel old."

"But a lot of little girls like me *want* to grow up, and now I'm stuck like this. Forever!" Alvina said, frowning. "I guess my body chemistry was already changing. I had just started full-on puberty, and the vampire blood accelerated the process. It sucks." As she explained, she sighed. "I might be getting acne. Even my vampire healing ability isn't strong enough to cure pimples."

I shook my head. I'd never thought about that before. The awkward teenage years, the social expectations, the peer pressure. Going through it for a few years was bad enough, but to be trapped at junior high or high school age for the rest of your life ... "Yeah, that sucks," I agreed.

Alvina continued, "I've chatted with hundreds of teen vampires online, and they all face the same problems. My blog community is a support group. We have a forum discussion, special guests that do interviews or guest posts."

"Sounds like you're shining a light on a problem even more important than the plight of the feral chickens," Sheyenne said.

"Going through a life-to-unlife transition is rough on everybody," I said, remembering when I was a regular guy, a private detective trying to make enough money to pay the rent. Then, *wham!*—Sheyenne got killed. And, *bam!*—I got killed. That's enough to mess up anybody's daily business. "I'm one of the lucky ones."

"My mom never understood any of that," Alvina said. "After I turned, she said I was a freak. I got bad grades in school because I couldn't go out in the sun for gym class. I couldn't try out for cheerleading. I was sleepy during my classes because I was up all night, but I'm *supposed* to be nocturnal! It's like my teachers didn't even know what a vampire was."

"Public school districts are required to make accommodations in cases like that," Robin said with a warning tone in her voice.

"Only if your parent or guardian files a request." Alvina was starting to sound bitter.

Sheyenne said consolingly, "You're here in the Unnatural Quarter now, Sweetheart, where you belong. You're with us. We're your new family."

"And we'll all be just fine," I added.

The kid brightened. "Does that mean you'll really read my blog?"

"Every entry," I promised.

Pleased, she went back to typing.

CHAPTER TWELVE

etting a good example for Alvina, I made up my mind I wouldn't stay out late drinking in the Goblin Tavern. Instead, I went early so I could meet McGoo for their special Unhappy Hour.

Unhappy Hour wasn't just a cute marketing gimmick. In her hoarse cigarette-and-scream damaged voice, Francine explained the logic as she poured our usual beers (nothing fancy tonight). "Happy people have nothing to worry about. *Unhappy* people, though, like to drink. That's why we have Unhappy Hour. It brings more customers into the tavern."

How could I argue with that?

McGoo seemed tired as he slouched on his barstool. "I've been wandering the beat all day, and my feet are sore. The chief is getting frustrated with all these reports."

"What's up? I thought everyone would be relaxed once we took care of the demon Obadeus. One big happy monster-filled city."

"You're right, Shamble. I wasn't expecting anything bigger than jaywalking tickets and domestic disputes, but we've had a rash of missing persons reports—at least fifteen mostly upstanding citizens just gone in the past week. *Poof!*" He raised his hands and almost knocked over his beer, which taught him not to be so enthusiastic with his gesticulations.

"Half your job seems to be finding missing persons," I said, recalling numerous previous cases. "They should hire a private investigator."

"I'll send them your way and get the work off my desk."

McGoo slurped his beer and wiped foam off his lips. "Chief told me to keep my eye out for any vanished people ... but how am I supposed to see them if they're *vanished?* That makes no sense."

"Send over the pictures, McGoo, and I'll keep an eye out too. I do a lot of aimless wandering around the Quarter."

"I thought you were doing detective work."

"That's what I call it. The cases don't solve themselves."

With so many missing people in the Unnatural Quarter from month to month, there had even been a reality show in development, "Missing Monsters of the Week," an exposé of the seedy underbelly in our society. But one of the producers had wanted to make it into a sitcom and the show fell apart due to creative differences. Now the UQPD—and helpful citizens like me—had to rely on spreading the word the old-fashioned way.

McGoo and I stayed for only one beer, feeling the unfamiliar weight of parental responsibility.

We left the Goblin Tavern with a farewell wave to Francine, but she was preoccupied with a dapper older vampire customer. He seemed enchanted with her company, and Francine wasn't going to miss an opportunity. Old One Fang, as we called him, had been coming in more often recently to strike up casual conversation with Francine. One Fang seemed lonely and oblivious to the fact that female bartenders are supposed to flirt a little with all customers. In Francine's case customers considered her flirting the equivalent of assault, but the dapper old vampire seemed convinced she was sincere, as did Francine. He even had one of the Monster Chow collectible numbered keychains, and he dangled it suggestively, as if hoping Francine would take the hint. Who was I to squelch a budding romance?

As we walked together down the street, McGoo wore a wistful smile. Tonight it was his turn to have Alvina. "You know, Shamble, I'm sort of looking forward to this. I like the kid. She's been trying to teach me checkers, but the strategy's complicated. I don't know why Rhonda had so much trouble with her. Alvina's clever, funny, and polite."

"Probably because Rhonda is none of those things," I said.

McGoo nodded. "That's it."

We passed an abandoned storefront. Inside, a small-statured fuzzy-faced werewolf was busy banging nails into two-by-fours and stringing rolls of chicken wire. I recognized Maynard Kleck from the AAA posters, and I could see his passion for helping displaced barnyard fowl.

"Everything all right in here?" McGoo said.

"Yes, yes, just fine. Doing a public service."

Kleck was a determined but scrawny werewolf with a pointed snout and fluttering paws. Despite his energy and determination, he had little talent for the carpentry work in which he was engaged. Only by inference did I guess that the ramshackle, off-kilter structures were supposed to be chicken coops.

"Welcome to my new flock flophouse," he said. "It's for the feral chickens. You might have seen our posters? My organization has many supporters, and I've raised enough money to buy this roll of chicken wire."

"You're building coops, then?" I asked.

"Think of it as a homeless shelter for birds. If you're a feral chicken, this is practically a luxury hotel. All those poor lost chickens with no place to go … What are we supposed to do with them?"

"You could eat them," McGoo suggested. "That would take care of the problem and solve world hunger at the same time."

Kleck recoiled in horror and dropped his hammer with a clatter on the floor. The chicken wire flopped loose and began to roll itself back up.

"My friend's just kidding," I said, then muttered in a lower voice, "There aren't nearly enough chickens here to solve world hunger, McGoo."

"Think of those poor birds, turned loose through no fault of their own, abandoned as eggs," Kleck said with a despairing groan deep in his throat. "Some well-meaning person turned them loose in the Quarter so they could be free, but we can't just leave them that way. We've got to do something about it. Once I get these coops done, the feral chickens can come here to roost."

I looked at the fuzzy-faced werewolf. His claws made holding nails and hammers difficult. "You look like a fox in a henhouse."

Kleck fumed. "Stereotypes. I hate stereotypes! I don't need to kill chickens in the wild. Monster Chow serves all my needs. I'm not even tempted, I assure you. But the work never ends, and funding is sometimes difficult." He turned a predatory glare at McGoo and me. "Would you care to make a donation?"

"I already gave at the office." I had done it to please Sheyenne and Robin, not out of any sense of moral obligation.

"So did I," McGoo said

I hate it when policemen lie.

Urging McGoo to leave before Kleck could apply more pressure, I backed out of the cluttered storefront. "Well, we have to be going, but we wish you luck, Mr. Kleck. When will you be open for business?"

He indicated the rickety tangles of chicken wire and collapsed two-by-fours. "Any time now."

McGoo and I parted ways at the corner, where he had to turn down the main boulevard to get back to his apartment. By now, Sheyenne would have taken Alvina over to wait for him, and he didn't want to make our daughter feel abandoned again.

I headed toward the Chambeaux & Deyer offices by my usual route, taking a shortcut into a long, dark, and narrow alley. It reminded me of the alley near the Basilisk nightclub where I'd been shot in the back of the head. I made the walk cheerier by whistling aloud.

Trash was strewn in the corners and gutters. Moisture dripped from the overhead eaves and trickled down rusty drainpipes, creating smears of fresh green algae on the brick walls. Rats scuttled along squeaking as they discussed the good garbage they had found.

I whistled the song "Spooky," which Sheyenne had sung for me at the nightclub. That was one of the many reasons I'd fallen in love with her. She carried a tune much better than I did.

Unfortunately, my whistling drowned out other noises ... scuttling, the skitter of claws, a strange and sinister clucking. I paused and listened as I spotted a flash of white feathers, then movement, a flapping of wings behind a dumpster.

A chicken heaved itself up to land on top of the dumpster, where it perched, looking more like a vulture than raw McNugget material. Feeling good, I chuckled. "Hey, chicken, if you're looking for a place to sleep, Maynard Kleck's opening a flock flophouse. You could be the first customer."

I didn't actually expect the chicken to understand what I was saying. I'm not stupid.

But the barnyard bird did respond to my voice. It raised its head, turned its yellow eyes toward me—glowing, monstrous eyes.

With a stir of clucking and bawking, another chicken emerged from the garbage bags inside the dumpster, flapping up to take a position next to the first chicken. Its eyes also flared with an evil light. The creature's beak looked like a sharp spear point.

Behind me in the alley, back the way I had come, more chickens emerged from discarded boxes. One carried a huge dead rat clamped in its beak.

In the eaves above, I heard more clucking. I looked up to see five feral chickens glowering down at me, as if I were road kill just waiting to be inspected. It looked like a full dozen.

"Easy now, fellas," I said, not willing to admit that I felt nervous surrounded by a bunch of chickens.

The first bird cawed at me like a battle cry, and in a wild, raucous chorus, all the chickens began a cacophony like a barnyard party. I slid my .38 from the pocket of my sport jacket, wondering how I would ever explain opening fire on a flock of chickens.

But as I looked into their nefarious glowing eyes, I realized this wasn't just a flock. No, that wasn't the right word for it. This was a *pack*, a vicious group of predatory birds that had no intention of laying eggs or being served up on a rotisserie.

Then they attacked.

The two chickens on top of the dumpster lunged, flapping their heavy wings in cumbersome flight. They battered me in a flurry of white horror. They pecked at me with their beaks, and I flailed my hands to knock them aside. I held the pistol in my right hand, hesitant to open fire, but I took off the fedora and swooped it from side to side.

More vicious chickens dropped down from above, leaping off the gutters and dive-bombing me, cawing and pecking, scratching with their claws.

Under such a fowl onslaught, I began to run. The chickens were merciless, pursuing me and looking for blood. They struck like a unified organism, going for the jugular—but for me the jugular just leaks, and I can always be refilled at the embalming parlor.

I fired my pistol twice, killing one of the chickens and winging another one. But that only made them more outraged.

Even though the loud bang scattered them temporarily, I kept running. I finally lurched out of the alley and into the wider street, bolting from the angry clucking and flapping of wings behind me. My jacket was covered with feathers and smeared with chicken shit.

When I reached up, I could feel all the little holes and tears in my gray skin. I was leaking from multiple wounds. The jacket wasn't the only thing that needed a touchup.

I was never going to donate to Maynard Kleck and his organization again. Those chickens were dangerous.

"Stupid peckers," I muttered as I hurried back to the office.

Chapter Thirteen

When a zombie gets damaged in the line of duty, who are you going to call?

The Unnatural Quarter has many service providers who combine the arts of taxidermy and mortuary science. After being killed the first time, I'd received the standard funeral touchup routine, appropriate makeup and fillers so that I looked more handsome than ever, although I was dead at the time. I awakened several days later and clawed my way out of my grave. Since then, I've been battered often enough that I knew my mortician/taxidermy provider quite well.

Miss Lujean Eccles had dedicated her life to preserving dead things. Her boutique business, the Patchup Parlor, was in a well-tended Victorian mansion landscaped with ominous-looking dead trees. The place had won Haunted House of the Year three times since the Big Uneasy.

Best of all, Miss Eccles made house calls.

After the vicious chicken attack, Sheyenne fussed over me, even though I was embarrassed by the ordeal. She called Miss Eccles, who came to our offices bringing her carpetbag full of supplies, her bottomless-pit repair kit with putty, spools of thread, flesh-colored rubber cement and covering tape, as well as wooden dowels for physical support.

McGoo arrived shortly afterward, quite worried, with Alvina in tow. The kid stared at me in disbelief. "You look terrible. That's worse than acne all over your skin."

"We'll get him fixed right up, don't you worry," Sheyenne said.

I found it heartwarming. "I don't mind when people worry about me. It shows you care."

"We all care, Dan." Robin emerged from her office, where she'd pulled an all-nighter and was about to start an all-dayer. "We have to file a complaint with City Fowl Control. This is getting out of hand."

Amused, McGoo crossed his arms over his blue uniform. "Let me get this straight, Shamble. You were attacked by a flock of—"

"A *pack*." I cut him off. "I was attacked by monsters. Let's just leave it at that."

"Whatever you say." He snickered, flapped his elbows, and said, "Bawk! Bawk! Hey Shamble—why did the zombie cross the road?" This wasn't a good time for humor. "To show the chicken that it could be done!"

Miss Eccles nudged them aside so she would have room to do her work. Lujean Eccles was in her late fifties with gray-brown hair piled in a beehive hairdo like a parasitic alien creature occupying the top of her skull. She came close and inspected my skin. "My, my! These look like they were caused by ... beaks."

"Yes, large killer birds," I said.

"Chickens," McGoo added, helpfully.

"That flock is still on the loose," I said. "I killed one, winged another."

"Man, I used to love chicken wings," McGoo added.

Robin frowned. "Maynard Kleck's organization says that the chickens are just unloved and misunderstood, that they all have good hearts."

"I like chicken hearts, too," McGoo said, "wrapped in bacon and broiled. I still say the best way to solve the feral chicken problem is to eat them."

Miss Eccles reached into her carpetbag and removed needles, spools of thread, rolls of patch-up tape, tubes of goop, and flesh-colored makeup. She set to work, dabbing at the holes in my face and my neck.

"While you're at it, can you plug the hole in his forehead?" Alvina asked. "It's kind of gross, makes him look like a pencil sharpener."

"I think it makes him look rugged and handsome," Sheyenne said.

"Yes, I can fill it," said Miss Eccles. I'd had it done before, and I knew the putty didn't last very long. Still, if it made Alvina happy … "Might be better if I filled the head cavity with straw, just to provide support."

McGoo couldn't resist a quick little sing-song, "If I only had a brain …"

"My brain works just fine, even with a hole in it," I said defensively.

Since I had to stay still while the mortician/taxidermist concentrated on her work, I needed to distract McGoo—not that I had to worry about laughing at his jokes, but if he even made me grimace, that would ruin the new makeup job. "Any word on Ma Hemoglobin and the boys? Did the rest of the delivery from Bubba's Bloodmobile get to its destination?"

McGoo, always a cop, got back to business. "They stole one crate of rare blood types en route to the blood bank, but the rest of the delivery was a commercial order for some vampire disco and meat market called Overbite."

"Never heard of it," I said. "Not that I have much cause to frequent vampire meat markets."

"Ma Hemoglobin and her gang are infamous," McGoo said, "but they aren't very competent for all that firepower. They waylaid the bloodmobile delivery, but didn't manage to steal much of the product. One raid on a bloodmobile isn't going to keep them satisfied for long."

"Maybe we could launch a flock of chickens at them?" Alvina suggested. "Just imagine if those birds could use their powers for good rather than evil! I think I'll blog about it … you know, civic responsibility."

"All teenage vampires need to learn about civic responsibility," I agreed.

"Hold still," Miss Eccles scolded as she dabbed on more makeup over the rubber cement that patched my skin. She added a glob of putty to the middle of my forehead, but it didn't quite match the rest of the color and merely drew attention to the missing bullet hole. She rummaged in her carpetbag, replaced the spools of thread, then pulled out a small lollipop and handed it to me.

She clicked her bag shut and paused, turning to me. "I've been meaning to ask, since you're a detective and all ... have you had any complaints about Cyrus Redfarb, the new representative of Monster Chow Industries?"

"We just saw him at the Chamber of Commerce yesterday," Sheyenne said. "Nobody's complaining about the free samples."

"The guy seems as bland and sweet as corn syrup," I said. "Has he been causing you problems?"

"Oh, no, no. He doesn't even know I exist, but ... have you watched his advertisements on TV? If you look in his eyes you'll see that one day they're blue, another day they're green. Yesterday they were brown. And other little details don't ring true, at least in my professional opinion."

"What sort of details?" Robin held her yellow legal pad, and the ensorcelled pencil hung poised to take notes.

"Oh, from a mortician and taxidermist's perspective. I considered taking him up on his offer to tour the Monster Chow factory, but I'm just an old woman, and I would never go alone." She looked at me. "Maybe you'd be willing to accompany me? In exchange for my services, of course." She gestured to the repair bag.

Sheyenne brightened. "Beaux, you promised you'd take me there on a date."

"I suppose that kills two birds with one stone," I said, then thought again of the bloodthirsty feral chickens that had caused me so many problems. "In fact, I'd like to kill a lot more than two birds, and I might need to use something bigger than a stone."

"Can I go along, too?" Alvina asked. "Maybe they'll give out free samples of Unlucky Charms."

Sheyenne flitted to her computer, called up the website for Monster Chow Industries. "I'll book us for a tour."

Chapter Fourteen

A tour of the Monster Chow factory might have seemed like an interesting date, but as our group grew larger it turned into a family outing. I took the keys to the company car— a battered, rusty old Ford Maverick we had dubbed the "Pro Bono Mobile"—and left Robin hard at work in her office, digging through piles of paperwork regarding the Talbot & Knowles blood bars.

With Sheyenne drifting at my side, I led Lujean Eccles and Alvina outside to where the car was parked. A zombie, a ghost, a vampire girl, and a taxidermist—it sounded like the start of one of McGoo's bad jokes. As we piled into the creaking Maverick, I couldn't help but think of those vacation comedy movies....

Barely able to contain her excitement, Alvina bounced in the back seat, making the suspension creak. "I like this car. It's a lot nicer than my mom's car."

"Very sorry to hear that." I started the engine, which coughed and popped, then purred like an asthmatic lion.

"Thank you for driving, Mr. Chambeaux," said Miss Eccles. "My reactions aren't as good as they used to be."

"Neither are mine, but I did qualify for my undead driver's license." On a scale of One to Awful, my driving skills were about average in the Unnatural Quarter. If the DMV could issue licenses to drivers with lobster claws and slimy tentacles that were barely able to grip a steering wheel or use the gear-shift lever, I wasn't a zombie anyone had to worry about.

The Monster Chow factory was a huge operation in the industrial district, and expanding rapidly as demand for various unnatural flavors continued to grow. Cavernous warehouse buildings and shipping depots sprawled around the main factory. New processing centers were being built on land that had, until recently, been a municipal park. A burly gray-furred werewolf drove a bulldozer, knocking down an empty swing set and climbing gym, then pushed the debris into a pile with smashed picnic tables. In the open warehouses, forklifts buzzed back and forth, lifting large family-size sacks of Monster Chow, along with boxes containing individual snack packets. Giant letters on the outer wall of each warehouse labeled that particular depot by the food it processed: Vampire, Werewolf, Zombie, Ghoul, Mummy. The largest warehouse said Miscellaneous.

The factory itself was a squarish brown-brick building with few windows, no landscaping, and three tall smokestacks that belched gray smoke into the air. It reminded me of a public school.

As I drove the Pro Bono Mobile across the parking lot, Lujean Eccles frowned at the widely separated warehouses. "I hope the tour doesn't take us to all of those. My joints would never manage so much walking—and neither would yours, Mr. Chambeaux."

"I get them greased up regularly whenever I go to the embalming parlor," I said. "Though I'm still a little stiff in the mornings."

"I thought you were a stiff all the time!" Alvina giggled at her own joke. Maybe she was McGoo's daughter after all....

I slid the Maverick into a space in Visitor Parking right next to a spot that said Unwelcome Visitor Parking, where the painted lines were too narrow to accommodate most vehicles.

As we climbed out of the Pro Bono Mobile, I drew a deep breath of the wafting roasty-toasty smell of the chow being produced in the factory ovens. Even though my senses were dulled, I found it tantalizing. "It almost makes you want to become an unnatural."

Miss Eccles sniffed the air. "Well, not exactly."

We strolled together up to the main glass door, which I held open for Sheyenne, Alvina, and Miss Eccles. After checking in with the receptionist and showing our printed tour tickets, we were directed to a "waiting parlor" where we joined a group of trolls, vampires, and human schoolchildren who had been bussed in on a field trip. Colorful labels of new products from Monster Chow Industries hung in frames around the room.

At the far end of the waiting parlor hung a portrait of the all-too-prominent company spokesman Cyrus Redfarb, whose handsome face wore an endearing smile, much like paintings of dictators from tinpot republics around the world. Considering that Redfarb had only recently taken over his position, he had already made an ambitious number of commercials and public service announcements in the factory's own video studio.

Alvina went over to go talk to a freckle-faced human boy about her age. "Are you afraid of monsters?" she asked, flashing her fangs.

The boy made a sound like "Meep!" and ran to his teacher, who glared at us.

"That's not helping calm fears among humans, Alvina," I pointed out.

"Just trying to be friendly," she said. "I thought he might like to read my blog. It's not just for teenage vampires, you know."

When it was time for our appointed tour, the door opened and Redfarb himself stood there in his signature V-neck argyle sweater. He briskly rubbed his long-fingered hands together, as if eager to have a new batch of converts, but his movements were somewhat uncoordinated, as if the right hand didn't know what the left was doing. That's a common thing in many large corporations.

When Redfarb smiled at us, I sensed something odd about his appearance, but I couldn't figure out what ... until I realized that his eyes were brown as opposed to the blue or green I had seen before.

"Welcome, neighbors! I'm here to show you our marvelous operation. You can already smell our delicious denatured meat-protein product, which is formed, seasoned, and carefully baked into oh-so-tasty morsels. At the end of the tour, you'll all get to sample species-appropriate meals." He looked to the teacher and the group of normal schoolchildren. "And for our human guests, we might be able to find a special treat or two!" The kids smiled uncertainly.

Redfarb continued, "Most of all, you'll be happy to know that with so many flavorful varieties, monsters certainly don't need to eat people."

"Even if they're delicious?" asked one of the trolls.

"The new Monster Chow is even more delicious and maybe a little addictive!" Redfarb replied with a calm smile. His face twitched as if he had indigestion, and then the smile settled into place again.

Holding up his hand so we could follow, he led us on through large swinging doors onto the factory floor, past warning signs that said Authorized Unnaturals Only. Redfarb gave the sign a dismissive wave. "I'll keep you safe, but remember this is an industrial area." More for the showmanship than for actual safety enhancement, he handed out hardhats, which Alvina and the other schoolchildren thoroughly enjoyed. Sheyenne had to use her poltergeist skills to keep her plastic helmet levitating in place.

The sealed concrete floor was striped with colored lines that extended in every direction, apparently designating paths, but to me they looked like the aftermath of an excessively violent Silly String duel.

High up on the walls around the factory floor were large television screens that displayed bland safety announcements, cheery inspirational phrases, and the local weather report. For special occasions, they could broadcast company-wide announcements from Cyrus Redfarb, possibly even sporting events.

Alvina trooped ahead with Sheyenne beside her, which made me ponder how Sheyenne would have been as a mother. Sweet and welcoming and warmhearted to everyone, my girlfriend showed a clear maternal instinct. For me, I wasn't convinced I'd have been much good as a father, but I found myself in that situation anyway. Alvina was growing on me.

Miss Eccles remained silent, concentrating on something. When I dropped back to walk beside her, I noticed she was more interested in watching Redfarb than the industrial operation. "What are you looking at?"

"The back of that man's head."

I looked at Redfarb's head, noting his dark hair, the high collar of his dress shirt that poked above the soft sweater. "It doesn't look all that interesting to me."

"Because you're not skilled in taxidermy," she said, but didn't explain further.

Redfarb led us first to a row of large metal basins that towered ten feet above the floor, deep round containers like huge bathtubs. He gestured to a set of reinforced metal stairs that ran up to a narrow walkway around the top of the basins.

"If you'll take turns, you can go up to see where the magic happens. These seed-material basins are the start of the process. We take denatured meat proteins and grow them rapidly into the delicious texturized substance that forms the basis for all of our chow. We call this the monster mash."

The group of schoolchildren trooped up the steps and then back down the other side. I let Alvina go ahead of me, and when I reached the top, I peered down into the vat to see a blobby mass of grayish dough that burbled and crawled as spinners turned it, kneaded it, popped it. It reminded me of a gigantic bread-making machine.

"That's a science experiment gone wrong," said Alvina.

Redfarb heard her. "No, this is a science experiment gone *right*. Each vat contains distinctive proteins tailored to a specific segment of our customer base. It's all entirely unnatural." He paused, waiting for a reaction. "Heh, heh. Just a little humor there."

"Just a little," I agreed. Alvina and I descended the metal stairs so the rest of the tour group could have a look.

"It's something like sourdough starter," he continued. "We use the original substance as a seed base, which is cloned, and the rest of the cells just grow and grow like a chia pet, enough to feed plenty of monsters."

Next, Redfarb led us along the factory floor to where the roasty-toasty smell grew thicker and the temperature increased. We passed rattling conveyor belts where pans of the dough slid under automated cutters and formers that pressed the dough into appropriate shapes.

"After we extrude the denatured protein into delicious bite-sized pieces, the dough goes into our ovens, where the kibble is baked to perfection and sent off to the packaging rooms. We have vampire flavor, werewolf flavor, and even zombie flavor." He glanced at me.

I asked, "Don't you mean flavors *for* vampires, werewolves, and zombies?"

Redfarb maintained his plastic smile and shrugged, with one shoulder moving differently from the other. "Our test-marketing groups didn't rate those labels as highly."

"I guess not everybody is as careful with words as I am," I said. Sheyenne let out a snort.

"Where does the starter material come from?" asked the freckle-faced boy that Alvina had frightened.

The boy's stern teacher gave him a quick slap on the back of the head. "This is an educational tour. You're not supposed to ask questions."

"Now, now, I don't mind," Redfarb said. "Our chefs and food specialists have done an enormous amount of research to get the flavors exactly right."

"But where does it come from in the first place?" the boy persisted, which earned him another smack from his teacher.

"I'm new here, young man. Only a few days on the job," Redfarb explained. "I'll have to get back to you on that."

I found it strange that the man didn't know such a basic answer, until I realized he was just being evasive.

For a few moments we watched the large toaster ovens that had come from old crematoriums put out of business by the Big Uneasy, before Redfarb moved us along again. "Now everyone, shall we go to the tasting room? We have many new exotic flavors, but nothing for the human children, alas." He paused with a sincere frown. "Except maybe … cookies!"

"Cookies!" cried the kids from the human middle school.

As we walked past the ovens, I bent down to retrieve something long and white caught beneath one of the conveyor belts. A feather—a chicken feather. I wondered if Monster Chow Industries was capturing and converting some of the Quarter's all-too-numerous feral chickens.

If so, I certainly wouldn't complain. We moved off to the tasting room.

CHAPTER FIFTEEN

The next day Alvina accompanied McGoo while he walked his beat around the Quarter, eager to tell him all about the Monster Chow tour. As they left our offices, McGoo cut a fairly impressive figure in his blue uniform and patrolman's cap, but even having such an adorable young girl at his side, I doubted anyone would give him an Officer Friendly award. She wore a floppy hat and lots of sunscreen, promising us she would stick to the shadows.

Robin watched them go, letting out a contemplative sigh. "We really are going to have to find some kind of daycare or a school for her."

"She's ten and going on puberty. I don't think daycare is the answer. Or nightcare."

"But Alvina's definitely school age," Sheyenne said as she straightened the papers on her desk, "and she will be for a long, long time to come. Imagine being stuck in seventh grade for decades."

"I didn't like seventh grade even once," I said.

At the end of the factory tour, after we had the option to taste samples of the various Chow flavors in little paper cups, we had compared the nibbles. Even the easily-spooked schoolboy took a tiny taste of Mummy Chow, which he claimed tasted like dust. The tour members unanimously agreed that the sriracha-lime Werewolf Chow was the best, the *au naturel* Ghoul Chow the worst ("It's species specific," Redfarb explained, "and something of an acquired taste.") Nothing in particular, not even the premium Zombie Chow, woke up my palate. At the end, Redfarb had insisted that we all take keychains as gifts, but I begged off since we already had one on Sheyenne's desk. Sheyenne and I loaded up on free samples of vampire-based breakfast cereals, thus providing Alvina with a feast for dinner, a midnight snack, and another snack in the morning. That seemed less dangerous than me trying to cook for her.

After the kid left with McGoo, I got ready to go wandering around the Quarter in my usual routine of solving cases. The flesh cement and stitched-up repairs from the chicken peck marks were blending in, but the putty-patched hole in my forehead was already starting to wear thin, partly because I kept fiddling with it. Alvina thought I looked good. Sheyenne thought I always looked good.

Before I could get out the door, though, a stranger barged into the office. Assuming it was a new client, I put on my most professional manner, only to have my hopes dashed.

He was an olive-skinned man with wavy black hair and a larger-than-average smile. His dark brown eyes glittered. He wore a pinstriped suit and held a briefcase. In his other hand, he carried a walking stick that served as a weapon as well as an affectation. On the back of one hand, a star tattoo signified that he belonged to the Necromancer's Guild; on his other hand, a tattoo of a hashtag certified that he was wise in the ways of social media and the online distribution of spells.

He stepped up to Sheyenne's desk with a formal nod. "Greetings, my satisfied customers. I am Alterro the Great, and I believe you're familiar with my wildly popular company Spells 'N Such?" He raised his eyebrows expectantly.

I recalled the flyer we'd received in the mail with the free sample spell. "Subscription service, right?"

"Mail order spells," Sheyenne said. "Yes, we got your flyer, Mr. Alterro. The demon-shattering spell proved surprisingly handy."

He brightened. "Indeed! I'd like to get a testimonial."

"Not a spell we're likely to use often, though," I said.

Resting his weight on his walking stick, Alterro set the briefcase on Sheyenne's desk and snapped it open with one hand. "I saw on the news how you used my magic to defeat that bloodthirsty demon." His tone became sterner. "I was disappointed you didn't mention the source. An acknowledgement would have done wonders for my business."

"It never occurred to me, sorry," I said. "I don't normally give testimonials."

Alterro rummaged around in the contents of his briefcase. "I've been spreading the word myself. I'd like to put your picture and a gushing blurb in my next mailing. It'll be great: Dan Shamble, the famous fictional detective, using one of my spells to solve a horrific case."

"Those stories are exaggerated," I said. "I'm just a normal, everyday zombie detective." I wondered how Mavis and Alma's ghost writer was going to dramatize this one.

"But you certainly realize how useful Spells 'N Such can be." Alterro was persistent. "I have a range of subscription plans. No doubt, you'll want our deluxe package?"

"Robin!" I called. "We need your expertise."

She hurried out of her office, looking stern. "Is there a legal emergency?"

"There might be," I said.

Alterro gave her a gentlemanly smile. "Ah, is this the lady of the house?"

That was the wrong thing to say. Her expression hardened. "No, it's the lawyer of the office. How can we help you?"

"I provided a free sample spell to advertise my monthly spell-subscription service. Since Mr. Chambeaux used it to destroy the demon Obadeus, I'd like to get paid for it."

"Paid?" I said. "It was a free sample."

Alterro brushed down the front of his pinstriped suit. "You don't understand anything about marketing if you think that a free sample means it's actually free. Didn't you read the fine print?"

"There was no fine print," Sheyenne said. "I read the whole flyer front and back."

He made a dismissive gesture. "The fine print comes in the next mailing. And you should know that a free sample incurs certain obligations."

Robin gave me a concerned look. "He expects some token form of payment."

Looking pleased, Alterro withdrew several flyers. "Now, let me describe my various Spells 'N Such plans. We have a specialized monthly option that contains love spells only...."

"Dan doesn't need those," Sheyenne said, a little too quickly.

He picked up another sheet. "Or we have joke spells that make any joke sound funny to your listeners."

Maybe I should get that one as a gift for McGoo.

Robin broke in. "No one in this office is an experienced magician or wizard of any sort. I'm afraid your service wouldn't be very helpful to us. Sorry."

"They all come complete with helpful phonetic pronunciations," Alterro said, sounding disappointed. "Not even a token payment for the free spell?"

Thinking fast, I snatched the free Monster Chow keychain from Sheyenne's desk. "Here, a genuine token. Now we're paid in full."

Alterro wasn't convinced. He flipped it over. "What's the symbol on the back?"

"Some kind of logo. Take it, it's yours. Might be a collector's item someday. See, it's numbered. They're rare."

He pursed his lips, then seemed pleased and intrigued. He pocketed the keychain and left his catalog on Sheyenne's desk. "Just in case you reconsider. Spells 'N Such might turn out to be useful. Four out of five dentists agree."

I frowned. "Why would dentists need spells?"

"You'd be surprised," Alterro said, then left the offices.

After I gulped down the rest of my cold, bitter coffee I retrieved my fedora and headed out. Wandering the streets of the Quarter, I passed the usual bustle and shamble of unnatural life: a laboratory surplus shop going out of business, a group of gossiping witches seated at a foldup table with plates of cookies, cupcakes, and brownies in a bake sale for the Pointy Hat Society. Inside a nail parlor that reeked of poisonous fumes, I saw a female mummy sitting in a chair with the bandages unwrapped from her feet while an intent vampire manicurist used steel files and a hacksaw to give her a pedicure.

I've grown quite fond of the Quarter. When I first hung up my private investigator shingle, it had seemed a motley and dizzying collection of strange creatures, cultures, and unfamiliar dangers. Now it just felt like home. I had grown color-blind and monster-blind. Unnaturals were all just people to me, some worse than others. But everybody has problems, and that was good for me; if nobody had problems, then Chambeaux & Dyer wouldn't have any clients.

I paused to look at a sign recently taped to a lamppost, MISSING, bearing a sketch of a thin accountant-looking vampire. Before I could read the details, I was startled to notice a tall hairy Bigfoot taping a sign on the opposite side of the lamppost. I hadn't seen him looming there.

He saw me staring at him and explained in a growly voice, "Even if people don't notice *us*, we hope they pay attention to these posters."

I read the complete sign. *"Please help us find my beloved husband, Ronald Skelton."* The sketch wasn't very well done, but vampires are at a distinct disadvantage in missing persons cases, because they don't show up on photographs. Ronald Skelton was thin, studious looking. The sketch looked a lot like that accountant vampire at the Chamber of Commerce meeting; in fact, I was sure it was him. Missing for two days and two nights, according to the poster. His coffin hadn't been slept in.

"A lot of people are going missing in the Quarter these days," I said to my hairy but somehow unnoticeable friend. I remembered the rash of cases McGoo had told me about. "Are they all vampires?"

The Bigfoot shook his head. "Zombies, werewolves, ghouls. Unnaturals of all types. Even some humans."

I felt a knot at the pit of my stomach, as if I had eaten some bad brains. "I hope we don't have another serial killer on the loose. Obadeus was bad enough."

I promised the Bigfoot I would keep an eye out, but as I walked away, the big guy lifted a plastic bucket and rattled it. I heard two coins jingling at the bottom. "Care to donate to our Visibility Society to help us gain some recognition?"

I pretended that I didn't notice him, and the Bigfoot believed me all too easily.

CHAPTER SIXTEEN

In less than an hour I ended up in the hospital. It was just a social call.

I decided to stop by and see how Travis Spade was recovering, although I had no intention of reading a draft of his script. My dedication to the case didn't extend that far.

According to the police reports McGoo had shared, two similar blood-rampage incidents had occurred in the Quarter, vampires gone wild for no apparent reason, not even spring break. I wanted to investigate whether that craziness had anything to do with Fletcher's case.

I entered the vampire screenwriter's room, where I found him sitting bored in the visitor's chair, the hospital coffin bed neatly made, the fine layer of generic soil raked smooth, the dirty pillowcases removed. Travis was dressed in street clothes instead of an embarrassing open-backed hospital gown. He had a spare laptop, which replaced the one he had smashed in his frenzy, and it was open on the rolling, adjustable table. Ignored, his meal tray held an unopened prepackaged cup of hospital blood-flavored gelatin dessert. The label said it was "buffered, with extra plasma for easy digestion."

Travis pecked away on his laptop, leaning close to the screen as he added more dialog. Hearing me enter, he looked up with a smile, but apparently I wasn't the person he had expected. His expression fell, and he let out a long sigh. "I shouldn't get my hopes up."

"It's good to have high hopes. What were you hoping for?"

"To get out of here. I'm all packed and ready to be discharged. I've been recovered since an hour after I arrived."

I took off my fedora, held it in the crook of my arm. "I came to see how you were doing, so I guess I caught you just in time."

"Not really. I was released eleven hours ago, and I'm still waiting for the discharge paperwork." He closed his laptop, fidgety and impatient. "I've written four whole scenes, and one of them is even good. Would you like to read it?"

"I ... ah ... no thanks. My attorney discourages reading manuscripts. I'll wait to see it on the big screen."

"We could read it together, run the lines, role-play the different parts. It's a poignant coming-of-age story in an age of monsters when monsters don't age."

"Are there car chases?" I asked.

"Of course." Travis sniffed. "It wouldn't be a poignant coming-of-age story otherwise."

Sadly, I thought of how Alvina would never have a normal coming of age now that she was a vampire. I made a suggestion to Travis. "For background, you might want to read a really good blog. It's called 'I Was a Teenage Vampire.' It might help you understand the underage unnatural."

Why not expand the kid's readership?

He brightened. "Oh, I follow it every week. That writer's a genius. Real insights into the human and inhuman condition."

I admit I felt a flush of pride.

I indicated his packed overnight bag. "The witch doctor says you're all right now? No aftereffects?"

"Apparently it was just a case of bad blood, and I'm over it now. Embarrassed more than anything else." Travis looked up, suddenly hopeful again as Zonda Nefarious appeared at the door. The witch doctor held her chart, considering all the numbers. "Mr. Spade, your tests came back clean." Distracted, she didn't even notice me, and for a moment I felt like a Bigfoot. Then she did glance at me. "Oh hello, Mr. Chambeaux. Continuing the investigation?"

"The cases don't solve themselves," I said.

"Neither do lab results. Mr. Spade's bloodwork is completely normal. Whatever contaminant caused his unusual behavior has been flushed out of his system. We'll never know what it was."

"Two more vampires went berserk in a similar fashion. Could it be spreading? Have you run tests on the other victims? Is it something in the water?"

"Fluoridation," Travis Spade said knowingly.

The witch doctor tapped on her clipboard. "Yes, I found trace elements in their blood, but the substance wore off quickly, as if burned out by standard vampire metabolism. The victims return to normal fairly quickly, although embarrassed."

"I'm normal," Travis said, "and embarrassed. *And* still waiting to be discharged." He said the last with a pointed tone.

Dr. Zonda continued to read off her results. "My lab Igors have been running tests. It seems to be a highly addictive substance."

"Like potato chips? No one can eat just one …" I recalled Cyrus Redfarb's conversations. "Or even like Monster Chow? Everyone in the Quarter is going nuts for the stuff, but that could just be marketing."

"I won't touch the artificial crap. Who knows what they put into the textured synthetic protein substances?" Travis said with a sniff. "I only want artisanal locally sourced blood products."

"Funny you should mention that, Mr. Chambeaux," said the witch doctor, ignoring her own patient. "I did analyze samples of the most popular Monster Chow varieties, but the tests were inconclusive because there are already so many additives present."

"I thought it was entirely unnatural," I said.

"That doesn't mean it's not sinister."

No longer interested in the analysis, Travis looked forlornly at his neatly made hospital coffin bed, his packed overnight bag. "So, I'm ready to go, right? A clean bill of health?"

"Absolutely," the witch doctor pronounced. "You are undead but in perfect shape."

Travis rose, relieved. "Thank you! I'm really anxious to get back home."

She waved a stern finger at him. "Not so fast. We have to get your discharge paperwork ready."

His expression fell. "But that was eleven hours ago."

Zonda made another checkmark on her clipboard. "Good, we should be ready to move on to step two. I'll alert administration."

Expecting the worst, he sat back down and opened his laptop. "I'll have time to write another scene, then."

I discreetly slipped out, glad that visitors didn't need to complete paperwork before they left the hospital.

O O O

Since it was time to remove the flesh-colored temporary tape and touch up the putty in the middle of my forehead, I made a brief visit to Miss Lujean Eccles in her Patchup Parlor. She had left quickly after our tour of the Monster Chow factory, and I hadn't had a chance to chat with her. (Alvina had been on a bit of a sugar rush after eating so many samples of the vampire breakfast cereal in the tasting room.)

Miss Eccles had said she was troubled by Cyrus Redfarb, and I wanted to know why.

The Patchup Parlor was a quaint Victorian mansion complete with dead trees and grim landscaping. I stood at the door under the shadowy porch beneath which dozens of bats nested, hanging upside down in the eaves and making a cheery flutter as I clacked the brass knocker. I heard a shuffling sound behind the door, which opened with a majestic groan of unoiled hinges.

A hodgepodge human stood before me, a young woman in a pretty dress that was stitched together much more evenly than she herself was. Sutures reassembled her arms in three places and attached them to her shoulders. Her head wasn't quite straight on her neck, and she moved with an awkward shuffle. Her lips formed a delighted lopsided grin when she saw me.

"Hello, Wendy," I said.

"Dan Shamble!" She giggled.

Wendy, the Patchwork Princess, was a heartbroken young lady who had tried to end her misery by throwing herself in front of an oncoming train. Tragically, the poor creature had revived as a disassembled zombie and found herself more miserable and heartbroken (and body-broken) than ever. Miss Eccles had taken pity on her pieces, gathered up everything she could find, and carried the poor girl back to her Patchup Parlor. It was a Humpty Dumpty-level project, but eventually the taxidermist/mortician had reassembled Wendy as best she could. Now the hard part was rebuilding Wendy's self-esteem.

I made a point of saying, "You look lovely today, Wendy."

She gave me the lopsided grin again, and her grayish skin even blushed a little. "Improving one step at a time. I see you're still wearing the jacket I fixed!" She sounded delighted.

I tugged at my collar, brushed down the front of my sport jacket where the bullet holes had been clumsily stitched up with black thread. Wendy had worked hard to fix it for me, and she had done the best she could with her clumsy fingers. "I wouldn't trade it for anything, Wendy."

She giggled, and I knew I had done wonders for her self-esteem. Besides, the jacket was sort of my trademark by now.

The Patchwork Princess gestured me inside. "Come into the Parlor. I'll find Miss Eccles."

I slumped onto the overstuffed velvet couch next to a ticking grandfather clock and Tiffany lamps that shed a muted glow. Wendy shuffled in carrying a plate of cookies. "I made them myself."

"I'm sure they're delicious." I politely munched one.

Wendy hobbled away as Miss Eccles came in, peeling off gloves. "Ah, Mr. Chambeaux. Are you in for a touchup already?"

"If it's not too much trouble. It's probably time to remove the tape and rubber cement." I tapped my forehead. "And Alvina says I should get the putty fixed, but I think I might go back to the natural look."

"You know the putty won't last," she said, clucking her tongue. "If you want my opinion, the bullet hole is rather distinctive."

"You mean like a beauty mark?"

She hesitated. "More like a trademark."

She snapped open her repair kit, fiddled with the array of instruments, and took out a pair of tweezers, with which she peeled off the flesh-colored repair tape and some of the excess flesh-colored rubber cement. She added makeup and cream to hide the leftover peck marks and finally used a pencil to dig around in the bullet hole in my forehead, cleaning out the old putty.

I decided that it was just too much trouble for her to rebuild the patch, and I'm not a vain zombie. I would just go back to being me. You can always tell when a guy combs over his hair to hide a bald spot, and he doesn't fool anyone. I was well known as a zombie P.I., and everybody knew I had a hole in the head. In fact, Howard Phillips Publishing had made it so prominent on the covers of their fictionalized cases it was part of my branding.

As she finished, I finally broached the subject that had brought me here. "You never told me your suspicions about Cyrus Redfarb." She continued to concentrate on her work, frowning but not answering. "What made you skeptical in the first place? You were paying close attention to the back of his head during the tour yesterday."

"And the front of his head," she said. "Did you notice his dead eyes?"

"I noticed they were blue one day and green another. Yesterday they were brown."

"I'm certain they're glass eyes," she said.

"Colored contact lenses would be a better explanation."

"No, they're glass eyes. Believe me, I've installed enough of them! Just finished putting two in a grizzly bear I'm stuffing back in the taxidermy workshop."

That surprised me. "Is there a market for stuffed grizzly bears?"

"It's for specialty collectors. Some people have ten or more, and the one I'm working on is a limited edition."

She kept working diligently on my appearance and finally answered about Redfarb. "He has thick dark hair, but when I looked closely I saw thread, lots of black thread. Tight little stitches. I recognize those things. He's been opened up and sewn back together."

"Maybe it was just a skateboarding accident," I suggested, remembering what had happened to Alvina.

"Not likely. I've seen this before, Mr. Chambeaux. As a mortician and taxidermist, I run into a lot of unusual things."

"I run into a lot of unusual things in my job too," I said. "What sort of *thing* are you talking about?"

She lowered her voice. "I think Cyrus Redfarb is a ... *meat puppet.*"

"That would explain a lot ... if I had any idea what a meat puppet is."

"He's just a stuffed shirt."

"I expected that. He's very corporate."

"No, I mean he's a bag of bones and skin, just the wrapper of a person. Stripped entirely out of the skin, the skeleton put back in place but the rest of his body stuffed with something else. Like the hand inside a puppet. It's the dark side of the taxidermy art."

I've seen plenty of strange creatures in the Unnatural Quarter, but that was a new one on me. That would explain how the corporate headquarters of Monster Chow Industries had come up with a perfect, congenial spokesman so quickly after the murderous Obadeus scare.

"But are they illegal? I might have to consult Robin."

"The law is unclear on the point," Miss Eccles said. "But I don't like it. I just don't like it. Who knows what's inside the meat puppet?"

"Who knows what's inside any of us?" I asked.

CHAPTER SEVENTEEN

When McGoo called, yelling about an emergency, I instantly jumped to the wrong conclusion. "What's wrong? Is it Alvina? How is she?"

"Cute as a button, but that's not going to help us here. It was a massacre, Shamble." He gave me the address of a private upscale werewolf smoking lounge called Fumes. "You've got to see this for yourself."

"A smoking lounge?" I said, even more concerned. "You're not letting our little girl go in there are you? It's dangerous."

"I'm with her, Shamble. Don't worry."

I was growing exasperated. "I mean the secondhand smoke!"

"Right. I'll have her wait outside."

The private club for smoking lycanthropes was located down a narrow dark alley similar to countless narrow dark alleys in the Quarter. Fumes was marked only by a red light over the door, with no sign, no advertising. I recognized the place instantly, though, because of the ten-year-old vampire standing in her pink sweater outside the door.

She brightened when I arrived, showing her fangs in a smile. "Good, you're finally here! Now you can escort me back inside. How am I supposed to help solve this case if I can't look at the clues?"

"Leave it to us," I said. "I'm the detective here, and McGoo is the cop."

"But what if you need the perspective of an underage vampire blogger?" She raised her eyebrows. "You never know."

Alvina had a point. "Just don't breathe," I warned. Together, we entered to find McGoo and several cops standing at the open door of a private airlocked smoking vault. Two gray-skinned goblin crime-scene investigators used sidewalk chalk to freestyle the outlines of imagined bodies on the floor. Other than the UQPD crowd, the vault was completely empty. Other goblin techs were stringing yellow crime-scene tape as if decorating for a forensic party. McGoo stood with his thumbs hooked in his belt, striking his best "I'm in charge" pose.

"What's the emergency, McGoo?" I asked. "I don't see any bodies. You said it was a massacre."

"The bodies are missing—that's the crux of it."

Inside the airtight chamber, a gray pall of cigar smoke still hung like a tobacco-based fog. The room held five overstuffed chairs, each one accompanied by a deep ashtray filled with flaky ashes like a drift of dirty snow. Balanced on each ashtray smoldered a fat brown cigar butt. They looked like amputated fingers to me, and I was glad I'd never taken up the habit.

"It's a locked-room mystery, Shamble. Five werewolves, members in good standing of the Lycanthrope Stogie Appreciation Society. They were sealed inside this chamber, smoking as they always do."

I looked around in an attempt to pick up clues, but my eyes burned from the thick smoke. "Alvina, you better get out of here. This is dangerous to your sensitive lungs."

"I'm a vampire. My lungs'll heal themselves," she said with a hint of defiance. "In fact, I might try smoking just to prove—"

"You will not," McGoo and I both said in unison, and she gave up the argument, though I could tell we hadn't heard the last of it.

McGoo continued filling me in. "This morning when the janitors came in to empty the ashtrays, they found that all five werewolves had vanished, leaving the cigars still lit. Three were Cubans."

"Cuban werewolves?" I asked.

"No, the cigars. No aficionado would leave them behind unsmoked. That's evidence of a real crime."

"And nobody saw them leave?" I asked. "How crowded was Fumes?"

"Nobody could tell. With the vault sealed, the cigar smoke is impenetrable. They disappeared without a trace." McGoo shook his head. "These missing persons cases are getting out of hand."

I nodded. "Yes, I saw a Bigfoot putting out posters all around town."

McGoo scratched his freckled cheek. "I wondered where all the posters came from. I didn't think Bigfeet existed."

"Apparently they do, and they seem very civic-minded for mythological creatures."

When the crime-scene goblins finished plundering and damaging the evidence, McGoo turned back to me. "I could really use your help, Shamble. I'll send over the new missing persons files."

"*We'll* be on the lookout," Alvina said and took my hand. "Can we go back to your office now? I need to post a new blog."

O O O

Just after I got Alvina settled in the conference room, a new client walked in. She was a pale-skinned, short-statured, middle-aged vampire woman with a brown pageboy cut and sensible domestic clothes. I didn't usually think of "housewife" and "vampire" in the same sentence, but I knew they existed.

Sheyenne offered the distraught vampire housewife her usual welcoming smile, but to no effect. "Welcome to Chambeaux & Deyer. Can I get you anything? We have some new Monster Chow blood shakes."

The woman began to sob. "You can get my husband back!" She pulled out a crumpled sheet of paper stained with palm sweat and teardrops. It was the same flyer with the crude sketch of the accountant vampire that the Bigfoot had posted. Ronald Skelton.

I consoled our new client, patting her on the shoulder. "You've come to the right place, ma'am. Tell us the details of the case, and we'll get started right away."

"My name is Regina Skelton, and my husband's vanished! Dear sweet Ronald never got into any trouble, never bothered anybody. But he just disappeared." She flared her open hands apart, mimicking a fireworks explosion. "Poof!"

While Alvina worked quietly in the back of the room, I led the weeping housewife to the other end of the table. "Tell me what happened. I've seen his posters all over town. Somebody's going to spot him."

"Yes, I paid someone to put those up ... I forget who." She shook her head. "I wanted to spread the word. I need to find my poor Ronald."

"I'm sure the *kidnappers* know where he is," Alvina piped up from the other end of the table. I don't think she realized she wasn't being very helpful.

"Kidnapped!" Regina squawked. "Are you sure he's been kidnapped? How can you tell?"

I tried to reassure her after giving Alvina a cautionary glance. "That's just a worst-case scenario, Mrs. Skelton."

"Worst case? I can think of worse cases."

I frowned. "Like what?"

"My Ronald could have run off with another woman. That would be much worse."

"At least he'd be safe," I pointed out.

"Not from me when I catch him," said Regina, and I conceded the point. She continued, "We've been married for a long time, ever since the Big Uneasy. Vampires have a reputation of being free spirits with loose morals, but some of us are monogamous. Ronald was always faithful to me. He went to his office, did his work, never complained."

"Where did he work?" I asked.

"He's a CPA with his own office," Regina said. "He specializes in blood inventory accounting for all the Talbot & Knowles blood bars, the hospital blood banks, even some specialty nightclubs."

That piqued my interest. "There's a lot of bad blood going around."

Regina fidgeted with her purse. "Ronald and I had a quiet life, mostly sitting around and watching TV, especially those old comedy spoof movies like *Night of the Living Dead* and *I Am Legend*. So ridiculous, you have to laugh!"

I looked down at the sketch on the poster again. "He does look familiar to me. Is he a member of the Chamber of Commerce, by chance?"

"Oh, yes. He gets most of his new business by networking at the Chamber meetings, but he also gets referrals on ChainedIn."

I tapped my finger on the sketch. "He was at the luncheon when Cyrus Redfarb gave a presentation about Monster Chow Industries."

"Ronald talked about that quite a bit, brought home some free samples—and a keychain."

"I had one of the keychains, too, but I gave it away as a token payment."

Alvina spoke up again, "Have a look at his client list." Having proved how smart she was, she went back to typing on her laptop.

"That's a good suggestion. Could I see who your husband's clients were? Maybe some part of his accounting put him in danger. In some cases, a misplaced decimal point could make all hell break lose."

She agreed. "I'll do everything I can to bring Ronald back. I miss him so much."

"If you think of anything else, Mrs. Skelton, please call me. You never know what clues might click together."

Clearly thinking hard, she swiped the back of her hand across her cheek to remove a tear. "Like a threatening ransom note? Would that be useful?"

I almost jumped out of my chair. "Of course! That would be vital."

"All right. I haven't seen one yet, but often the mail is delayed." Then she snapped open her purse and reached inside. "Here's a matchbook from the Overbite Lounge. I found it in Ronald's pockets when I did the laundry."

"Overbite?" I asked. "Isn't that a ... seedy place? Some kind of edgy nightclub?"

"It's a vampire meat market, I believe, but I'm sure Ronald just went there to meet a client. That makes the most sense. He does accounting."

I took the Overbite matchbook from her, thinking Mrs. Skelton might be a bit oblivious to her husband's extracurricular activities. Suddenly I remembered where I'd heard the name of the place before. When Ma Hemoglobin and her boys knocked over Bubba's Bloodmobile, part of the shipment had been bound for the Overbite Lounge.

I slipped the matchbook into the pocket of my sport jacket. "I'll investigate this thoroughly, ma'am." I decided to ask Sheyenne what she was doing that evening.

CHAPTER EIGHTEEN

Despite Regina Skelton's claim that vampires could be monogamous, the clientele at the Overbite Lounge suggested otherwise—in an extreme fashion.

Sheyenne and I arrived at the Overbite on a makeshift date, hoping to poke around inside to see if anyone had seen the missing vampire accountant. As we approached the door, I suggested, "Could be that Ronald just had a matchbook from this place because they're his clients."

"Sure, no other reason to be hanging out at a seedy vampire meat market," Sheyenne said with the most skeptical of expressions. "Overbite doesn't have a good reputation."

For a place to get a bad reputation in the Unnatural Quarter, it had to be really bad.

"Let's see for ourselves."

The entrance to the Overbite Lounge was in yet another back alley. The city planners had installed a labyrinth of back alleys in the Quarter, since alleys were such prime real estate. Overbite had only a small sign on the brick wall next to the door, as if it were a black-market dentist's office for illicit orthodontia. (Yes, there is a market for illicit orthodontia. Many vampires secretly get laminates or implants because of self-esteem issues, believing that size really matters.) A second small sign promised "What happens in Overbite stays in Overbite."

"We might have trouble getting information from the clientele," Sheyenne warned.

Robin had taught me about loopholes, though. "Read the words closely. All we have to do is go *inside* the lounge and interview them there. Then their information really does stay inside Overbite."

When we opened the door, we were immediately blocked by an enormous golem guard. Worse, from inside we were bombarded by pounding, throbbing techno music of the kind preferred by German vampires. The monotonous deafening beat was so loud and the flashing strobe lights from the dance floor so intense that I didn't at first hear the gruff challenge the guard threw at me.

"You're not welcome here," he said again. "Exclusive club. Vampires only."

If Robin had been with us, she'd have slapped the entire club with a discrimination lawsuit before the cocktail waitresses could finish serving their current round of drinks. As a private investigator, however, I didn't turn to legal recourse right away. I preferred deception and fast thinking.

And it's not terribly difficult to think faster than a golem.

"It's all right. We have a pass." I fished inside my sport jacket and pulled out my private detective's license, holding it up in front of the gray clay behemoth. "See, right here. There's my picture. Read the words." I tapped the license with my finger. "It says free pass to Overbite Lounge, plus one guest."

The golem squinted at the license, trying to decipher the letters (which said nothing more than my name and mailing address). I waited patiently as the golem stared and scrutinized.

Puzzled, Sheyenne hovered next to me and followed my lead. "My boyfriend and I have been so looking forward to this."

The golem used his fat clay fingers to take the license away, which concerned me because if I lost that thing, I couldn't solve cases—not legally. After long contemplation, he handed it back. Golems require long contemplation for even simple decisions.

"All right, go on in." He stepped aside to let us enter the hell of industrial pounding techno noise, flashing strobe lights, and pheromone-drunk vampires on the make.

"How did you do that, Beaux?" Sheyenne shouted in my ear, although it was meant to be a whisper.

"I've learned a lot of things in my time as a private detective. Like the fact that most golems can't read."

A flashing mirror ball sent dizzying shards of light in all directions. Every wall was covered with mirrors, which seemed unusual. Fletcher's Basilisk Nightclub prided itself in being "a place without mirrors" so that monsters could have their privacy. Here in this meat market, the vamps crowded the dance floor or sat shoulder to shoulder at the bar, but when I studied the mirrors the place looked entirely empty without their reflections Sheyenne and I seemed to be the only people there.

"What happens in Overbite stays in Overbite," I muttered. "Thanks to all those mirrors, nobody can see what the vampires are doing, who they're hitting on, and who they slink off with."

She slipped her spectral arm through mine, then leaned closer, giving me a stern look. "I'm not here to help you flirt with any vampire women."

"When have I ever flirted with vampire women?"

"Ivory certainly had the hots for you."

Ivory was a full-bodied, full-throated, and full-breasted vampire diva at Basilisk who had an insatiable taste for life and a list of victims to match. She'd made no secret that she wanted me as a romantic hors d'oeuvre. The vampire diva had been annoyed with Sheyenne stealing her thunder as a singer, so when Sheyenne was poisoned to death in the nightclub, I'd figured Ivory as a prime suspect, but that was a false alarm.

"You've got nothing to worry about, Spooky. I'd leave a bad taste in her mouth."

Three vampire bartenders worked the long, polished bar, serving vampire customers. The bartenders used arterial foam dispensers, filling shot glasses from spigots marked with various blood types. Top-shelf virgin's blood was the most expensive. Fancy cocktails seemed to be in great demand. The shipment from Bubba's Bloodmobile had seemed like a huge amount, but seeing how fast the vampire bartenders were serving, I doubted all the blood in the truck would be more than one night's supply.

Vampire cocktail waitresses in extremely short and extremely slinky dresses strolled among the patrons seated around small tables designed for intimate conversations and the exchange of phone numbers or gravesites.

Several hookup apps catered specifically to unnaturals. Some were simple dating services for lonely monsters in search of a lasting relationship, while some—especially one called Fangr—made no bones about the fact that they facilitated sexual hookups. Judging from the crowded floor in the Overbite Lounge, though, traditional vampires still enjoyed an old-fashioned meat market where they could trace sharp fingernails across cold white skin and use competing glamor spells. We watched vampires pairing off and slipping out secret exits. "Your coffin or mine?"

Sheyenne squeezed intangibly closer to me. "Let's do what we came here for."

We nudged our way up to the bar, each carrying one of the MISSING posters showing the hand-drawn picture of Ronald Skelton. A plump white-haired vampire woman on the next stool turned to give me a predatory look. "Hello there, big dead boy. Want to buy me a drink?"

Honesty is always the best policy. "Not really." I showed her the flyer. "Have you seen this man? He's a vampire accountant named Ronald Skelton."

"I can read, dear boy," she said.

"Not everyone here can," I responded, thinking of the golem door guard.

She took her half-empty drink, a crimson blood martini and ignored me as she searched for a different mark.

Up at the stage, a scrawny Goth vampire hunched over a mixing board in search of even more obnoxious music from his music library. He had plenty to choose from.

I caught the attention of one of the bartenders, who frowned at my appearance. I was the wrong sort of undead. "We serve only blood, finest quality," he said. "No brains or embalming fluid for zombies. And no spirits for her."

"We're just here to watch," Sheyenne said. "And we're looking for this person. He disappeared, and we found an Overbite matchbook among his things. His wife very much wants him found."

"Maybe he doesn't want to be found," said the bartender. "If he came here, maybe he got lucky."

"Missing persons aren't usually lucky."

The bartender barely glanced at the flyer. "I couldn't say. I look in the mirrors, so I don't really see the customers. I just mix the drinks."

"Could you have another look?" Sheyenne said, using her charm, which was more potent than any vampire's glamor spell. "Please?"

Before the bartender could respond, the Goth music maestro twitched, made a loud scratch sound effect, and his equipment let out a shriek of intense feedback. It took me a few seconds to realize it wasn't part of the song.

At his mixing board, the gangly DJ vamp picked up his half-finished blood cocktail and hurled it into the crowd, smashing it against the head of a vampire dancer. The DJ picked up the mixing board with a roar. His fangs turned into tusk-like canines three inches long, springing out of his mouth like something from an overzealous makeup department.

He smashed his mixing board, and the feedback mercifully fell silent only to be replaced by loud, angry screams that rippled among the dancers and other patrons of Overbite. Like a madman, he hurled the remains of his mixing board into the crowd where it shattered among several dancers. They went berserk, too, tearing the equipment to pieces, flinging shattered scraps of plastic, knobs, and metal in all directions.

Yowling incomprehensibly, the Goth maestro spread his arms and flung himself from the raised stage, as if diving into a huge mosh pit. No one on the dance floor saw him coming, and he crashed to the floor as the dancers turned on each other. They all grew ultralong fangs and sharp claws, which they used to tear at one another, ripping out throats, drinking each other's blood, shredding cocktail dresses and slick blazers.

This was a hundred times worse than when Travis Spade had lost control of himself at the blood bar.

Even the bartender across from us transformed into a wild man. He grabbed a bottle in each hand, smashed them to make jagged weapons, and dove over the bar to attack the nearest cocktail waitress. She screamed and slashed out his eyes with her claws.

Even during the fight, the vamps healed quickly before attacking each other again. With their unnatural constitution, vampires can recover from just about any physical injury, given enough time.

Zombies can't, though, and the feral chickens had already damaged me enough for one week. As the frenzy grew worse, screaming and sucking and tearing, Sheyenne waved me frantically toward the door. "They can't hurt a ghost, Beaux, but you'd better get out of here."

We both bolted for the exit, caroming off wild vampires. Since my embalming fluid didn't have the same cachet, the vamps paid little attention to me as a victim. We reached the exit as the frenzy built to a crescendo behind us, louder even than the music had been.

The golem guard blocked the door with his back to us, facing the alley outside and waiting to challenge any new customer trying to get in. I shouted to him, "Can't you hear the screams back there? The vampires are going crazy and causing lots of damage. Do something!"

"Not my job," said the golem.

"You're a guard!" Sheyenne said. "Go break up the brawl."

"I'm just here to keep people from getting in who aren't supposed to be in."

Behind us, we heard screams and shattering glass ... and feeding. Loud, rude feeding. Vampires can be real slobs when they lose control.

I gestured back into the club. "You really don't hear that?"

"Doesn't sound much different from what they usually play on the dance floor," said the golem, and I couldn't argue with him.

We pushed past the golem, glad to be out in the dark and shadowy streets where we felt safer.

"What happens in Overbite stays in Overbite may be *their* motto," I said, "but I've got to let McGoo know. Dr. Zonda is going to want to take samples and run tests."

CHAPTER NINETEEN

For an undead person, I'm fairly sociable. I enjoy spending time with Sheyenne, and Robin, McGoo, and now Alvina. But sometimes after a hectic day—like a massacre at a vampire pick-up joint—a zombie just wants a little alone time. Many guys have what they call a man cave, a retreat from the world like a kids' clubhouse, a place to sit around and contemplate important things.

In the Unnatural Quarter, most of the real caves had been rented quickly by nocturnal or subterranean creatures, and I couldn't afford a cave of my own. Instead, I settled for a different private haunt—the Ghoul's Diner.

Neither Robin nor McGoo particularly liked the food, and Sheyenne didn't like the service, so I could get away completely by myself if I wanted. I could claim a seat at the counter, put my elbows up on the flecked Formica, and tolerate a cup of terrible-tasting coffee. Even when the place was crowded, the other customers generally left me alone. Albert the ghoul was always there cooking something indefinable. Sometimes the rowdy monsters called sarcastic or supposedly flirtatious comments at Esther, and the harpy waitress would respond with predictable vehemence.

But I could read the newspaper without being bothered, do a crossword puzzle, sit as long as I liked. It was a nice place to hide from the world.

When I pulled open the door now on this particular evening, I saw that I was going to be more alone than I had expected. Even though it was the usually slow early night shift, the diner was as quiet as a tomb, and not in a good way. All the booths were empty, the counter was vacant, a half-empty pot of coffee steamed and snarled on a burner. There was no sign of a waitress, polite or otherwise.

"Are you closed, Albert?" I called out.

"No," came a slow phlegmy voice. "Just deserted." Albert shuffled out from the grill and stood behind the counter. His stench preceded him, but I knew what to expect from the ghoul's personal hygiene as well as from his cooking.

"Then I'll be your only customer." I took a stool at the counter closest to Albert. He gets more decrepit each day, and I didn't want to make him move any more than necessary. "What's good tonight?"

The question stumped him. "Never said anything was good."

"What's the special tonight?"

"Today's special, soon to be tomorrow's special," he said. "It's currently in transition."

"I'll have that, please. And a cup of coffee if it's willing to leave the pot."

Albert glanced at the nasty black oozing substance as if he wasn't sure. "Pour it yourself. I'm the only one on duty tonight. Esther had a date."

I immediately felt sorry for the poor beau. I doubted she got many second dates. "You can handle the rush, Albert."

He muttered as he lurched back to the hot grill and the bubbling cauldrons on the stove. "Feeling a little overwhelmed right now."

I swung off the stool and walked to the coffeemaker, picked up a white ceramic cup with disappointing brown stains inside, and wrenched the coffee urn free. When I upended it, the bubbling brownish-black liquid seemed like a living thing. It refused to come out of the urn and slid around the curve of the glass. I gave up and switched to decaf instead, which seemed more cooperative.

Albert shuffled back out, holding a plate that dripped a greenish gelatinous substance, which looked different from the usual gray gravy. "Is that a new recipe?" I asked.

The ghoul seemed proud as he set the plate in front of me. "All organic." There were cubes of some kind of meat, whip-like tendrils that might have been vermicelli. Maybe because I was his only customer and he had a little time to do a creative gourmet flourish, Albert had given me a tiny sprig of parsley.

"Looks delicious." I picked up a fork and attacked the dinner, afraid it might fight back.

Albert stood there, disheartened. "I hope somebody else tries it. Business was slow today, slow yesterday."

I looked around, puzzled. "Where are all the customers? Did you get a poor health rating?" Here in the Quarter, I doubted that would drive customers away.

"Nobody goes out to dinner anymore. Monster Chow is ruining everything. It tastes good, and people want the convenience. Zombie Chow, Werewolf Chow, Vampire shakes, Mummy Chow. I even tried some of the Ghoul Chow, and like the advertisement says, it tastes just like human." When he let out a sigh, mucus dripped from his nose onto the counter. "How can I compete with that? All I have is home cooking."

Vending machines had cropped up around the Quarter, so that people could buy a pack of their favorite chow and eat it on the go.

"Nobody takes time to sit down and enjoy a meal." Albert shook his head, shuffled back to the stove, and returned with another plate of his green mystery special for himself. He stood eating it in front of me. More mucus dripped from his nose onto his plate; apparently that was where the green coloring came from.

"Your regular customers will still come in. This place is a tradition in the Quarter."

"Thanks." Albert looked around again at his empty diner. "Might have to close down soon."

I ate the rest of my meal in silence, and Albert didn't seem to mind.

O   O   O

Feeling neither nourished nor satisfied, I left the diner. In the quiet and sleepy hours of the early evening, when the day-dwellers were heading home to their families and the raucous nightlife hadn't gotten up steam, the Quarter was relatively quiet.

Minding my own business, I walked past the deserted storefront where Maynard Kleck and his misguided charitable heart had fixated on saving the feral chickens. I no longer had a warm fuzzy feeling for the displaced fowl.

I paused, saw scattered white feathers in the window and on the doorstep. I wondered if the chickens had come home to roost. Since the fowl flophouse was dark inside, I assumed Maynard had given up on his carpentry efforts after taking a realistic assessment of his skill as a craftsman.

The feathers bothered me, though, and I recalled the stray feather I'd found on the floor of the Monster Chow factory. Those chickens were everywhere. The werewolf Samaritan insisted that the barnyard fowl were just misunderstood and needed a home and a little love. I didn't buy it.

Seeing the door ajar, I pushed it open and had a look inside. I smelled blood and fur. Poor Maynard Kleck had discovered the true nature of those vicious chickens.

The werewolf do-gooder had left out bowls of water and a bin of chicken feed, but the feral creatures preferred the taste of Maynard Kleck. The poor guy lay sprawled amid feathers and blood, tangled in rumpled chicken wire as he had thrashed about. Maynard had been attacked—*murdered*. His furry hide was torn to shreds, his eyes gone, his throat ripped open. He had suffered the death of a thousand beaks.

Standing there, I felt angry and sickened. The gullible werewolf had only wanted to help, and the creatures turned on him. I agreed with McGoo's suggested solution to the problem: a Quarter-wide chicken barbecue. This was murder, plain and simple.

I called it in and waited for McGoo and the coroner squad to respond.

The UQPD would put out an all-points bulletin to arrest any feral chickens found on the street, although I was willing to bet they'd all have alibis. How could we prove which chicken or chickens had attacked Maynard?

Maybe there would be incriminating blood in their beaks.

Chapter Twenty

e might have to approach the law in a completely different way," Robin said to Fletcher's ghost. "That's how we solve intractable problems around here."

Fletcher hovered in front of her, concerned and frustrated. "But I've tried everything, Ms. Deyer! I don't know what you mean."

I translated for her. "She's saying we might have to break the law, but she's speaking in legalese."

Robin's eyebrows rose. "That's not what I'm saying at all, Dan! I would never even suggest that." Her indignation was for Fletcher's benefit and maybe for her own conscience, but I wasn't fooled. She continued, "I just mean we have to think outside the box."

"I've been outside the box ever since I clawed my way from the grave." I gave Fletcher a confident nod. "Leave it to us. I have an idea how we can snoop on the Talbot & Knowles Board of Directors. Didn't you say there was a Board meeting this morning?"

"Yes, but it's behind closed doors and I'm forbidden to attend. Even though I can walk through the walls, the Board resolution was clear."

Robin nodded. "If Fletcher's caught spying on the Board meeting, it could ruin our entire case."

I inhaled deeply (for effect, not because I needed to breathe). "Good thing private investigators have an entirely different set of morals than lawyers. Fletcher isn't the only ghost around here." I smiled. "Meanwhile, Sheyenne and I are going to Talbot & Knowles headquarters to fill out job applications. One of their stores must be in need of a zombie or ghost barista."

O O O

I had cleaned and patched my sport jacket after the chicken attack, so I looked somewhat less "vintage homeless person," but I was too fond of the garment to get rid of it. I dusted off my fedora, shaped and reformed it, and set it on my head. The bullet hole at the hat line was clean as a whistle, now that I had given up on Miss Eccles's putty. After Sheyenne straightened my collar and adjusted my hat, I felt like a very distinguished job applicant.

Looking beautiful as usual, she wore her best conservative job-applicant dress. She had never actually applied at Chambeaux & Deyer Investigations, because it was so obvious that we needed her and she was so perfect for the job. After I had solved our mutual but connected murders, she'd just stayed on. The last time she'd interviewed for a real job was to Fletcher Knowles himself at the Basilisk Nightclub. Now, she and I would both fill out applications to become Talbot & Knowles blood baristas. If nothing else, it was a fallback job in case the whole detective agency thing didn't work out.

And it gave us an excuse to get inside the headquarters.

We arrived at 10:00 AM, around the time when the top secret, closed-door Board meeting was taking place in the administrative conference room.

She and I emerged from the elevator on the thirteenth floor, facing an expansive reception desk that held several phones, three computer screens, and the Talbot & Knowles logo. A perky young vampire woman busily answered phones in a polite and professional manner.

There were two sofas in the waiting room and a coffee table displaying a stack of magazines, including a full year's worth of

Phlebotomy Today and another with a vampire holding a goblet of crimson blood, smiling as he made a toast on the cover of *Artery Aficionado*. There was also a tourist's guide to the Unnatural Quarter produced by the Chamber of Commerce. (Chambeaux & Deyer was listed in the ads in back, since Sheyenne had insisted.) We'd have plenty of reading material while we waited.

A dispenser held a large jug of chilled premium blood along with plastic cups, "For our valued customers," while a pitcher of lukewarm tap water sat beside it, labeled "For our other visitors." Together, we stepped up to the reception desk, and the vampire woman glanced at us between phone calls. "How may I help you?"

"We'd like to apply for a job as blood baristas."

She frowned at us. "You're not vampires."

"But we're very competent," Sheyenne said.

"This is corporate headquarters," the receptionist replied in a scolding tone. "Job applications are taken at individual store locations. This is most unusual."

"And we're most unusual job applicants," I said. "We decided to come straight to corporate central where we'd have a direct chance at getting a job."

"Do you have any experience?" the receptionist asked.

"None whatsoever." I tried to make it sound like a positive thing. "That means we aren't entrenched in the wrong way of doing things."

"We want to learn the Talbot & Knowles way," Sheyenne added.

The receptionist seemed prepared to continue arguing, but decided that her simplest course would be to let us fill out job applications, which she would probably discard as soon as we left. It didn't matter to me. I didn't have my hopes pinned on this job anyway. It was just a diversion.

The receptionist handed us each a form on a clipboard along with a pen topped with ridiculous black flowers to ensure that no one would walk off with them. I sat down on the sofa with the clipboard and made a point of pouring a cup of the murky tap water just to take advantage of their hospitality. Sheyenne sat primly beside me with another of the silly pens and a clipboard.

I lowered my voice, "Fletcher was good friends with Harry Talbot, but there must be something sinister going on in their corporate management. Once we find out what's really happening in that meeting, maybe Robin can take action."

I glanced down the hall at the prominent closed doors of the large Board room. Two burly guards stood outside the doors so no one could enter, both of them monthly werewolves who looked just as intimidating in human form as they would when they sprouted facial and body hair during the full moon. I imagined what ominous activities might be taking place inside, what grim decisions were being made.

Some blood baristas had been complaining about the corporate treatment of employees, how Talbot & Knowles had offered them healthcare (which they really didn't need, being vampires who could heal from just about anything) and bargain-basement no-coverage afterlife insurance, while refusing to provide dental care, which was a real sticking point.

Sheyenne filled in a few blanks on her employee application. I looked at my watch and glanced at her, nodding. "You're up, Spooky."

She set the clipboard aside and wafted up to the receptionist desk. "Excuse me, I need to use the restroom."

Talking on the phone, the receptionist jotted something down in a calendar, called up a screen on her computer, and casually gestured Sheyenne toward a side hall. Then she tucked the phone receiver against her shoulder. "You're a ghost. Why do you need to go to the bathroom?"

"So I can restroom in peace. Is there privacy?"

With a sigh, the vampire receptionist waved her down the hall adjacent to the dark-windowed and guarded conference room. As a ghost, Sheyenne could simply drift through the opposite wall and spy on the Board proceedings. Fletcher could have done the same thing, but not legally (not that Sheyenne's current activities were strictly legal either).

Not wanting to raise the receptionist's suspicions, I continued to fill out the job application, amazed at how many private details they required. I suppose making elaborate concoctions to please high-maintenance customers was equivalent to being an industrial chemist. The form asked for my blood type, and I wrote "embalming fluid." They asked for my *preferred* blood type, which I assumed meant what the potential employee would consume during breaks on the job. I listed my birth date, my death date, my last known address at Greenlawn Cemetery, and my current address.

The second page was a complete psychological profile, and I thought I might even learn something about myself; the Talbot & Knowles Corporation was certainly learning a lot about me. I began to wonder whether I really wanted to be a blood barista after all.

Before I could get into the depths of my personal problems, shouts exploded from inside the Board room. The heavily caffeinated guards sprang into action, yanking handguns from shoulder holsters and whirling to stare at the closed door as if it might explode. One burly guard cautiously pulled it open, agitated, as if he might sprout fur right then and there, even though it wasn't that time of the month.

Inside, Board members were yelling. A harried-looking man popped out. He had shadows under his eyes, and his face was gaunt. I recognized Harry Talbot from photos Fletcher had shown us, and I knew him from when I had worked with him in early days. He didn't look smug and dominant to me; in fact, Talbot looked as if someone had been grinding him down.

Behind him in the room stood four gangly hayseed young men munching on Danishes. In the back, I caught a glimpse of a squat, frumpy woman as attractive as a blacksmith's anvil.

Ma Hemoglobin and a few of her boys.

Harry Talbot cried, "We saw a ghost!"

The guards relaxed. "Everybody sees ghosts."

"This was a real ghost," Talbot insisted. "We're being spied on! A woman popped through the walls to eavesdrop on our discussions. We'd just revealed a top-secret new unicorn frappé made with real unicorn blood!"

The security guards barged into the conference room, shoulder to shoulder.

I knew Sheyenne could escape easily, so I decided to get out of there as quickly as possible, too. I filled out the rest of the application, marking my psychological profile as Severely Disturbed, and handed it in to the receptionist. "I'll wait for your phone call. My hours are flexible." I bolted before she could acknowledge me.

The elevator dropped me down to ground level, and I left the corporate headquarters building just in time for Sheyenne to emerge from the solid wall of the building near the street. "I didn't hear much, Beaux, but Ma Hemoglobin and all four of her boys have taken over the Board of Directors! It looks like they've got Harry Talbot hostage."

As Sheyenne and I hurried away, I reached into the pocket of my sport jacket and realized I had accidentally walked off with one of their ugly pens.

It was the first step in getting even.

Chapter Twenty-One

Since Ma Hemoglobin was on the Unnatural Quarter's Most Wanted list after the bloodmobile heist, McGoo rushed with a group of UQPD officers to stake out the Talbot & Knowles headquarters building, hoping they could nab some of the gang as they left the Board meeting.

Sheyenne and I hurried back to the Chambeaux & Deyer offices. Her phone rang just as we entered, and she swooped forward, glad to get back to normal business, although "normal" business is broadly defined, considering our cases and our clientele.

Her voice was bright and professional. "Yes, Mr. Alterro. No, Mr. Alterro. No, we haven't changed our mind. Yes, that's absolute. We have no interest in subscribing, thank you." She continued to smile, even though he couldn't see her face. "No, I don't think so. Not even at a reduced rate. Not for promotional purposes, no." Then she handed me the phone. "He wants to talk to you, Beaux."

The pushy proprietor of Spells 'N Such was the last person I wanted to talk to. "Can I fight another bloodthirsty demon instead?" I asked in a low voice. When she shook her head, I grudgingly accepted the phone. "Hello, Mr. Alterro. How can I help you today?"

"I'm calling with some exciting news." He sounded bright and cheery, undeterred despite Sheyenne's firm rejection. "I deciphered that interesting rune, and I know what it is. I'm going to include it in my spell catalog, thanks to you. I've never seen anything quite like it before." He paused, giving me time to understand what he was saying, but he didn't wait long enough. "So, ahem, do you think we can get a mention of our close teamwork in the next Dan Shamble novel? It would really help my business."

"The novels haven't helped my business much," I said. "Those are fictionalized adventures. The Wannovich sisters have a ghostwriter." I stopped myself from giving him the entire well-rehearsed rebuttal. "Now, which rune are you talking about, exactly? What kind of spell?"

"It's a delayed carnivorism spell," he said. "Very interesting. Deep demonic origin, I think."

"What's a delayed carnivorism spell? Something that makes you a vegetarian in the morning, but then you can eat meat for a late-night snack?"

Alterro clicked his tongue. "No, it's specifically used for meat transference. A magic user can whisk anyone holding this rune away from wherever they are, so they can be eaten later."

I frowned. "I still don't know which rune you're talking about, Mr. Alterro. Where did you find it?"

"You gave it to me, Mr. Shamble, on the keychain. As your token payment, remember? The design is imprinted on the plastic. You thought it was just a logo for Monster Chow Industries."

I tried to wrap my head around that. "You mean with this rune somebody can snatch a person, a monster, a vampire, or a werewolf...."

"A *meal*," Alterro interjected. "The body is transferred elsewhere for the purposes of consumption and digestion. It's not just any kidnapping spell. It's very specific."

"That puts an entirely different light on the concept of 'Meals to Go,'" I said.

I recalled all the people gone missing around the Quarter, the vampire accountant Ronald Skelton, the werewolves in the Fumes cigar lounge. And if Cyrus Redfarb was handing out those keychains at Chamber of Commerce meetings and to anyone who took a tour of his factory ...

I also knew that Ronald Skelton had attended the Chamber luncheon and taken one of the keychains.

I hung up, put on my fedora, and turned to the door. "I'm going to the police station. I've got to talk to McGoo about this right away."

"The telephone works just as well," Sheyenne pointed out as she settled behind the desk.

"I know, but when delivering grim news or an exciting break in the case, I like to see the expression on the person's face." And I wanted to see if McGoo had had any luck cornering Ma Hemoglobin.

By now, I was a familiar sight at UQPD headquarters. I shambled in through the doors and headed toward McGoo's desk among the cubicles in the rear. Against the far wall were many holding cells reinforced with silver or mirrors or spell markings designed to hold unnatural creatures.

I barged past the front desk, without recognizing the small uniformed frog demon on duty. The little, speckled amphibian leaped to her feet, flicked out a long, forked tongue. "Excuse me, where do you think you're going?"

"To the back," I said. "To see Officer McGoohan."

"Did he arrest you?"

"No, we're best buddies. I'm helping him on a case."

"Then why aren't you on the stakeout with him? This is most irregular."

"I have information on the missing persons he asked me to look into. I—"

Two patrol cars screeched up to the curb out front, sirens wailing, dome lights flashing. Riding shotgun in the first car, McGoo sprang out and went to the back to wrestle out a handcuffed suspect. The lanky young man wore a flannel shirt and patched jeans with a towel over his head to hide his identity.

"Come on, Ben," McGoo said, pulling on the suspect's arm. Since the young man had a towel on his head, he stumbled into the squad car door. Two other cops rushed to grab his arms, thinking (or hoping) that he might be resisting arrest.

"Watch your step," McGoo said, dragging him into the precinct building. "Right this way."

I held open the door as McGoo perp-walked the suspect into the station. "You got one of Ma Hemoglobin's boys."

"The others slipped out of the Talbot & Knowles headquarters before we got there," he said, "but this one stayed behind to have an extra blood drink. We got him just in time."

"I haven't done anything!" Ben said.

"You shot at us when you held up Bubba's Bloodmobile," I said. "That counts as doing something."

"It was in self-defense. I was standing my ground. It's within my constitutional rights."

"You were robbing a blood-delivery van. There are wanted posters for you all over the Quarter."

"Prove it!" Ben said defiantly. "You can't match my photograph because you can't take a photo of a vampire, and that sketch doesn't look anything like me."

McGoo said, "We have your driver's license. We know who you are."

Ben Hemoglobin sputtered, trying to think of some other excuse as McGoo manhandled him to the booking station. "I'm not gonna talk! I won't say anything about my Ma's operations. I won't tell you where her hideout is, unless we work out some kind of deal. Do you want to make a deal? I'm flexible."

"We'll talk about it in a little bit," McGoo said. "First, you're going into a holding cell."

Ben struggled until the towel disguise finally fell off his head. I could see his features, and it was a face only a mother could love, which was probably why he and his brothers formed such a tight-knit family gang. Their relationship would have been touching enough for one of those sappy movie channels, except without the robbery, murder, and mayhem.

"I'm not going to talk," Ben snarled. "I won't tell you about the additives my Ma is sneaking into the blood supply as a test stimulant. I absolutely will not explain how they intend to use the Talbot & Knowles blood bars as a distribution system. Not until I get immunity. Not until I get my phone call." He huffed. "Not until I get a drink of water."

"We'll ask the questions later," McGoo said, "and you're going to talk. You'll give us clues or else."

"That's a threat," Ben wailed. "I'd never turn on Ma or any of my brothers, even though they all deserve to be in jail a lot more than I do. Len is the one you want. And Dewey … you should see his internet search history!"

"I met Huey and Louis on another case," I said, "but there wasn't much conversation after they were dead."

"They're the ones who did it," Ben said. "Blame it on them."

"They were dead by the time your gang knocked over the Bloodmobile."

"We didn't knock it over. It was still standing upright, just a little shot up."

After McGoo wrapped up the booking paperwork and a tech finished fingerprinting Ben, the young man looked sick and fidgety. "I'm not saying another word, I swear. I'm never turning on my family."

"We'll let you think about it for a little while," McGoo said as he nudged the vampire gangster into a holding cell with silver-plated bars.

"I want my Ma!" he cried. Ben grabbed the bars to rattle them, but yanked his hands back, staring at his smoking palms after touching the silver. "Ow! This is cruel and inhuman punishment!"

"We're allowed to use inhuman punishment on inhumans," McGoo said then smiled at me. "That was a nice way to improve the day. Good to see you, Shamble. Did you come to buy me a drink or a cup of coffee?"

"I came to share a vital clue," I said.

"It seems more productive if we do that over a beer at the Goblin Tavern," McGoo said.

"It's only early afternoon."

"If you talk slowly, it'll be 5:00 p.m. soon enough."

I agreed that wasn't such a bad suggestion after all.

CHAPTER TWENTY-TWO

Since the Goblin Tavern was having Early Bird Trivia Night, our watering hole was less quiet and sleepy than McGoo and I preferred. Unnaturals gathered in teams to demonstrate their knowledge of obscure and inconsequential things. In the age-old rivalry, a full-furred werewolf team had squared off against a vampire team, with a third interloping team of swarthy monthly werewolves, who were equally hated by both sides.

The racket increased as we claimed our usual stools at the far end of the bar. "It'll be a little loud for us to discuss the case," McGoo said, "but at least it's better than Scottish dancing night."

I groaned. "Anything's better than Scottish dancing night."

McGoo considered. "The Irish singalong is awfully loud too, especially when the banshees come." He put his elbows on the bar. "Hey, Shamble, what comes out of a ghost's nose?" He didn't even wait for me to guess. "Boo-gers!"

Before I had to decide whether to pretend to laugh, the monthly werewolves howled, arguing over the correct answer as to how many Wolfman movies Lon Chaney had starred in.

"Lon Chaney wasn't in *any* of them!" one of the monthlies snarled. "It was Lon Chaney, *Junior.* Lon Chaney, *Senior* was in *Phantom of the Opera* and *The Hunchback of Notre Dame.* Lon Chaney, *Junior* was in *Abbott and Costello Meet Frankenstein.*"

"He's right," I muttered.

McGoo frowned at me and shook his head. "You don't want to get into that fight, Shamble. You can't win."

The vampires argued that Abbott and Costello movies didn't count. The full-furred werewolves insisted that the Wolfman wasn't a *real* werewolf and that his portrayal was morally offensive, to which the vampires replied that it was another time and another place, and one couldn't apply current standards of political correctness.

The trivia degenerated from there.

"Wait until they start arguing about the Hammer Dracula films," McGoo grumbled. "Then there's the debate over Bela Lugosi versus Christopher Lee, Frank Langella versus George Hamilton, and on and on."

"At least you and I concern ourselves with more consequential things," I said, thinking of Ben Hemoglobin, who was stewing in the holding cell. "Are you going to have a full-fledged interrogator work Ben over? See what information you can squeeze out of him?"

"We do have torture specialists," McGoo said. "We hire the ghost of the Marquis de Sade as a consultant, but I don't think we'll need that. Did you see the look on Ben's face? He's blabbing already. We'll just let him sit behind silver bars for a while. Pretty soon he'll be singing like a chicken."

"Have you ever *heard* a chicken sing?" I asked. "It's horrifying."

"I give him a day, and his goose is cooked."

"You're just full of the fowl clichés, aren't you, McGoo?"

He tried to hide his smile behind his beer glass. "There are so many of them."

I got down to the matter of Alterro's revelation about the keychain. "I learned about something called a delayed carnivorism spell. It might be the root cause of all the disappearances."

I told him about the rune on the keychain. McGoo asked, "Do you still have it? So we know what to look for?"

"Looked like a magic symbol to me. It shouldn't be too hard to get another keychain. Cyrus Redfarb was handing them out everywhere."

Deep in thought, McGoo slurped his beer. Francine had served us without even asking. The trivia shouting was getting too loud for us to order anything different. I saw that she was again preoccupied with the older vampire gentleman. One Fang seemed to be sweet on her, and I also noticed she wore a high-collared shirt to hide her neck. I wondered what hanky-panky those two might be up to after hours, but I realized it was none of my business, and good for Francine.

"I'll need proof so I can get a warrant," McGoo said. "Then we'll take a team to search the Monster Chow factory."

"You don't need a warrant," I said. "Just sign up for one of the tours and keep your eyes open."

"You took a tour, Shamble. Did you see anything?"

"I found a chicken feather," I said. "It seemed incriminating."

McGoo nodded slowly. "If we learned that Redfarb was illegally harboring the murderous chickens that killed Maynard Kleck, we could shut him down. That guy deserves justice. No good deed goes unpunished."

He surprised me by changing the subject. I knew something must be troubling him because it had been five minutes already and he'd only finished half of his beer. "Is the Quarter really a place where we want to raise a little girl, Shamble? Monsters on every corner. Delayed carnivorism spells. People getting pecked to death in homeless shelters for chickens."

"What choice do we have, McGoo? Rhonda dumped Alvina on our doorstep and then disappeared. Now the kid's our responsibility. Besides, she's a vampire girl, so she'll fit in here better than most. She seems to be well adjusted."

With a snort, McGoo took a long draw on his beer, draining the rest of it. "She must have supernatural powers if she can stay normal, cute, and good-natured after growing up under Rhonda. Compared to that, what's a few monsters?"

I nursed my beer while McGoo tried to attract Francine's attention for a second one. The bartender was wiping down spotted glasses while refreshing One Fang's drink. She didn't notice McGoo, nor did she react when the full-furred werewolf team pounded their paws on the table to their correct answer of the Japanese actor who had starred as the giant monster in *Frankenstein Conquers the World*.

"Neither of us is cut out to be a single dad, McGoo, but we don't have to be."

"Yeah, we've got each other," McGoo said.

"I'd shudder to think if the two of us were Alvina's only role models. But she's got Sheyenne and Robin too, and I don't think you could ask for better than that."

"Are they watching her now?" McGoo asked.

"Yes, Robin had about ten bankers' boxes of old files and she needed someone to organize them. Sheyenne couldn't do it herself, because picking up all those papers with her poltergeist powers gets exhausting."

"Glad you have a little office helper," McGoo said. "If she's good at it, the precinct has about ten years of sloppy records."

I finished my beer and decided to get back to the offices. I hadn't spent enough time there in the past few days, and I wanted to check in on Alvina.

O O O

By the time I arrived, Sheyenne and the vampire kid had already worked their way up to the letter C in all the files that had been stored in randomly disorganized bankers' boxes. A naturally efficient person, Robin was thrilled to be tying up loose ends on so many old cases.

"I'll be spending the next month typing up final reports," Robin said, "but it's best not to leave anything unfinished."

I nodded. "And we have an agreement with Howard Phillips Publishing. The Wannovich sisters are supposed to have access to all our cases, and they'll want the final details to give to their ghostwriter for the next novel."

"Not that they pay attention to the details," Sheyenne said. "Some of the ridiculous dialogue they put in those books! I would never say things like that, and neither would you, Beaux."

Robin tapped her lower lip. "Officer McGoohan would, though."

Alvina was particularly interested in the summary of our case with Jody Caligari, the young mad scientist boy who dreamed of becoming a talented supervillain someday. Without Jody's help in his guise as Dr. Darkness!!!, we would never have defeated the evil slum underlord Ah'Chulhu.

"He's cute." Alvina looked down at his photo. "Is he coming back?"

"Oh, he's cute," I said, "in an off-the-charts blood-sugar-rush sort of way. He'll be back for next year's junior mad-scientist camp." Alvina seemed to consider that a good thing.

Together we all worked through the night, and the awkwardly paternal part of me thought that it was time to send Alvina to bed. But she pointed out in a patient, logical, and far-too-mature way that she was a vampire and therefore nocturnal. "This way, I get life and career experience here in the offices."

"I second that," Sheyenne said and was pleased to move on to the first storage box with the letter D.

An hour before dawn, Fletcher's ghost arrived to talk about what we had discovered at the Talbot & Knowles Board meeting. He seemed both delighted and appalled by what we told him. "Harry Talbot would never get into business with someone like Ma Hemoglobin! We've had our issues in the past, but never anything like that!"

"That might not have been a discretionary act on his part," I said. "Ma has a way of getting what she wants."

Fletcher hung his spectral head. "Ma Hemoglobin will ruin the Talbot & Knowles reputation!"

"The high prices already gave you a bad reputation," I pointed out.

"When we started the blood bars, our intention was to provide only the highest-quality product, and that leads to high prices." He seemed miserable. "How do we extricate the company from the control of that gangster lady? I was sure my friend hadn't betrayed me."

"We're using every possible legal method," Robin said.

"And we do have one of her sons in lockup," I pointed out. "McGoo will be interrogating him soon."

Alvina finished stuffing a folder and put it into place alphabetically. "I love Talbot & Knowles. I never get to go there because my mom said it was too expensive—and because they were too far away."

"I'll have to take you there someday," I promised her.

Fletcher brightened. "I happen to have several coupons for a free high-end blood drink during Happy Hour. I may be expired, but the coupons aren't." He fished them out of his spectral pocket.

Alvina lit up. "Can we go? Can we all go?"

I looked at the time. "It's almost dawn, when most of the vamps will be heading back to their coffins. Happy Hour starts at sunrise." I took the coupons from Fletcher.

"We're all going," Robin said. "We've been working hard, and we deserve a break."

CHAPTER TWENTY-THREE

Fletcher still felt uncomfortable going to one of his own blood bars when he was persona non grata on the Board of Directors, so Robin, Sheyenne, and I accompanied Alvina for her well-earned treat. During Happy Hour we would just sit and have a pleasant, friendly conversation, watching a little girl drink blood.

"You've all been working so hard on the filing," I said. "The offices have really needed that extra organization."

"And a facelift. I brought in a potted flower," Alvina said. "It brightens up the place."

"And the files are only done up to the letter D," Sheyenne said. "We've still got an alphabet full of adventures to go."

"And when we get to the letter O," Robin pointed out, "there's a big new file under Obadeus."

"But we finished Ah'Chulhu," Alvina pointed out. "And Tony Cralo and his black-market body parts business."

"But you haven't gotten up to the Jekyll Beauty Products and Necroceuticals," I said. "Or Snazz the pawnbroker gremlin, or Missy Goodfellow and the Smile Syndicate."

After we entered the blood bar, Alvina stood looking at the extensive wall menu with a confusing variety of incomprehensible arterial drinks, each one originally developed by a team of mad scientists and phlebotomists. True connoisseurs could argue the subtle gourmet differences of positive and negative blood, the richness of type O, the piquant refreshing quality of A negative and the uplifting aftertaste of B positive. But straight blood, whether hot or on ice, whether mixed with half and half or soy milk, with artificial sweetener or pure cane sugar—none of that was what Alvina wanted. She read down the entire menu amazed and excited by the different varieties.

"A fresh supply in just this morning, young lady," said the cheery blood barista, looking down at Alvina. He was a young vampire with heavy eyebrows, a skinny face, and a skinny chin, as well as a taste for the mellow sounds of tuneless jazz to promote low blood pressure.

The line began to build behind us as Alvina carefully considered her options. She finally settled on the new and wildly popular unicorn frappé, made with real unicorn blood. And because she had the coupons from Fletcher, she added an extra shot of virgin's blood. I was certainly glad for the coupon because the actual price for the small drink was over $20.

The unicorn blood frappé was the most difficult type of drink to make, and by the time the barista had delivered it to a smiling Alvina, nine people were lined up behind us, impatiently flashing their fangs, tapping long fingernails on the countertop. But when Alvina turned around with her hair in pigtails, her freckled face showing delicately pointed baby-tooth fangs, she melted their hearts.

Since the sun had barely risen, we decided to sit outside under the deep red awning. The girl slurped through her straw, beaming with delight.

"We're glad you're staying with us, Alvina," Robin said. "I want to reassure you that we have your best interests at heart."

The girl's expression fell. "I know that tone of voice. You're going to send me to school."

Robin was taken aback. "That was my lawyer tone. I always talk like that."

"She does," I said.

Alvina wrapped her small hands around the cup with the swirling red rainbow colors of her unicorn frappé. She enjoyed the expensive drink and drained it within seconds. "Can I have another one?"

"I'm not sure you should have that much caffeine," I said. "Or sugar. Or artificial colors." I realized I was sounding like an overprotective parent.

Sheyenne broke in, "But we do have another coupon. Why not treat her, Beaux?"

Of course I couldn't object to that. "Sure, why not. I'm still in my spoil-the-kid phase." Alvina was delighted.

"I'll get it." Sheyenne took the second coupon and went to stand in line. I knew she would be a while, because the customers waiting in line behind us had seen Alvina's unicorn blood frappé, and each person decided they wanted one, too.

With all the high-maintenance orders, the harried blood barista looked as if he might go berserk himself. Alvina slurped the last foamy pink remnants of frappé, drawing hard on the straw to show the sheer sucking power a vampire could bring.

Watching Alvina, I still found her adorable. I was starting to think of her as at least half mine.

"We might make this a regular thing," I suggested, surprising Robin. "Depending on how much money we have in the petty cash fund. We want you to have a good childhood."

"So you're bonding with me over blood?" Alvina smiled. "At least you're trying."

"Blood ties are supposed to be the strongest."

We hadn't asked the girl much about her home life with Rhonda, but I wasn't sure I wanted to hear it, because the details would just make me angry. Since my embalming fluid is at a steady state, I don't have trouble with blood pressure, but if Rhonda had treated this little kid badly, I might do things I'd end up regretting.

"Don't worry, you're doing a good job," Alvina said, as if she felt we needed reassurance as much as she did. "You'd be surprised how resilient little kids are, and because I'm a vampire I can bounce right back." She looked away, toyed with her empty cup, and grew serious. "But being trapped in a little girl's body and still facing accelerated puberty ... that does get me down sometimes."

She looked mournfully at her empty frappé glass. I wished Sheyenne would hurry, but when I glanced back inside, the line had only moved forward by one customer.

"The teenage years are always awkward," Robin said. "I didn't fit in either."

Alvina was surprised, "But ... but you're beautiful, and you're perfect. You're smart. You're even a lawyer!"

"I admit I'm a lawyer, but I make the best of it. I had good schools, nice clothes, and my parents wanted everything for me. They wanted me to be an athlete and kept pushing me to join sports teams, track and basketball. But who goes to law school on a basketball scholarship? I wanted to help people, and with the law you can defend the defenseless. You can help the downtrodden. And after the Big Uneasy I saw a whole new class of individuals who needed my help. Monsters were treated badly. The laws had to be changed, and I meant to do it all myself."

"Robin's a real crusader, Alvina. You'll get used to it."

The vampire girl looked up at my partner with admiration.

"I'm not just a crusader," Robin said. "I'm an *attorney.*"

Alvina's expression flickered, and she frowned down at her empty drink. "You had everything, but I've been bounced around. I didn't even know who my father was until just recently, and then I met both of them. In fact, I still don't know which one's my father."

"It's either me or McGoo," I said. "You can flip a coin if you like."

"Or be content with both of them," Sheyenne said as she finally returned with another colorful and sickeningly sweet blood concoction. "And you can have Robin and me, too. We're a blended family—and that's better than a family on the rocks."

I groaned, "That joke was worthy of McGoo, Sheyenne."

"Just a little bartending humor after our experience at the Overbite Lounge the other night."

Alvina happily slurped her second drink.

"What do you think, Alvina?" Robin asked. "Do you want to be a lawyer? I can help you."

"Or maybe a private investigator," I suggested. "What do you want to be when you grow up?"

I saw tears appear in Alvina's eyes. "What do I want to be when I grow up? I won't grow up! I am what you see. I'll never be an adult, just forever stuck as a kid that nobody treats with respect. I won't have a boyfriend. I won't have a job. I won't get married. I'll never be taller than I am now. I ..." She sniffled, and her whole body started shaking. "I won't be able to have a normal life. I really am a freak, just like Mom said."

She was growing more and more upset, ready to explode.

"Now honey, don't worry. We'll help you get through it," Sheyenne said.

Alvina knocked her precious unicorn blood frappé aside. Her arms were shaking. Her nails started growing longer, and she jabbed them into the table top. Her face reddened. Her lips drew back to display alarmingly long fangs. "Never normal!" she shouted, her voice building to a raw, wailing scream. Her eyes grew red, and she thrashed out of her seat.

I grabbed her, and Robin caught her other wrist, but Alvina was like a dervish, yelling wordlessly. The other blood bar customers backed away, astonished. Several set their unicorn frappés on the counter and fled.

I tackled Alvina, trying to hold her down. "I've got you. I've got you!"

Sheyenne was already calling an ambulance. Now Robin took hold of the vampire girl's feet. She twisted and snarled, spitting, raving, and I expected green vomit to spew out and her head to rotate all the way around her shoulders. Her twin pigtails bobbed about.

"No, Alvina. No!" She was certainly strong for a little girl, but after one last convulsion she slumped on the ground, silent and still. Her hands fell limp. Her fingers sprawled out. Her eyes closed, and she was completely unconscious ... as if she were dead.

The ambulance couldn't come soon enough.

CHAPTER TWENTY-FOUR

The sound of the banshee siren wailed in my ears, loud enough to make my skull ring as the ambulance screeched up to the Emergency Room entrance. EMTs rushed forward to take care of Alvina, who was strapped on a stretcher, but the banshee in the shotgun seat up front kept wailing and shrieking. Robin finally shook the creature by the shoulders, making her shut up. "We're here. No need for the siren!"

The banshee blinked, embarrassed. "Sorry. I was just so upset about that poor little lass."

"We all are," I said and rushed after the gurney as the emergency technicians rolled Alvina through the hospital doors. On the long, noisy ride careening through the streets of the Quarter, Robin, Sheyenne, and I had huddled in the back with Alvina, feeling helpless. The kid was entirely comatose, her skin paler than usual, but at least her oversized fangs had reverted to the small pointed baby teeth. But she wouldn't wake up.

"She's so cold," Robin said.

"She is a vampire, ma'am," said the EMT, hooking up a drip bag of plasma with extra vitamins.

"If she needs fresh blood I'll offer mine," Robin said. "I can spare it."

The techs hooked up diagnostics, writing down details on the charts. "We're giving her plenty of fresh blood, which was effective on the other similar cases. But this one doesn't seem to be responding...."

"She's a strong kid," I said to Robin and Sheyenne. "She'll pull through."

Dr. Zonda Nefarious met us in the emergency room, bustling forward in her black pointy hat and wearing a deeply concerned expression. "Is it another case like the other blood rampage? I'm not sure what we can do other than let her sleep it off. Did she get fresh blood?"

"Look at her! It's not like all the others," I said. "She's still in a coma."

The witch doctor shone a penlight into Alvina's slitted and unresponsive pupils, tried to take a pulse, but couldn't find any. "Everything seems normal," she said. "So now we have to figure out what's wrong."

In overlapping urgent conversations Sheyenne, Robin, and I described what had happened after she'd finished her overpriced blood drink.

"Clearly the culprit is the blood bar," Robin said. "It was something in her unicorn blood frappé ... but Travis Spade just had straight blood with a dollop of cream."

"And artificial sweetener," I said.

"Hmm, and artificial sweetener," said Dr. Zonda. "I have to run more analysis. I have a full staff of Igors on call."

"Just keep the kid safe," I said. "Please."

Sheyenne hovered in front of Robin. "It's not just Talbot & Knowles, because the biggest incident of blood rampage was at the Overbite Lounge."

Dr. Zonda poked and prodded Alvina, but the little vampire lay completely motionless. "Hmm, yes, I was brought in on the Overbite case, too. All those victims had an extremely adverse reaction to some contaminant in the blood. Inside the lounge, though, I could only use my portable analysis devices, and I was limited to the blood spatter around the dance floor and the bar area."

"You didn't test any victims directly?" Robin asked. "That seems a vital step."

"I wasn't allowed to. Each victim was anonymous. Most of them disappeared as soon as they recovered, and I couldn't even take samples back to the hospital."

I nodded, understanding. Sheyenne met my eyes and said, "What happens in Overbite, stays in Overbite."

Two other emergency room physicians joined in, consulting with Dr. Zonda, discussing the kid's charts and the readings on the bleeping machines. The witch doctor scuttled off with her colleagues, wheeling Alvina's gurney with her. Dr. Zonda waved back at us, "Stay in the waiting room. As soon as we've treated her, we'll take the girl to the intensive care unit. You can spend the night with her, if you like."

"We like." I said. It sounded like I'd been reading a Facebook post. "No, I don't like—not at all, but we'll be here for her. We need to call McGoo."

They whisked Alvina back into the treatment center, and the doors flapped shut behind her with finality.

The waiting room was a drab and depressing place filled with old magazines that no one had wanted to read when they were new. A vending machine displayed a variety of Monster Chow products, along with a few token candy bars and snack chips for the human patients or their families. A coffeemaker held an old bitter brew that smelled even worse than what I'd had at the Ghoul's Diner. Two mummies were playing checkers. A stale talk show droned on the television set.

As the hour stretched out, I paced the room, shuffling back and forth. When I sat down, Robin got up to take her turn pacing, after which Sheyenne drifted around aimlessly.

McGoo finally burst in, his face flushed, his blue cap askew. "I came as soon as I heard. What happened to Alvina? Is she all right?"

"We don't know, McGoo," I said. "The kid went into seizures like one of the vampires going berserk, but she hasn't snapped out of it like the others did. She's still in a coma."

He looked angry and helpless, then took his turn pacing the room.

Finally, the witch doctor came out to talk to us. Her pointy hat was straight on her head, and her wild black hair stuck out in all directions. She wore a grave expression. "We've stabilized your daughter for now, and she's in a private room in the ICU. You can go see her now, but I don't know how to treat her condition until I run more tests. There was some sort of toxin in the drink she consumed, as with the others … but the others woke up much sooner than this. Something's different with this sweet little girl."

"Are you sure it wasn't artificial dyes?" I asked. "Those unicorn blood frappés were unnaturally bright."

"I'm afraid that doesn't line up with the other data points," Zonda said. "We think it's in the base blood supply, in some random shipments to Talbot & Knowles, and other outlets."

McGoo clenched and unclenched his fists. "I'm going to confiscate everything down to the napkins and the stir sticks in that blood bar. We'll shut it down as a health hazard."

Sheyenne said, "Let's go see Alvina. That's most important right now."

In the private hospital room, my dead heart broke to see the kid stretched out in a pint-sized coffin bed. Dozens of monitors filled the room like surplus equipment from a mad scientist's lab, and they produced an odd assortment of beeping, whistling, and pinging noises, which made Alvina's condition seem even more serious. Two bags of blood hung on a metal tree on each side of her hospital bed; one tube led to a needle poked in her arm and another dangled down like a straw tucked between her lips.

I looked at McGoo, and he glanced back at me. It was apparent how much both of us already cared for the kid. "I'll give blood, if she needs it."

"I already offered," Robin said.

"But I'm her father," McGoo added.

"Maybe," I said. "Or maybe we can give her half and half."

"That isn't the problem," Sheyenne said. "The witch doctor said this is something different. Alvina's reaction isn't like the others."

We sat in sullen silence for a long moment until McGoo said, "In a situation like this, we have to face another difficult decision."

Robin straightened, wondering if there was some legal testament or parental consent form we had to sign.

McGoo didn't take his eyes off of me. "One of us has to call Rhonda."

"She's already abandoned her daughter," Sheyenne said defensively. "We're the ones watching out for Alvina now."

"Her mother still deserves to know," I said. "But Rhonda's phone no longer works. Disconnected."

McGoo made a disgusted sound. "Rhonda's been disconnected for a very long time."

"There may be ways we can track her down," Robin said, sinking her teeth into the legal problem. "I could even file a motion to make *her* pay child support. She's turned over the care and wellbeing of her daughter to you two. She can pay some of the expenses."

"I like the sound of that," I said. "But not right now. We'll be vindictive later, when we have time to enjoy it."

Dr. Zonda bustled into the room, still checking her readings and still frowning. "We've discovered why this patient is reacting differently from the other victims. It's because of her accelerated puberty chemistry. Going through the vampire metamorphosis at this particular point in her development seems to have altered the chemical reactions. The mystery contaminant drove other vampires berserk, and they recovered quickly. But in Alvina … this is serious."

"As if puberty wasn't already a big enough pain in the butt," McGoo grumbled.

"Did anyone else at the blood bar have the same reaction?" Robin asked. "A lot of other customers ordered unicorn blood frappés."

Dr. Zonda shook her head. "No other cases so far. That contaminant is hit or miss, only in certain samples … like a widespread test."

Robin was determined. "If it was Talbot & Knowles, their base supply must be corrupted. Fletcher is going to be disturbed to hear that, even if he's been ousted from the Board."

I couldn't take my eyes away from Alvina in the ICU coffin bed. "We know that Ma Hemoglobin is involved. They must be poisoning the blood in the supply chain, adding some strange chemical. I bet that's how it got to the Overbite Lounge, too. The Hemoglobin gang tried to knock over Bubba's Bloodmobile, and that shipment was on its way to the Overbite. It was the nightclub's supply."

McGoo frowned. "But they only stole a few bags before they fled. They took forever dinking around, but didn't accomplish much. How could they be responsible?"

I held up a finger like a stern professor. I imagined myself in a real "the butler did it" moment. "What if that raid was just a diversion? Maybe they weren't trying to *steal* the blood after all. They could have taken that time to *add* something to the blood supply. After the gang got away, the shipment was safely delivered to the Overbite ... and we all saw what happened."

The witch doctor made notes on her clipboard. "I'll take all that into account. We'll do everything we can for your little girl, I promise." She patted Alvina on the cold forehead. The medical monitors kept beeping, whistling, and humming. Blood continued to pump into the little girl's mouth and into her vein. She didn't move.

McGoo clenched his hands on the rail at the side of Alvina's bed. "When I got the call, I was interrogating Ben Hemoglobin in the holding cell, and I think he was about to crack. He might tell us everything we need to know." I had never seen McGoo so angry or so determined. "When I get my hands on Ma Hemoglobin, I'm going to tear her limb from limb, I swear."

"You don't get all the fun, McGoo." I felt just as angry. "We'll each take an arm and leg and pull. It'll be just like a chicken wishbone."

McGoo smiled. He liked that idea. "And I bet we'll each make the same wish."

CHAPTER TWENTY-FIVE

We stayed in the ICU all day. Robin made phone calls. I made phone calls. McGoo used his phone to play Skull Crush.

Finally, after dark I was growing restless and impatient. "I don't want to leave Alvina, but I can't just sit around. The cases don't solve themselves, and I'll do better if I'm wandering. Who knows what I might bump into?"

Robin came to a decision. "I'll go with you, Dan. Fletcher has to know what happened with the unicorn blood frappé, and there's a lot of legal work I can do. I want to file a motion to close the blood bar stores for health concerns until we can figure out what's causing the bad blood."

"There'll be riots," I said. "Putting a tourniquet on the high-end gourmet blood supply in a city full of vampires is going to get ugly."

McGoo rose from Alvina's bedside. "And I need to go squeeze some answers out of Ben Hemoglobin."

Sheyenne hovered by the bedside. "I'll stay here, but I'll call the instant anything happens."

Leaving the hospital, Robin and I strolled through the comfortably dark streets, and even though Alvina's condition weighed upon us like a dark swamp fog, we preoccupied ourselves with the business at hand. Robin had sunk her teeth into the problem of finding Alvina's mother and making her accountable.

Robin's a dedicated lawyer, ruthless in serving the interests of her clients.

"It's not right for a woman just to abandon a sweet child like that. I hope Alvina pulls out of it." Her voice suddenly hitched. "She only got up to the letter D in our filing boxes, and I know she dreamed of finishing the alphabet someday."

"She'll finish, Robin. Don't worry."

We turned down another one of the long, narrow alleys strewn with garbage, bones, discarded bags, and discarded unnaturals snoozing comfortably among the debris. As dark alleys went, this was a main thoroughfare, a shortcut that would take us to the main business district and to our office building. I knew the city like the back of my gray undead hand.

As she brainstormed her brief, Robin cited chapter and verse of numerous legal precedents that I couldn't follow, but I found the sound of her voice soothing. A homeless zombie in tattered clothes huddled against a slimy brick wall, gnawing on a bone he had found. He smiled and wished us good evening as we headed deeper into the darkness.

Robin switched subjects, suggesting that the proof of contaminated blood was not only sufficient justification to shut down the Talbot & Knowles operation, it was also a way to assert that without Fletcher's wise guidance on the Board of Directors, the company's business practices had gone astray.

"We can turn the tables and oust Harry Talbot," she said. "Put Fletcher back at the head of the Board."

"Then would he have to go to meetings with Ma Hemoglobin?" I asked.

"I propose we start an entire new company administration with the whole Hemoglobin gang behind bars." She huffed.

Once again I thought of the poor vampire kid lying in a coma. "Or sending them to the electric chair would suit me just fine."

I was so focused on imagining the sizzle and pop as that vile woman and her bottom-of-the-gene-pool sons turned into a Justice Department, afternoon barbecue that I didn't notice the rustling in the debris, the burbling clucking sounds.

"There's another exception in the case of Karloff versus Krueger," Robin was saying, pulling out obscure legal paragraphs as if to comfort herself. "We can—"

In a burst of white feathers, razor-sharp beaks, and blood-red wattles and combs, the chickens were upon us. They clucked and cackled, flapped their wings, and struck with their plump rotisserie-designed bodies. Their claws were outstretched on chicken feet that would have been too tough and gamey for even the cheapest Chinese dim sum.

Robin lifted her hands to cover her face as a dozen chickens swooped in. Demonic and ruthless, their intent was obviously to kill. I smacked one of them off of Robin's shoulder with my bare hand. Another had gotten tangled in her hair, and she flailed at it.

The chickens were upon me too, clucking, hissing, scratching. I grabbed one by the wing and threw it against the brick wall with enough force that the evil creature made a sound like a deflating bagpipe. Robin swung her briefcase and smacked another chicken, making feathers fly.

But they kept coming.

Beaks punctured my skin, claws tore my sport jacket, a wing knocked my fedora askew. I saw blood on Robin's smooth brown skin, and it made me really angry. I couldn't stop thinking of how Maynard Kleck had been pecked to death in his feral chicken homeless shelter. He had befriended them, and they had committed murder most fowl.

It was kill or be killed. I finally seized one and did what any hillbilly grandmother knew how to do; I wrung the chicken's neck. It gave a last defiant squawk and fell limp, then I held the chicken by its flopping neck and swung it around like a barnyard cudgel.

Barely able to fly, another chicken dive-bombed my head, knocking the fedora loose, and I swung the limp-necked carcass hard enough to batter the other chicken out of the air in a spray of white pinfeathers. Though marginally effective, the dead chicken was not a good enough weapon to scatter the entire flock. I had a better one in my pocket. My .38.

Robin shouted for help at the top of her lungs, but she went unanswered. Screams were not uncommon in dark alleys in the Unnatural Quarter.

I drew my pistol and fired. I caught one of the feral chickens full in the chest splitting it through the wishbone before I'd even had a chance to make a wish. Blood and feathers sprayed in all directions.

"That's two dead chickens," I said, "with a whole pack to go."

I shot another one. The cawing and clucking had reached a crescendo, and Robin and I were being driven back. We took shelter next to a dumpster, and I knew this was our last stand. The chickens kept coming. I thought of that movie *Zulu Dawn*, and I knew how the British soldiers must have felt under the onslaught of wave after wave of angry tribal warriors.

"I've got your back, Robin," I said. "We'll get out of this."

"Don't lie to me, Dan," she said.

"It's not a lie. I'm being hopeful," I said. "We'll get out of this because Alvina needs us." I shot and killed another chicken, but I knew I didn't have enough bullets to kill them all.

"A little help would still be nice. Where's the cavalry when you need it?" Robin said, holding up her briefcase as a shield.

The cavalry did arrive in the form of looming, shaggy monsters that lumbered down the alley, knocking garbage bags and empty boxes and snoozing homeless creatures aside. A pair of hulking, yeti-sized yetis appeared, grabbing chickens by the feathers and throwing them into the air. The demonic birds squawked and cackled, turning their attention from us.

"Are those Bigfoots?" Robin asked.

"*Bigfeet* is the correct plural," I said. "And, yes they are."

When the hairy Wookiee-like creatures scattered the flock, the feral chickens knew they had met their match. They retreated, flapping furiously to lift their barnyard bodies up to the roofs of the buildings on either side of the alley, where they disappeared into the darkness overhead.

Four chickens lay dead in the alley. Robin and I were battered and scuffed. She bled from half a dozen peck wounds on her cheeks, neck, and arms. I heaved a long sigh and looked up at our towering furry rescuers. "You certainly came out of nowhere."

The Bigfeet glanced at each other, then back at us. "We've been here all along. You looked like you needed help."

I pondered, trying to capture the stray thought just at the end of my mind. "Haven't I seen you somewhere before?"

"You have," said the Bigfoot. "We keep trying to make an impression."

Robin brushed pinfeathers from herself, attempting to regain her dignity. She touched some of the bleeding wounds. "Those were the most aggressive chickens I've ever seen."

The two Bigfeet bent over and picked up the dead chickens. "We'll take these, if you're not going to use them."

"Be my guest," I said. The two hairy beasts gathered their prizes and shuffled off. They were gone before I remembered to thank them.

CHAPTER TWENTY-SIX

Robin had faced many a ruthless opposing counsel in a courtroom, but she had never before experienced such an attack. The incident certainly ruffled our feathers.

I got her safely back to our offices, where she insisted, unconvincingly, that she was all right. She brushed feathers and chicken poop from her jacket and skirt. "Don't worry, Dan. We're safe now. I'll clean up."

"You always clean up very nicely." I looked at my hands, surveying the numerous peck marks in my sport jacket and my skin. "I hope Ms. Eccles gives quantity discounts." I touched my forehead, glad that I hadn't bothered to keep the putty plug. That thing was more trouble than it was worth.

"The Wannovich sisters need to work their rejuvenation spell on you again," Robin said.

"I've certainly earned it." The witches at Howard Phillips Publishing performed a monthly touchup spell in return for being allowed to use my name and case files for their fictional zombie detective, but I suspected that a roving pack of predatory feral chickens might be too ridiculous even for their ghost writer.

"I'm not worried about my physical condition right now." I straightened out my jacket, then straightened out my face. I flopped my fedora and reshaped it before putting it back on my head. "Alvina's in the hospital. Ma Hemoglobin's gang is on the loose, and some deadly contaminant is being introduced in the blood line. Somebody's got to pay for that." I drew a breath. "And I don't intend to accept credit."

I left the offices again, knowing that Robin would stay there and remain safe. My first target was to return to the scene of the crime, where Alvina had been poisoned: the Talbot & Knowles Blood Bar where we had spent so much time together (mostly waiting in line to get her unicorn blood frappé). That was the source of what had sent our little girl into a coma. Immediately after the incident, the Unnatural Quarter's Health & Decay Board had closed down that specific location, but I suspected the contaminant had spread in a similar vein throughout the chain. And Ma Hemoglobin, now on the run, had something to do with it.

The store was closed and shuttered, as it often was during daylight hours to protect their vampire customers, but now yellow police tape dangled around the doors, and a crowd of surly protesters had gathered outside from all walks of monsterdom. Zombies milled about (more than usual), along with werewolves, restless ghosts, and even a troll family that was using the angry protest as an instructive family outing. The Suck Dynasty brothers/cousins were also there, showing off their extravagant beards, pot bellies, plaid shirts, and trucker caps.

I doubted I would get much quiet investigating done, given the crowd, but it was entertaining to watch. Raising their signs, the mob members shouted, "You're poisoning us!"

"And charging an arm and a leg!" cried a zombie who was, in fact, missing an arm and a leg and was propped up by two of his friends. They shouted at the dark, empty building, and I wondered who was there to hear.

Fletcher's ghost appeared, passing through the sealed door and raising his spectral hands. "Please, please! I promise we'll work this out. Talbot & Knowles uses only the highest-quality ingredients."

"And the highest-cost ingredients," complained one of the vampires. "With the price of blood drinks, how is an aspiring writer supposed to get a play written?"

"We do offer Happy Hour specials and coupons," Fletcher said.

"Who the hell are you?" grumbled Ernie, the head of the Suck Dynasty. "And you're a ghost. What do you know about blood?"

"I have a college degree," Fletcher said. "My friend Harry and I formed Talbot & Knowles Blood Bars as a service to the community."

"Some service," muttered another vampire. "You drove up blood prices across the Quarter. Even a plain cup of blood at the Ghoul's Diner costs twice as much as it used to."

"It's a matter of supply and demand," Fletcher explained. "Truly, we're investigating. We're trying to make this right."

"By poisoning us all," Ernie muttered again. He raised his fist, bellowing to the gathered protesters, "The only way to be sure the blood is pure is to drink it right out of a human throat—the way it was meant to be. No straws."

His brothers/cousins agreed. "Yeah, drink fresh from the source."

"We need more humans. It's the only way to be sure."

That was an alarming turn of the conversation, although the rest of the crowd seemed to think it was a good idea. Fletcher's ghost spotted me in the crowd. "Dan Chambeaux! Help me here. We have to get this situation under control."

I shambled up to stand beside him. "I thought you weren't even a member of the Board anymore. Why are you here defending Talbot & Knowles?"

"I still feel a sense of obligation. This company's my baby. Harry and I built it from scratch, after we put aside our differences. If it's been taken over by a corrupt organized crime influence, then we have to take a stand, even if it does get bloody."

"It's Ma Hemoglobin, no doubt about that," I said. "Though to describe her crime as 'organized' might be a bit of an exaggeration."

Behind us, the yellow-taped door to the blood bar opened, and a thin harried-looking man stepped out. He had a goatee like Fletcher's, but his was dark brown instead of bleached blond. He was mostly bald, with his remaining fringe of hair trimmed short. Fletcher spun in the air and looked at him with surprise and delight. "Harry! I haven't seen you in ages. Tell me what's going on since you ousted me from the company."

"It was bad advice." At least Talbot had the decency to look embarrassed. "It was a hostile takeover, and I don't do well with hostility. Now we've got to save our company. You and me, Fletcher. Like always." He stepped next to his partner's ghost and faced the protesters. "I'm Harry Talbot and this is Fletcher Knowles. Even though neither of us is a vampire, you might say our names are written in blood." He sniffled, deeply ashamed. "Something terrible has gone wrong with our product. We appreciate your patience while we look into this unfortunate matter."

"How did the poison get into the blood in the first place?" demanded Ernie. "If your baristas drained it fresh from humans right there at the store, then your customers could see that quality standards are imposed. That's the way you should do it."

I was surprised the guy knew so many big words.

"The administration of Talbot & Knowles has recently undergone a few dramatic changes." Talbot glanced at the ghost beside him. "Sorry, Fletcher, I didn't mean to do it. It was out of my control." He turned back to the crowd. "We were influenced by a ruthless criminal known as Ma Hemoglobin, but she is on the run and the police are after her. That means Talbot & Knowles can go back to providing the expensive gourmet blood drinks you've come to expect."

This elicited a mixed round of cheers and boos as the protesters reacted to different parts of his statement.

"*He* looks like fresh blood," said Ernie, and his brothers/cousins agreed. "Let's all have a drink. One sip each."

The vamps snarled, showing their fangs and easing toward Harry Talbot.

"What about the little girl who was poisoned?" asked a middle-aged housewife vampire. "How do we know that won't happen to all of our kids?"

Talbot said, "Our blood baristas are highly trained, and every job application has a complete psychological profile. This won't happen again, I assure you."

"I'll help you make sure it doesn't," Fletcher said. "I'm onboard now. In the past I spent too much time running the Basilisk Nightclub, but this is my company too. I shouldn't have left you by yourself, Harry. If the two of us had stuck together, best friends forever, Ma Hemoglobin never could have wormed her way in."

Talbot was about to cry.

"We shouldn't have had a falling out," Fletcher continued. "I'm sorry I left you with all the responsibilities."

"And I'm sorry you got killed by a slimy tentacle demon," Talbot said, and that was enough for them to bury the hatchet. The two stood together. "We are Talbot and Knowles, and we take full responsibility."

"Good," yelled the protesters. "Get 'em!"

Sensing an untapped market in the gathering mob, a local produce vendor from the equally overpriced gourmet grocery chain of Less-Than-Whole Foods had set up a cart of rotting vegetables, rancid meats, and clotted and sour dairy products. Protesters purchased the items at discounted prices then used the materials as ammunition. Rotten tomatoes, overripe cantaloupes, green moldy yogurts, and decomposing meats showered the two men standing in front of the blood bar entrance. Even the zombie spectators got into the fun by throwing rotten brains extracted from internet trolls, which were considered too poisonous and vitriolic to sell even in the deep-discount bin.

Seeing the oncoming barrage of unpleasant groceries, Fletcher swooped in front of his partner to protect him from the onslaught. He held up his hands to block the flying garbage, but since he was a ghost, Fletcher provided very little physical protection. The rotten tomatoes, cantaloupes, yogurts, meats, and internet troll brains passed right through him and splattered Harry Talbot, who dodged with little success.

"Wait, wait!" he cried as the protesters continued pelting him. "I'll make it up to you."

I wanted to prevent this from erupting into greater violence, but I also remembered poor Alvina's face as she writhed in convulsions, going berserk from the colorful and overly sweetened unicorn blood frappé this very store had sold her. I couldn't feel too bad about it.

Splattered with muck and stinking debris, Talbot pawed at his pockets and yanked out a sheaf of small paper cards. "I have coupons! You can all have coupons! One free high-end blood drink—a $40 value!"

This remarkable offer quieted the angry mob, which turned into a different sort of mob stampeding forward to snatch the coupons out of his hands. After the feeding frenzy was over and the protesters dwindled into the streets, a distressed Harry Talbot collapsed onto the cement step in front of the police-taped door.

"That was a lot of coupons," I observed. "That offer might bankrupt your company."

Fletcher hovered next to his friend, trying to wipe away the rotten tomato stains and the gloppy yogurt, but his intangible hand passed right through.

"Were they the usual coupons?" Fletcher asked.

"Yes, thank goodness," Talbot said with a sigh. "We'll be fine."

I gave them a curious look. "What does that mean?"

"The coupons are good only for today and only at this store—which has been closed by the police. We'll be out of here before they read the fine print."

"You always were a good businessman, Harry," Fletcher said. "Glad we teamed up. Should we go back to the Basilisk Nightclub? I'll buy you a drink. We have a lot to catch up on."

"That would be fine with me." Talbot looked relieved. "Are you sure it's safe? That tentacle monster is gone?"

Fletcher gave a dismissive gesture with his ghostly hand. "That was only a temporary monster."

I wasn't ready to relax. "Before you two sit around the campfire and roast marshmallows, my daughter's in a coma because of whatever chemical was in your blood. How are we going to stop that from happening again?"

"Simple enough," Talbot said. "Just stop Ma Hemoglobin and everything will be fine."

"Good," I said sarcastically. "I like easy solutions."

CHAPTER TWENTY-SEVEN

The basic principle of Harry Talbot's solution was sound, and I already had a big enough beef with Ma Hemoglobin and her boys to supply an entire chain of hamburger stands. The problem was catching her, and stopping her.

McGoo had her son Ben locked up behind silver bars in a holding cell back at the UQPD. I decided to help with the interrogation. I'm good at twisting arms, or any twistable body part. The boy had already demonstrated his penchant for spilling his guts, and we needed to make him spill some more.

At the Unnatural Quarter precinct headquarters, I strode through the tall doors beneath the loitering stone gargoyles. Again, the young frog demon at the reception desk looked up at me, flicked out her long, forked tongue, and said "Hey, you can't go back there!" I ignored her, waving to the other beat cops I knew, detectives working on cases, handcuffed perpetrators waiting to post bail, and shark attorneys waiting to pick up clients (including one literal shark demon, with big fangs and hard gray skin in a pinstriped business suit).

Above McGoo's desk, which was empty, I paused to note the poster of Hairy Harry, the legendary vigilante werewolf cop who took the law into his own paws. I had met Hairy Harry in person when I solved the case of his missing hellhound. That werewolf cop set an example—not necessarily a good one—for the UQPD.

When McGoo interrogated Ben Hemoglobin, he probably intended to go all "Hairy Harry" on him.

And I wasn't going to object. After Alvina's ordeal, this was personal for us. We'd play Bad Cop-Bad Cop on Ben, whether or not he needed it.

I headed for the holding cells in the back of the building, a secure area with cinderblock walls painted a queasy shade of seafoam green. I could hear McGoo's voice growing angrier and louder. "You'll talk, or else."

"No!" the vamp prisoner cried. "I'll talk!"

"Not so fast. What's happening to the blood supply? What is your gang doing to it? I've got a little vampire girl in intensive care because of what you did!"

"I want a lawyer," Ben whined just as I shambled up to the bars of the holding cell.

"I can suggest one," I said, getting tough to double-team the already-intimidated vampire. "Robin Deyer is the best lawyer representing unnaturals in the Quarter." I gave him a hard smile from the other side of the bars. "Robin just spent hours at the bedside of that vampire girl you poisoned, but I'm sure she'll be objective and do her best for you."

McGoo looked at me from inside the cell, ran his eyes up and down my rumpled, battered form, noting the peck marks, the traces of pinfeathers, the smears of gray-white poop. "You look like shit, Shamble."

"I look like chicken shit, actually." I explained about the second attack of the feral barnyard fowl.

Ben Hemoglobin sat on the cot and put his head in his hands, moaning. "I can't stay here! I'm claustrophobic. I can't even sleep in my own coffin without leaving the lid open." He burst into tears. "I want my mommy."

"Your ma is definitely a wanted woman," McGoo agreed. "We want her too. We'll even put her in a holding cell next to yours so she can reach through the bars and wipe snot from your noise with a tissue."

Ben brightened. "That would be nice."

McGoo let me into the cell so the two of us could do a tag team interrogation. I said, "I saw those vamps go berserk at the Overbite Lounge—because of the blood you contaminated. What did your gang do to the supplies in Bubba's Bloodmobile?" I demanded.

"We just added a little enhancement," Ben said. "Ma's been testing it. Since she was on the Talbot & Knowles Board of Directors, we wanted to make the blood more addictive so vampires would go out and buy it more often."

McGoo scratched his red hair. "That doesn't make any sense. Vampires already need to drink blood. What's the advantage of making it more addictive? That's like making air addictive, or water. Or coffee. Things we *require* to live."

"No, not simple blood," Ben said. "But the high-end beverages, the foamy oxygenated arterial macchiatos, the blended iced blood drinks, half-clotted venous blood, a light pink latte with fewer antigens. The really expensive ones."

I added, "The ones that take forever to make."

"Exactly," Ben said. Once the miserable vampire started talking, it was as if we had fed him spoiled Mexican food and his confession came out like diarrhea. "Ma's always been working on ways to make things more addictive. It's a hobby of hers. She came up with a really potent substance called Simply Irresistible. It adds a certain special something to the base blood and pumps the vampires up. Each batch is home made, and sometimes the formula is off and triggers a few side effects."

"Yeah, we've seen that," McGoo said.

"How did Ma Hemoglobin invent such a thing?" I asked. I couldn't picture the battleship in a dress as a research chemist.

Ben blinked up at us. "Oh, Ma's always whipping up something in the kitchen, a few spices here and there, some cleaning chemicals, a secret ingredient. She's been at it a long time. She started out trying to get her munchie clients addicted to something so they would be her customers forever."

"What munchie clients?" McGoo asked.

"Originally she worked in the snack food industry. Ma's first success was with potato chips, adding extra salt and artificial flavorings so that no one could eat just one." Ben nodded to himself, waxing nostalgic. "After the Big Uneasy we got into the black-market blood-supply trade. It was a family business."

I frowned. "It's because of seedy black-market blood vendors that the Talbot & Knowles blood bars took off in the first place. Vampires didn't want to buy questionable supplies from back alley pushers or street corner dealers. It's a clean business now, reputable. Harry Talbot and Fletcher Knowles made things better for everyone."

"Right," Ben said. "That's why Ma had to fix it. Those two do-gooders almost ruined the entire market, but Ma has a good business head on her shoulders."

"And what do you boys bring to the operation?" McGoo asked.

"Muscle," Ben said, "or at least body weight. All of us together can do a lot of shooting, and that's what Ma needs."

"Where's your gang hideout?" McGoo wanted to know. "Where can we find your Ma?"

"It's a safe and secure place," Ben said defiantly. "You'll never find it."

"How do you know we won't?" I asked.

"Because even I can't find it. That's why I always stay with the group. I used to have the address written on my hand." He held up his palm and frowned. "But I washed my hands yesterday and now I have no way of knowing." He squirmed on his cot. "Do you have any blood? All this talking sure makes me thirsty."

I could see the signs of withdrawal on his pale gray skin, the sweat on Ben's brow, the jitters. I suddenly made a mental leap, although such things often turn into a mental stumble for me. "You drink the contaminated blood yourself! You've been sipping some of the bags with the Simply Irresistible chemical in it."

"No!" he shouted. "Never! Only on weekends ... not very often. Not since last night." He began to whimper. "Are you sure you don't have any?"

"We only have Monster Chow blood shakes from the vending machine," McGoo said. "But it'll come out of your prisoner account."

"Do they have the raspberry one?" he asked, sounding resigned.

"I'll check the vending machine once we get more answers," McGoo said.

The interrogation was going quite well, but the bomb interrupted the flow. A loud explosion blew out the back of the holding cell.

The loud roar and boom broke out the entire wall, blasting chunks of concrete bricks toward us and out into the alley behind the station. McGoo banged his head on the silver bars, and I took countless cinderblock shards to the chest and face, which did even more damage than the pecking chickens had. Smoke and dust filled the cell.

From outside, I heard shouting voices. "Move, move! Use the chain, Louis. Rip out the wall!"

A thick chain with a grappling hook clanked through the blasted hole and caught on the edge of the cinderblocks. A winch groaned loudly as the chain tightened, ripped out more concrete bricks, and caused the whole wall to topple. As the smoke and dust cleared, I picked myself up and saw figures rushing in from the alley to help the jailbreak operation. An expanded hearse served as a getaway car. Ma Hemoglobin waved her plump arms and bellowed, "Ben Hamanubin, you come to your mother right this instant!"

Ben blinked, confused, as if wondering what he should do.

"This instant, boy, you hear?"

Charlton, one of the human sons, yelled, "Come on Ben. Don't be an idiot."

Coughing, Ben scrambled around and tripped on the rubble on the cell floor. Two cops rushed to the closed bars, yelling, "He's getting away!"

I lurched forward to stop Ben just as the young vamp suddenly realized that, yes, he was actually supposed to be escaping. His vampire brother Len jumped through the ragged hole into the cell and cuffed his brother on the side of the head. "You'd lose your testicles if they weren't stapled on. Now get to the hearse quick!"

From the outside, other cops rattled the silver bars of the holding cell, but no one had thought to bring the keys. "Hey you! No escaping!"

I started throwing cinderblock chunks at Ben and Len as they dove through the blasted wall, but my aim was poor. There's a reason why you rarely see zombies on softball teams.

Outside in the alley, the rest of the Hemoglobin gang opened fire, peppering the wall of the cell, striking ricochet sparks on the silver bars. I had to duck from the barrage of bullets; luckily, McGoo was already sprawled flat on the floor. The other cops scattered out of the way.

Ma Hemoglobin cackled loudly as all of her boys piled into the hearse and she swung herself behind the wheel.

I crawled back to the hole in the cinderblock wall and poked my head out just in time to see the getaway hearse peeling off with a squeal of tires, leaving a black rubber stain on the pavement.

McGoo sat up and groaned.

Now, with Ben gone, we had no way of knowing where to catch Ma Hemoglobin and find the substance that had poisoned Alvina.

CHAPTER TWENTY-EIGHT

e were all a little busy when the escaped ambulatory skeleton burst into the offices, begging for help. It was just one more thing at the end of a very long and turbulent day.

The UQPD was in an uproar, as usually happens whenever a most-wanted criminal gang leader blows out the back wall of the holding cells. Medics tended McGoo for cinderblock-explosion-related injuries. He had bandages on his forehead and his hands. One of the busybody medics kept trying to put his arm in a sling, even though he had no injury there. "But I need practice doing my slings," whined the medic, so McGoo let the man try, but when it was done, he slipped his arm out again and let the empty sling dangle like a noose around his neck.

When Robin called me about the unexpected visitor, I was still waiting for the dust to settle at the police station. Her voice sounded agitated. "Dan, there's a skeleton here to see you. Says it's important."

After she gave me the bare bones of the situation, I told McGoo I had to go. At the time, I didn't realize that the escaped skeleton was connected to our other important cases.

When I walked through the office door, covered with cinderblock dust as well as chicken shit, I saw the skeleton sitting naked in a chair near the receptionist desk. Skeletons aren't usually uptight about being naked, but this one seemed embarrassed, even frantic. It's difficult to read expressions on a skeleton's face, but I used my intuition. "Hello, sir. I'm Dan Chambeaux, private investigator. How can I help you? You look very concerned."

"I *am* concerned! Look at me." He held up his bony hands, which were wet and slick with traces of red on many of the bones, gristle around his joints.

I dutifully looked at him. "And what am I supposed to be seeing?"

"*Me!* Does this look normal to you?"

"It is if you're a skeleton," I said.

Robin tried to sound reassuring. "I assure you, sir, we'll do our best to help ... whatever the problem is."

"The problem is that I'm not supposed to be a skeleton. I'm a vampire!"

How could I not have noticed the fangs in his bony jaw?

With the distal phalanx of his forefinger, he tapped the front of his dental work, which was now exposed for all to see, including several old crowns in the back of his jaw that otherwise wouldn't have been noticeable.

I sat down in the chair at Sheyenne's desk, facing him. "You'd better start at the beginning. Tell us the whole story. How did you lose your skin?"

"Not just my skin, but my meat and my internal organs, too. Are you blind? I'm the one without eyes." Using his same bony forefinger, he tapped the empty orbital sockets above his nasal cavity.

Robin got her yellow legal pad and let the magical pencil take notes. "Our regular receptionist isn't here right now, but Dan and I will take care of you. What's your name?"

"Ronald. Ronald Skelton."

I perked up. "We know you. You're famous."

"Yes, my posters are all around town. That's how I knew to come here, but I've been disoriented for days. The posters say Chambeaux & Deyer is in charge of the case."

"We haven't had any calls so far," Robin said.

"Maybe because you don't look anything like your picture," I added.

"I looked like that before my face was peeled off!" Ronald's jawbones clacked together as he talked with greater urgency.

"If you haven't always been a skeleton, then how did this happen to you?" I leaned closer. I was glad he couldn't see very well, because I was a mess after all I'd been through in the past 24 hours.

"I'm just your average vampire," Ronald said. "I'm the bookkeeper for quite a few businesses in the Quarter." He raised his skull. "You should consider hiring me to do your business accounting. It shouldn't be left to amateurs."

"I don't think we have enough clients to worry about complicated bookkeeping," I said.

Robin quickly interjected, "What Dan means is that we do a lot of pro-bono work."

"That's what the clients call it when they don't bother to pay," I added.

"I always pay my bills. I have an impeccable credit rating."

Reassured, I got back to his case. "We'll do our best for you, sir. To the problem at hand—let me get this straight, you were a vampire when you went missing, but now you're a skeleton?" By making such an astute observation I hoped to impress him with my detective skills.

Ronald sniffled loudly, which indicated some remaining wet tissue inside his empty sinuses, although he didn't have lungs, and that made sniffling more difficult in general. "I was sitting at my office, minding my own business. I had finished doing a profit and loss statement for the Overbite Lounge, which was quite a challenge. They had very sloppy recordkeeping, but I straightened it out. It was two days after the Chamber of Commerce luncheon." He raised his skull again, turned it toward me. "We met there, didn't we? You were with that lovely ghost."

"Yeah, she's out of my league," I said, "but she's my girlfriend anyway."

"I sent you an invitation to connect on ChainedIn," he said. "Maybe we can share our network."

"I think we should start by determining what happened to your body," Robin said. For a vampire who had lost most of his corporeal existence, Ronald Skelton certainly seemed distractible.

"Well, I don't know exactly. As I said, I was in my office at my desk, going over ledgers, when suddenly I felt strange. I found myself transported in the blink of an eye."

"Did you still have eyes then?" Robin asked.

"Yes, I was me." He used his bony fingers to touch his rib cage. He felt his curved bones, tapped on his clavicle, and shook his head in dismay. "Now I'm just all … empty inside."

"You said you were transported somewhere?" I asked. "Where did you end up?"

"It was a factory of some kind, a big industrial slaughterhouse. I was stunned and disoriented—who wouldn't be?—but I saw vats of meat, fresh blood everywhere. I could *smell* it. As a vampire I'm attuned to things like that." He tried to inhale deeply, but his sense of smell was impaired due to his skeletal condition. Puzzled, he ran a clawed fingerbone around in his sinus cavity, as if trying to pick a nonexistent nose. "I had appeared on a narrow walkway high off the floor, around the edge of one of the vats.

"There were other vats with other unnaturals standing around the edges, and they all looked just as confused. We'd all just been minding our own business, and then we were whisked there. A group of full-furred werewolves reeked so strongly of cigar smoke I could smell it even over the blood and meat." As he continued his story, he shuddered, which made his bones rattle. "I suppose we should have run, but we didn't know what was going on."

"That sounds like the Monster Chow factory!" I said.

"Yes, that's it! Now I remember. I saw that nice man who gave a talk at the Chamber of Commerce. Cyrus Redfarb. He was watching it all from the floor below, looking up at us." The skeleton would have frowned, but was at a disadvantage without lips. "He's not nice after all. He didn't do anything to stop what happened next!"

The suspense was killing me. "And what happened next?"

"The werewolves started asking questions, but before we could get our bearings, some troll night watchmen took us by surprise at each of the vats. The werewolves went in first. The guards pushed them over the edge and into the soup, then Cyrus Redfarb turned on the machinery from a control panel below. It was horrible! Metal paddles and claws and rakes started spinning, churning the dough and blood, and the werewolves were sucked down and shredded into bite-sized pieces.

"The big guards were like quarterbacks, running along each metal walkway. In a flash, they knocked all of us into the separate vats—zombies into one vat, mummies, ghouls, and vampires into different ones. And I was thrown in. It all happened so fast."

Robin looked sickened. "But how did the unnaturals get transported to the Monster Chow factory in the first place?"

I remembered Alterro and the delayed carnivorism spell he had told us about. "You took one of Redfarb's keychains at the Chamber of Commerce meeting, didn't you?"

"Of course. It was a nice collectible."

"It was imprinted with a magical symbol, a spell used to kidnap and transport victims for the purpose of feeding. Redfarb must have activated it and transported you and a handful of victims into the Monster Chow factory."

"I don't remember any spell," Ronald said. "But I seem to be losing track of a lot of things. My brain is pretty much gone, you know."

Robin gasped. "The seed material in the factory! All that talk of how he uses texturized flavored protein, and he claimed it was one hundred percent unnatural. He has to get the meat starter material from somewhere, so he can grow it into the monster mash. Real zombies get separated into the zombie vat. Real werewolves go into the werewolf vat."

"And I went into the vampire vat," said Ronald Skelton.

It was all becoming clear to me now. "Using his chemistry sets and his mad scientist equipment, Redfarb uses that material to create more of the starter dough that he processes and forms and bakes into delicious Monster Chow kibble."

Robin's face twisted. "That's disgusting."

"I thought it was disgusting before, but now it's criminal. That solves the case of the missing unnaturals. Just as I suspected. That'll be all the proof McGoo needs for his warrant."

"So glad I could help," said Ronald. "Now can you help me? Even though I'm no longer missing?"

"You haven't explained how you escaped."

"It was a spot of good luck, that's for sure," he said. "When I was knocked into the vat along with two other vampires, I tried to swim. We were all clawing our way toward the side, but the paddles and scoops and meat-tenderizing forks grabbed at us. Both of the other vampires were sucked under by the vortex and chopped to pieces. I got caught with one of the claws, and I felt the skin rip right off of me. Another set of forks peeled away all of my muscles. But I still tried to swim.

"Just then, there was a problem at one of the other vats. The whole group of werewolves had gone in at once, which clogged the choppers—all that hair! While the troll security guards rushed to deal with the problem, I used the distraction to escape." He tried unsuccessfully to sigh. "By this point, all the meat had been stripped off my bones, and I was just a skeleton. But I'm a tough skeleton. When they were looking the other way, I managed to climb out."

I was impressed by his survival story, and I recalled the mayhem and the massacre at the Overbite Lounge, after which the mangled vampires had managed to heal. I wasn't surprised that Ronald Skelton could keep moving, even in this condition.

"It was as disorienting as the transportation spell in the first place, but I kept running. All I could think of was seeing my dear, sweet Regina again. We're monogamous, you know."

"We've heard," I said. "Unusual for vampires."

"We're a special couple. I came right here, Mr. Chambeaux. You have to stop what's going on at the Monster Chow factory. All those poor unnaturals!"

"There's no worse fate than ending up as snack food," I agreed.

"It's horrible," Robin said, her expression dark with fury. "Cyrus Redfarb has been on a goodwill tour, handing keychains to his audiences in an effort to identify potential victims that he can dump into his vats whenever he needs to replenish his seed material."

"He must need it a lot," I said. "Monster Chow is selling like crazy. I'll call McGoo right now, and he'll round up the UQPD for a raid, though they're a bit busy after the jail break."

"I don't want to cause any trouble," Ronald said, "but this is sort of an emergency."

"Ma Hemoglobin will have to wait," I said, shaking my head. "I'm heading right back to the police department."

"Ma Hemoglobin?" said Ronald. "Oh, she was there at the factory too, came running in all flustered."

Now he had my full attention. "Ma Hemoglobin was at the Monster Chow factory, too? What was she doing there?"

The skeleton turned away. "I didn't stop to talk with her, since I was fleeing for my life and my eyes were gone. But I'm certain it was her."

I couldn't understand what the gangster ma and the Monster Chow spokesman had in common. She had become a hostile silent partner in the Talbot & Knowles blood bars. Was she expanding her portfolio?

I hadn't even taken off my fedora, and now I was heading out again. "Robin, call Regina Skelton and let her know that we've solved the case. Her husband is safe." I paused, looking at the stripped vampire. "Well, at least tell her that her husband is *present*."

"I want to help," said Ronald. "Let me go with you. I feel obligated."

"No, you need to get back to your wife," I said.

"It's Regina's backgammon night. She won't be home anyway."

But I was already out the door. As long as I had my best human friend and the entire UQ police force, I didn't need the help of an ambulatory skeleton.

CHAPTER TWENTY-NINE

When I returned to police headquarters, McGoo had his arm back in a sling, apparently having been scolded by the earnest medic. The cops were still swarming over the broken rear wall, trying to build up temporary barricades to ensure that no well-meaning criminals attempted to break in and surrender themselves through the back door.

That wasn't my biggest worry at the moment. "McGoo, we've got to get to the Monster Chow factory. I've solved the case!"

"Which one?" He slipped his arm out of the sling again much to the disappointment of the busy medic.

"All of them," I said. "The missing persons around the Quarter, the contaminated blood supply, what's really going on at the Monster Chow factory, even where Ma Hemoglobin is hiding. She's connected to all this, and so is Cyrus Redfarb."

"I never liked that guy," McGoo said. "He seemed too trustworthy." He settled his patrolman's cap on his head again, checked both of his Police Special revolvers. "Let's go. I'm calling for backup right now."

"You haven't even left the station." I gestured to the cops all around us. "Why not just ask them?"

"Gotta follow the proper procedures, and it'll take them a while to process the request. Everyone's busy wrapping up the jail break."

All I could think of was Alvina. "We can't wait, McGoo. More kidnapped unnaturals could be fed into the monster mash vats any minute now, and if we don't get there in time, Ma Hemoglobin might escape! We need a sample of that Simply Irresistible so Dr. Zonda can whip up an antidote. She's got an excellent staff of lab Igors."

"That's the most important thing," McGoo said, "but what does Redfarb have to do with it?"

I suddenly remembered what the taxidermist-mortician had told me. "Miss Eccles thinks Redfarb is a meat puppet. A stuffed shirt, and there's no telling what's really inside."

"If he had anything to do with what happened to our little Alvina, we're going to pop a few of his buttons," McGoo growled.

We rushed out of the precinct station as soon as McGoo had filled out and submitted an emergency form for immediate official backup. The frog demon receptionist called after us, saying that we couldn't leave without checking in first, but we were already out the door and heading for his patrol car.

Normally, McGoo likes driving with the lights flashing and sirens blaring, but this time we needed to be more stealthy. As we pulled out, several other uniformed officers waved, promising that they would come as backup soon, though I suspected it would take a while to cut through the red tape. McGoo and I would handle it ourselves, for our daughter.

"This is like one of those buddy cop movies," I said as McGoo roared toward the factory district at top speed.

"I'll be the heroic cop. You be the sidekick," he said. "And you know the sidekick always gets killed in the movies."

"I've already been killed, so we're one step ahead of the plot," I said.

It was the middle of the night, and we saw no school buses in the parking lot, no senior center vans or other tourist vehicles. The Monster Chow factory was in full private production mode.

McGoo screeched the patrol car to a halt in a Visitor parking space in front of the ominous industrial building. The looming smokestacks rose high, belching exhaust up against the full moon, and a pall of smoke hung in the air, thick with the savory roasty-toasty aroma of baking Monster Chow.

"Something smells funny," McGoo said.

I sniffed. "I think there's a batch of ghoul chow in the ovens right now."

As we climbed out of the patrol car, I drew my .38 and McGoo pulled his police extra-special revolver with silver bullets. "We don't know what we're up against, and silver bullets will kill real humans just as dead as regular bullets will."

"Just don't go shooting people until we get information that'll help Alvina."

Side-by-side and pumped up to take on the world, or at least the dark forces behind Monster Chow Industries, we charged into the factory through the visitor's entrance. We were ready for anything.

Except for the guards. Two huge pebble-skinned trolls wearing nighttime security uniforms nabbed us within seconds. We barely got through the front door. They gripped my arm so hard I feared they would tear it off, which would put me at a distinct disadvantage. They seized McGoo and relieved him of both of his revolvers, then disarmed me as well.

"We should have gone in the employee entrance," I said.

One of the troll guards glowered at us. "It's not visiting hours. You aren't allowed inside."

"We're here on official business," McGoo said. "We need to see Mr. Redfarb and Ma Hemoglobin. We know those two are in cahoots." He struggled to break free, but the troll guard squeezed tighter.

"If you don't behave, I'll pop you like a pimple," said the guard.

"Gross," McGoo said.

"We're taking you to the office," said the larger troll without releasing his grip on me. I was reminded of being sent to the principal's office back when I'd been in a public school very much like this building.

The troll guards duck-walked us across the manufacturing floor, where we saw giant metal-walled vats, heard paddles and tenderizing forks whipping around, scraping and kneading the base material. Before the end of the night I would probably end up in the vat as seed material for zombie chow, and that was not a digestive fate I had ever considered. The big TV screens on the walls around the factory floor showed a cute kitten dangling from a branch, with the words "Hang in There!" offering encouragement.

McGoo leaned close. "Don't worry, Shamble. We've got backup coming any day now."

Above us in the high bay, four figures emerged onto the upper catwalk above the packaging line. I recognized Ben Hemoglobin and his nearly identical vampire brother Len, along with Dewey and Charlton, the two human brothers. They all wore faded flannel shirts, and they were all about the same size. Instead of doing hand-me-downs, the Hemoglobin boys probably just saved time and did hand-me-arounds. Seeing us escorted across the manufacturing floor by the troll security guards, Ben pointed and laughed. His brothers also hooted and snickered with such enthusiasm they nearly lost their balance and fell onto the assembly line, where they would have ended up neatly packaged, though probably mislabeled.

No such luck, though.

We followed the bright orange line painted on the floor amidst the tangle of other lines. The trolls stared at their feet, making sure they didn't lose track. "O for orange. O for office. That's how we remember."

"I'm surprised you can read and spell," I said.

The trolls angrily snorted. "We're not *golems*."

After crossing the industrial floor, we reached the primary admin offices not far from the in-house video studio where Cyrus Redfarb filmed his little public service announcements. One of the trolls knocked politely on the door, and we heard Redfarb's avuncular, slightly nasal voice. "Do come in. It's office hours."

After crashing open the door, the troll guards shoved McGoo and me into the room. We stumbled forward, and the trolls followed, setting our confiscated guns on Redfarb's desk, before bowing out.

The Monster Chow spokesman frowned at us as we stood rumpled and sore from the manhandling. McGoo was indignant. "We know what you're doing here, Redfarb. We know about the delayed carnivorism spell."

Redfarb wore a tan V-neck sweater over a white dress shirt. He rested his well-manicured hands on the desk. When McGoo accused him, he twitched. Redfarb looked at us, and I saw he had one brown eye and one blue eye.

"You've got your eyes mixed up," I said.

He frowned, reached up to pop a glass eye out of his left socket and held it in front of his right eye. "I hate it when that happens." He opened a desk drawer and removed an entire tray of glass eyes, like a collection of miniature billiard balls. Redfarb scrutinized them until he selected an appropriately blue one, which he popped back in. "Thank you for pointing that out. It's all about keeping up appearances, isn't it?"

His movements were jerky, and it took him several tries to seat the eyeball property in its socket. "Ever since I became a spokesman for Monster Chow Industries—ever since I was *created*—you have to admit I've done a remarkable job in a very short time. You wouldn't believe how many public appearances and customer service talks I've given. All those tours to make the naturals rest easy and for the unnaturals to eat lots and lots of Monster Chow."

"We know where your seed material comes from," I said. "You're kidnapping unnaturals with a delayed carnivorism spell and throwing them into your meat vats."

When Redfarb chuckled, his mouth opened and closed excessively. He reached up with a hand to straighten his jaw. "Yes, that's our secret ingredient. It's such an obscure spell though, I'm surprised you figured it out."

"We know at least two obscure spells," I said, thinking of the first free sample we had used from the Spells 'N Such mailing.

"Do you have one that's designed to rescue meddlesome spies from their well-deserved fates?" he asked. "That's the one you need right now."

"Hasn't there been enough killing?" McGoo asked.

He frowned in puzzlement. "Of course not, there's never enough killing. It's so much fun, a real hobby of mine. And I do like to keep score in nice, round numbers." His hands twitched and jerked. I noticed another white feather on the floor in front of his desk.

"Even if you get rid of us, Redfarb, we have a witness who can testify about what you're doing here in the factory. One of your victims escaped the vats."

He jerked and squawked. "A witness? How could there possibly be a witness?"

"One of your vampire victims climbed out and survived," I said. "He told us his story, and now we've uncovered the rest."

Not to be upstaged, McGoo added, "And we know you're in league with Ma Hemoglobin and her contaminated blood supply. You'll pay for that. Our daughter's in a coma because of it."

Redfarb jerked again and shook his head like a swimmer with water in his ear. "Oh, we had nothing to do with the bad blood. Ma Hemoglobin came with an interesting business proposition, suggesting that we use her Simply Irresistible concoction to make Monster Chow more addictive. She's my kind of person, an ingenious entrepreneur, but I would only allow the smallest amount of additives for now." He reached up to scratch behind his head, and when he tugged, his thick mat of perfectly combed hair shifted from side to side like a wig. "Please excuse me, gentlemen. Something's not adjusted right."

"We know you're a meat puppet," I blurted out, hoping Miss Eccles was right. "Who are we really dealing with? Who's running the show?"

His glass eyes were already glassy but now he chuckled. "Someone who likes to kill very much—and someone who would very much like to kill you two! You have caused me a great amount of misery, although it did turn into an opportunity. Ah, how I miss my den with all the pretty trophies, but I still like killing. I'll go up on the wall of fame in the Fifth Pit of Hell."

Frustrated, Redfarb fiddled with the back of his neck, and his flaccid face squirmed and reshaped itself. Then his entire body slumped forward on the desk as his hands kept moving, bending at odd angles to reach a spot in the middle of his back. His neck and the back of his head were sloppily sewn up with thick black stitches, and his hands fumbled with the knot, finally undoing it. His twitchy hands pulled the loose thread, unraveling it with a purring sound like a farmer opening a feed bag. The stitches went all the way down his back, behind his soft V-necked sweater.

Cyrus Redfarb, the meat puppet, opened himself up, and squirming things began to emerge. Disgusting, unearthly things ...

white-feathered things. The first demonic head poked out of the gap: a beak, a red wattle, white feathers, glaring yellow eyes. A feral chicken crawled out of Redfarb's body, followed by another and another. Each of the monstrous barnyard birds looked flattened and moist, crammed and crowded inside the skin suit they had inhabited.

"Chickens!" McGoo squawked. "What the hell are chickens doing inside a company exec?"

The last bird emerged, leaving Redfarb as an empty meat puppet, just a flabby spineless suit of skin wearing impeccable clothes.

All eight of the glowering and angry chickens stood on the desk, fluttering their wings, pointing their beaks toward us, glaring with yellow eyes. They cackled, then spoke in unison, a rumbly and all-too-familiar voice. "We're not just chickens. We're *demon-possessed* chickens." They bobbed their heads in a monstrous and threatening way. "We are the great Obadeus!"

I groaned, realizing that the demon-shattering spell must have merely *broken* the monstrous serial-killer demon into bite-sized pieces that scattered and possessed the nearby flock of feral chickens.

CHAPTER THIRTY

Under normal circumstances I like chicken. It's a ubiquitous meat, easily raised in concentration-camp-style farms, appropriate for almost any type of seasoning, delicious in many forms, whether grilled, battered and fried, or processed, fused, and pressed into convenient nuggets.

Demonically possessed chickens, though, were an entirely different story.

In the closed admin office, McGoo and I faced eight of the evil barnyard beasts. After squirming out of the flaccid meat suit that had been Cyrus Redfarb, they clucked in eerie unison. Their eyes flashed with an awful power, not to mention Obadeus's festering anger at being cooped up in his fine feathered friends. With strangely synchronized movements, like poultry in motion, several chickens hopped onto the desk. One jumped onto the credenza near an old coffeemaker. One left a gray-white smear on the telephone message pad.

"Now we have you," the chickens said in a wobbly echo from numerous wattled throats. "We'll get our revenge for what you did to me!"

"You don't like being multiple chickens, then?" I asked.

The demon-possessed chickens ruffled their feathers. "Have you ever tried laying an egg?"

"He has," McGoo answered helpfully.

"It's better than being stuck in the Fifth Pit of Hell, but not by much," Obadeus said. "As a serial killer, it's a lot harder to torture and slaughter victims when you're just a bunch of chickens."

"You attacked me twice," I said, indicating my battered sport jacket.

"And you killed poor Maynard Kleck," McGoo added. "That guy was just trying to give you a coop to call your own."

"Do-gooder!" cried the chickens all cawing at once, as if that were an inexcusable crime. "Kleck wanted to be warm and fuzzy, but we're cold and feathery. We didn't want his homeless coops. We wanted his blood!"

"And his eyes," one of the independent chickens said.

"And his flesh," said another.

"Tasty," said a third.

As the birds grew agitated, the voices came out sporadically rather than in perfect unison. Three of the chickens wandered around the office pecking at the carpet or digging in the trash can. I wondered if Obadeus had more of a split personality than usual.

I fidgeted. "The demon-shattering spell I used against you was a last resort, but we thought it had worked. I should never believe the claims in junk-mail advertisements." I remembered another lesson from my private eye school: always keep the chickens talking.

"We should have cleared all the feral chickens from the vicinity before shattering you," McGoo said. "That was our first mistake."

"Maybe not our *first* mistake," I amended, "but a significant one, nevertheless."

The voice of Obadeus came from several directions. "My components spread out into the air, and I possessed this entire flock. These magnificent birds are useful minions who will help restore me to my glory, now that I've taken over Monster Chow Industries."

"Pretty ambitious for a bunch of chickens," I said.

"We are very ambitious chickens."

McGoo said, "You possessed a flock of wild chickens—and now you've become a corporate executive? That's not a typical career path."

"Corporate spokesman," said the various birds. "We found this empty meat suit discarded in the alley. People are always leaving things lying around, and when I saw it, I had a wonderful idea. After we adjusted ourselves inside the meat suit and figured out how to walk, we made our grand plans. I'm a demon who dreams big!"

Two chickens squabbled over a paper clip they found on the carpet.

I casually tried to sidle closer to the desk where our guns had been placed, but the chickens spotted my move. Four of them jumped onto the desk and glared at me, jerking their heads and flashing their beaks in a highly threatening manner.

"We wanted to kill lots of people," said the chickens. "And Monster Chow Industries gave us the opportunity to do it."

"Monster Chow is supposed to help unnaturals, not kill them," I said.

One chicken emerged as the primary voice of Obadeus. The main bird flapped white wings, flashing razor-sharp pin feathers. "That was before Ma Hemoglobin came up with her ingenious idea."

I wasn't sure anything about Ma Hemoglobin could be called ingenious, but I let the chickens keep talking.

Redfarb's office door burst open, and I hoped it was the troll guards bringing refreshments. Instead we saw the far-less-attractive sight of Ma Hemoglobin herself. Frumpy and stern, she looked like the worst Sunday School teacher in the world. Her legs belonged on sturdy furniture. Her body was like a loud scolding wrapped in flesh, and her black dress was mercifully shapeless. She wore a pillbox hat as if she were going to church or to a funeral and would have been just as happy with either. "My boys said you had visitors in here, Cyrus." She looked around, saw the scattered chickens and the flaccid meat suit, and clucked her tongue in rebuke. "I thought we agreed you weren't going to disassemble in public."

"It was cramped in there, and we needed some breathing room," said the multiple chicken voices. "We won't leave any witnesses, don't worry."

I was, in fact, worried about exactly that, but I didn't comment. Len and Ben, her two vampire sons, stood next to her, grinning. They wore similar flannel hand-me-around shirts, looking like bad photocopies of each other. Dewey and Charlton jockeyed for position behind them, but their two vampire brothers knocked them aside.

"Can we help, Ma?" said Dewey. "If you're going to kill them, it's our turn."

"You'll screw it up," said Ben.

"Oh?" Charlton snorted. "Says the idiot who got arrested at Talbot & Knowles headquarters because he just *had* to sneak another free blood drink."

"I escaped after all," Ben said indignantly.

"Because we rescued you!" Dewey and Charlton yelled.

The chickens squawked and grew louder, more agitated. "When there's killing to be done it's *our job*. I am Obadeus!"

The Hemoglobin boys were crowded at the door close to their Ma, blocking any chance for escape. Cyrus Redfarb had left his tray of glass eyes for all occasions on the desktop, and they seemed to stare at us with disgust or impatience. The eight possessed chickens flapped their wings in unison, reminding me of the flying monkeys from *The Wizard of Oz*.

"There is work for your minions to do, Ma Hemoglobin," Obadeus said from his multiple beaks. "Our meat suit needs cleaning. See to it!"

Ma and her boys trembled at the thunderous command from the chickens. She snapped her fingers toward her two human sons. "Dewey, Charlton—see to it. Take the meat suit and rinse it out."

"Clean out all the feathers this time," said one of the chickens.

"And scrub all the little nooks and crannies."

Dewey frowned, poked at the flaccid empty husk of Redfarb's skin. "It stinks like chicken shit in there."

"One of us had an accident," said the main bird perched on the desk, and all of the furious demonic eyes turned toward one of the chickens, who cringed. "You can smell it. Imagine being sewn up in there."

Charlton grumbled, "Why can't Len and Ben do the work? They never do anything."

"Because we're vampires," said Len and Ben in unison, like the chickens. "We're better."

"They were always your favorites," Dewey grumbled.

"No more sass from you boys," said Ma Hemoglobin. "Do your chores without complaining and maybe you'll get pudding for dessert."

As the two henpecked human sons wrestled the flopping meat puppet from behind the desk and out the office door, Ma snapped at vampire sons, "And you two, get the spells ready. Good old Cyrus here gave away more of those keychains, and we have a big order to fill tonight. We need more seed material for meat. Use the next thirty numbers from the collectible list, and that should give us a good mix. Once you activate the delayed carnivorism spell, we'll fill up the vats with fresh werewolf, vampire, and zombie material. Those are Monster Chow's bestsellers."

"We'll stop you," McGoo said.

"I agree with the basic idea," I added, although I wasn't sure how we'd manage it.

"You have to kill people to feed people," Ma said. "Supply and demand. Cause and effect."

"Bait and switch," I added.

"Those few monsters that go into the vats are the start of something beautiful ... and *lucrative*, now that we've taken over the company and are producing our own special Monster Chow varieties. We'll add my addictive additive to more and more of the product, increasing the dosages across all the packaging lines. We've just been experimenting so far, but you can already see how much the customers like our special recipe with only a little bit of the stuff. Sales are going through the roof, and it's just the beginning."

Ma leered at us as if she derived an S&M-quality pleasure from revealing her evil plan. She backed away and almost stepped on a chicken who squawked and instinctively pecked at her support hose. "Obadeus is skilled at luring people into a false sense of security. Cyrus Redfarb is a wonderful creation."

"Why, thank you," the chickens said.

"But *I'm* working behind the scenes to dominate the entire food and beverage industry throughout the Unnatural Quarter. *I've* been adding a special test Simply Irresistible cocktail to the blood we distribute through Talbot & Knowles, and we'll increase the amount of Simply Irresistible in all Monster Chow brands." She smiled, showing off smeared lipstick on her teeth. "Once they taste the new enhanced Chow, the unnaturals will find it absolutely delicious. They'll eat more and more of our product, and they won't be able to stop."

"Sales will be terrific," said the cackling chicken voices. "And then we'll take over the world."

CHAPTER THIRTY-ONE

ven with the four Hemoglobin boys off doing their separate chores, Redfarb's office felt tense and stuffy. A heavyset gangster woman and eight demon-possessed chickens would have made things uncomfortable under the best of circumstances.

For all her maternal instinct, not to mention the production of far too many sons, Ma Hemoglobin still fit the standard villain mold, in that she was so proud of her complicated schemes that she reveled in revealing them to her intended victims, like McGoo and myself. Even the demon-possessed feral chickens seemed intrigued, clucking like a cheerleading section as she explained. They acted as if they had never heard her grand plan, but I supposed that their chicken-sized brains didn't have much long-term memory.

While we stood as helpless hostages, Ma Hemoglobin lifted a sequin-encrusted clutch purse, snapped it open, and used her pudgy fingers to withdraw a glass bottle that looked like it contained a cheap perfume. "Here it is, Simply Irresistible, my own special concoction combining the best elements of cologne and aftershave, with real toilet water, a bit of sassafras, bacon drippings, and other good things." She held up the bottle, looked at it. "This is for my own personal use, but we have many gallons to pour into the Monster Chow vats tonight. After my boys use the delayed carnivorism spell to bring in more seed material, we'll add Simply Irresistible to the batches, and the unnaturals will have a feeding frenzy."

"You know that chemical has terrible side effects," I said in a scolding tone.

Ma Hemoglobin didn't seem concerned. "Haven't you listened to drug commercials on TV? We'll add fine print to the packaging labels. 'May cause excessive enthusiasm, high blood pressure, flatulence, increased heart rate, with a chance of stroke or possible death and delayed resurrection. Some patients have reported skin rash, inability to sleep, loss of appetite, loss of sexual interest, headache, dizziness, possible weight gain or weight loss, hair loss, change in skin tone, acne, cold sores, appendicitis, curvature of the spine, or warts. Please consult your physician.'" Ma rattled off the words so quickly that even I couldn't grasp most of them. "We'll play cheerful music so it won't affect sales."

The eight demonic chickens scampered around. They seemed thrilled rather than concerned about the side effects. Obadeus cackled through eight different chicken throats. "By eating Monster Chow, everyone will be eating their own unnaturals."

"Cannibalism should be a choice," I said, sounding overly politically correct.

"They won't mind at all," Ma Hemoglobin said, clucking her tongue. She admired her perfume bottle full of Simply Irresistible in one hand and snapped her clutch purse closed with the other hand.

Then accompanied by an explosive triumphant shout, the office door burst open. With a clatter of bones, an ambulatory skeleton burst into the crowded office. "I've got a bone to pick with you!"

"Ronald Skelton!" I shouted. "You were supposed to stay at the offices where it's safe."

"I had to help, so I broke in," Ronald lifted his bony finger. "I do have a skeleton key."

McGoo said, "Is that the missing accountant vampire? That doesn't look like his picture at all."

"This is the stripped-down model," I said.

The vengeful skeleton charged into the office, and the chickens scattered, flapping their wings as they pulled together and prepared to attack.

I used the distraction. I was close enough to the desk that I snatched one of the glass eyeballs from Cyrus Redfarb's display case, a green one. It looked intent in its stare. I cupped the glass eye and threw it straight at Ma Hemoglobin.

Flinching, she lifted her hands to protect herself. One hand held the clutch purse, while the other held the bottle of Simply Irresistible. Fortunately, I aimed for the correct target. The glass eye smashed the glass bottle and both shattered. The broken eye served little purpose, but the broken perfume bottle elicited a rather dramatic reaction. Simply Irresistible spilled all over Ma Hemoglobin's frumpy dress. She spluttered, sniffed, and fluttered her hands in disgust. "That was a five-dollar bottle!"

The smell of bacon, aftershave, and sassafras wafted into the air like a cloud. The chickens circled, ready to attack the skeleton, me, and McGoo.

Ma Hemoglobin scowled at the stain on her dress.

McGoo snorted. "I don't think the chemical works, Ma. You're no more irresistible now than you were a minute ago."

Ronald Skelton stood in the doorway trembling, a pile of barely assembled bones. His jaws clacked as he spoke. "I, uh, thought you two would take it from here?"

The chickens, though, reacted strangely. They perked up, clucking and bawking. Their monstrous eyes glowed like embers. They jerked their heads, clacked their beaks—and turned toward Ma Hemoglobin. They fluttered their wings, spraying loose white feathers.

Ma sensed her peril. "You chickens stop looking at me like that!"

The barnyard birds cackled and began to move toward her, paying no attention to me, McGoo, or the ambulatory skeleton. Instead, they closed in.

Ma backed away, struck the desk, knocking Cyrus Redfarb's tray of glass eyes to the floor, where they all clattered and bounced around. The predatory fowl pack lunged toward Ma.

"Stop it this instant!" she cried. "We're partners. We have plans. We have complex schemes. We have—"

Unable to resist the Simply Irresistible, the demon-possessed chickens attacked, converging on Ma Hemoglobin. Obadeus wanted to satisfy his bloodlust.

Pecking and pecking, the eight chickens did their worst to the rather substantial body of Ma Hemoglobin. Sharp beaks flashed up and down, stabbing like Norman Bates on a full day of knife-wielding practice.

Ma tried to defend herself. McGoo and I weren't overly inclined to do so ourselves. We're normally chivalrous, but this woman was responsible for the contaminated blood that had put Alvina in intensive care. She swung her clutch purse, and the sequins scattered. She screamed and fell to the floor, and the chickens kept pecking as if someone had dumped worms all over the carpeting.

Within minutes, they tore Ma Hemoglobin to shreds. I said, "I've played *Angry Birds* before, but it was never so realistic."

The evil gangster woman was soon no more than a pile of dripping red meat, tatters of flesh, and an exposed, sturdy-looking skeleton.

"Now you know how it feels," snapped a bitter-sounding Ronald Skelton.

I retrieved my .38 from the desk along with both of McGoo's pistols. "Which one do you want? The Police Special or the Police Extra Special?"

"I'd like a gun," Ronald said. "Haven't I earned it?" I handed him the regular pistol. He wrapped his bony fingers around the grip, placed a phalange on the trigger.

We needed to defend ourselves against the demon-possessed chickens before we could fight our way out of the Monster Chow factory. The troll security guards shouldn't cause much of a problem; like the golem at the Overbite Lounge, they were paid to keep people from breaking in, not from getting out.

"We could run," I said as the chickens finished gorging themselves.

McGoo scratched the side of his head. "I'm enjoying the moment. She was a real pain in the ass."

But something strange began to happen. The eight chickens, each possessed by one-eighth of a shattered bloodthirsty serial-killer demon, had eaten the entire body of the large woman, stuffing themselves. Unable to stop because of the Simply Irresistible, the eight supernatural birds had nearly doubled in size, waddling around like feather pillows on chicken feet. The blazing eyes looked dull and stupefied. The chickens could barely walk. And we've all seen a stuffed chicken before.

"I can't believe I ate the whole thing," they said in unison.

They pecked listlessly at the remainder of Ma's bones, then looked up at us, seeming to pull together the presence and personality of Obadeus. In a slurred, ponderous voice that wasn't at all threatening, they said in unison, "I am Obadeus! Tremble at my might!"

They nearly collapsed, trying to waddle toward us in a threatening manner.

When they had attacked me in the alley, I'd killed a few of the feathery bodies. The demon from the Fifth Pit of Hell might be scattered among a number of bodies, but those bodies were still just chickens.

"We could wring their necks," I suggested, then hefted my handgun. "But why bother wasting time?"

I shot one of the chickens, which died in a spray of feathers. The lumbering birds tried to flee, but they had neither the energy nor the constitution to do so. They were too overstuffed with Ma Hemoglobin, and completely vulnerable.

"I always said there's one way to get rid of the feral chicken problem in the Quarter." McGoo fired his police extra special. The silver bullet killed another murderous chicken.

Ronald Skelton cackled, sounding much like the demonic birds, and squeezed the trigger with a bony finger.

With a rain of gunfire we soon turned all eight of the demon chickens into nugget fodder.

McGoo looked down at the scattered feathers among the bones of Ma Hemoglobin. "Right now, I think I'm hungry for a nice steak. Hold the chicken."

CHAPTER THIRTY-TWO

With Ma Hemoglobin's bones picked clean and multiple dead chickens strewn across the carpet, the office looked like a scene out of the Texas Chainsaw Chicken Barbecue. Ronald Skelton stood quivering, his bones rattling with relief or rage. A layer of skin on his face would have made it much easier to determine his expression.

I squared my shoulders. "We're not done yet, McGoo. Len and Ben went out to activate the delayed carnivorism spell. We've got to stop them from bringing another dozen victims as starter material for the monster mash."

Sometimes it feels good to be a real hero.

Ronald looked at the bloody ruins of Ma Hemoglobin. "She didn't just take the shirt off my back, but the skin off my bones. Look at me! Do you know what this'll do to my marriage to Regina?" He touched his empty ribs, his scooped pelvis. "And my sex life?"

"Your wife still loves you," I said. "Regina came to our offices quite distraught and explained all about monogamous vampires."

"I sowed my wild oats back in the day," the skeleton said. "I was like a vampire version of John Travolta in *Saturday Night Blood Fever*, and I practically lived in clubs like the Overbite Lounge."

I remembered the skinny accountant vampire I'd met at the Chamber of Commerce meeting. "I'm sure you were."

Grim and determined. Ronald held up McGoo's Police Special revolver. "Ms. Deyer already called my wife to let her know that I'm somewhat intact. I really want to go home, but we can't let these terrible people get away with their crimes. We've got to shut down this Monster Chow factory!"

The office door popped open again and Dewey and Charlton entered with the flopping, flaccid, dripping Redfarb skin suit. The boys looked preoccupied and moist, having splashed soapy water on each other.

"We got it all clean, Ma!" Dewey was grinning like a puppy.

"Inside and out," Charlton added. "Even scrubbed the inside of the feet down to the little toes. You'll be so proud."

Then they saw the torn shreds of flesh, the tatters of Ma's frumpy black dress, her sequined clutch purse, and her pillbox hat that had been smashed in the feathery frenzy. Dewey wailed, unable to find words for his horror. His voice sounded like a police siren that went louder and trailed off in waves. "Ma! Ma! Ma!" He looked at his brother and nudged him with an elbow. "They killed Ma."

When Charlton finally figured out what he was seeing, his mouth fell open. The two Hemoglobin boys dropped the meat suit and turned white as ghosts. "Ma! Ma! Ma!" Dewey wailed.

"It was sort of an accident," I said.

Ronald Skelton was so angry at the abuse done to his body he was ready to snap. "It was my revenge!" He pointed his borrowed gun at the two humans. "You'll all die!"

Rather than going through the rest of the five stages of grief, Dewey and Charlton turned and bolted screaming into the factory. We could hear all the processes of the production, manufacturing, and packaging lines ramping up.

"How are we going to shut down the whole factory?" McGoo asked.

I looked at the discarded skin suit, then at Ronald Skelton. "I've got an idea."

O O O

Glad to be fully armed again, McGoo and I got to work. He had taken back his other revolver, and now we marched out onto the factory floor like government revenue agents on a moonshine raid. A handful of night shift workers in jumpsuits were standing in various positions along the assembly lines.

We hurried past the rattling conveyor belt from the oven where the freshly baked roasty-toasty Monster Chow kibble rolled along to the packaging lines. The ovens were in full flame. We ran, desperate to arrive before any new delayed carnivorism victims could be added to the mix.

On the high walkway around one of the primary vats towering above us, a whiteboard and erasable markers stood on a flimsy tripod easel. Huddled together, Len and Ben were drawing a complicated spell symbol with colored markers. I recognized the design embossed on the back of the Monster Chow keychains Redfarb had handed out so liberally. The brothers were arguing, drawing one line, erasing it, adding it in a different direction.

Ben insisted, "No, it goes kitty-corner like that, with a loop on the end."

"It's not. It's angled this way," Len said. He drew the new line and waited with diminishing confidence. When no magical eruption occurred, he sullenly agreed to try his brother's suggestion. They drew a different line with a loop, but still no spell happened. I wondered if they had gotten their original design from Alterro's Spells 'N Such.

"We've got to be forgetting something," Ben said.

"Oh wait, there's a period at the end of the sentence!" Len said and put a dot on the other side of the spell symbol.

Suddenly, the air began to crackle and hum. The two vampire gang members stood back, holding the frame of the whiteboard so it wouldn't fall off of its flimsy easel and into the vat. I could feel the magic building, the power rising in the air, static electricity, thin bolts of lightning. "Hurry, McGoo!" We rushed across the floor, but Len and Ben were high above us.

The magical transportation routine latched onto the next batch of victims who had taken token keychains, yanking vampires, werewolves, mummies, zombies, and miscellaneous monsters from their beds, jobs, or bowling leagues. The air flickered, and the new victims began to solidify on the narrow walkway around the different vats.

As Len and Ben stayed by their easel and whiteboard, Cyrus Redfarb unexpectedly tottered out onto the process floor. His V-necked argyle sweater was rumpled and splashed with Ma Hemoglobin's blood. His loafers were on the wrong feet, and he walked awkwardly, as if drunk. His voice sounded different too.

Across the humming process floor, the night-shift workers looked up when Redfarb bellowed, "Attention on the floor! We are shutting down the factory this instant. It's an emergency. This place is hazardous to your health. Evacuate immediately." Gaining momentum, and a sense of balance, Redfarb strode forward. "You hear me? You have the night off! Evacuate. Run for your very lives! Take a free vacation day!"

The factory workers obeyed, though I couldn't tell whether they were more excited about the imminent danger or the promise of time off. As the workers bolted, including the guards on the walkways around the high vats, Len and Ben looked alarmed and disappointed. Just as the shimmering bodies became solid on the precarious edge of the vats, their support thugs disappeared, leaving just the two Hemoglobin boys by their magical whiteboard.

"Hey, where are you all going?" Len shouted. "Don't listen to him!"

But the Monster Chow employees couldn't punch the time clocks fast enough as they fled into the night. Cyrus Redfarb came up to McGoo and me. "How did I do?" asked Ronald Skelton. "This skin suit is really uncomfortable."

"You did just fine," I said. "They believed you."

He tugged at his fingers, then adjusted his face, pushing the skin from side to side. "I didn't stitch myself up very well in the back of the neck."

"You did what was necessary," McGoo said. "The production lines are shutting down."

"Not good enough." Ronald managed to fashion a determined expression on his uncooperative, unfamiliar face. "I'll go to the corporate studio down the hall, make a selfie video, and broadcast it across the Quarter. Everyone needs to know what's really happening here." He nodded, still adjusting his chin. "They'll believe me because they think I'm Cyrus Redfarb, the most trusted spokesman in the Quarter."

"And your wife will be impressed to see you on TV," I said.

He wobbled off at an unsteady run toward the studio.

McGoo and I looked up as a dozen zombies, werewolves, and vampires materialized in place around the high vats. I was surprised to see the kindly old vampire who often flirted with Francine, the guy we had nicknamed One Fang. He looked disoriented, tentatively extending a hand as if he'd been holding a drink. He and four other vampires stood on the precarious edge of the Vampire Chow vat.

The monsters were separated by species, and confused, dizzy, and speechless. Among the Miscellaneous victims stood a small, gray-skinned figure, the over-eager troll real-estate agent, Edgar Allen. Even before the other monsters around him had come to their senses, he had managed to distribute business cards.

"Stay away from the edge!" I called upward. "Watch out!"

The two Hemoglobin boys faced six werewolves on the narrow walkway encircling the vat where they had erected their whiteboard. None of the fresh arrivals was guarded, because the rest of the crew had taken an emergency night off.

Exasperated, Len and Ben glanced at the group of furry lycanthropes who stood around them, confused but growing angry. "We can't do this all ourselves." When they looked down and saw only me and McGoo standing on the factory floor, they were clearly confused.

"What have you done?" Ben said. "Where's Ma?"

"Can you give us a hand?" Len asked.

As the kidnapped unnaturals began to realize where they were, I shouted a warning from far down on the floor. "Protect yourselves! These two plan to dump you into the vats where you'll be chopped up, formed, fused, and extruded as Monster Chow kibble."

The werewolves growled in confusion. The vampires turned about, and doddering old One Fang nearly fell off the edge, but he managed to grab his neighbor with a sigh of relief. The zombies were completely disoriented, as they usually were. Edgar Allen had already introduced himself to all of the other unnaturals around the Miscellaneous tank.

As they understood where they were, the victims-to-be reacted with growing anger. Werewolves tend to get emotionally volatile—something to do with their monthly cycle. Len and Ben took a step back as the hairy beasts looked down into the swirling, churning vats, with their meat paddles, flesh rakes, chopping knives, and tenderizing hammers. They didn't like what they saw.

"You meant to throw us in there?" growled one burly, black-furred male.

From down on the floor, we couldn't quite see what was going on, but it was obvious that the lycanthrope victims decided not to donate their flesh to the starter dough. Instead, they seemed to think Len and Ben might be more appropriate starting material for the next batch of Monster Chow.

The four werewolves surged forward in a mob, but they had to move single file because the walkway was narrow. Ben picked up the spell-scribbled whiteboard and used it as a shield to block the pushy werewolves.

"Get 'em, Ben! Hold 'em off!" Len shouted as he retreated behind his brother, backing away as far as he could. But since the vat was circular, the more he retreated clockwise, the closer he came to the tail end of the angry werewolves moving counter-clockwise. The vicious, furry monsters saw Len and charged after him in the opposite direction.

"Take them into custody," McGoo shouted up to the top of the high vat. "We'll see that they face justice."

"Okay," said the big black-furred brute. He swung a massive paw and knocked the whiteboard out of Ben's hand, then shoved Ben backward into the vat. He plopped into the thickening dough, squirming and struggling, and we heard him sucked under. The meat paddles and flesh rakes ground audibly against new starter material.

Coming the other way around the circle, the last werewolf in line saw what his comrade had done, decided that was a good idea, and knocked the other Hemoglobin boy in to join his brother.

"We wanted to take the boys into custody," I muttered.

"Saves time and taxpayer money," McGoo said.

With a roar of sirens and a squeal of tires, police cars rolled up to the visitor's parking lot outside the Monster Chow factory. Our backup had finally arrived.

CHAPTER THIRTY-THREE

Within minutes, uniformed cops swarmed through the Monster Chow factory to rescue McGoo and me, long after we actually needed rescue. It was an assortment of human law-enforcement officers along with fresh-faced unnatural rookies. McGoo walked among his comrades on the force, smiling and exchanging high fives.

"It's a zoo out there," said a burly female minotaur with a decorative ring through her nose. She wore a parking-enforcement uniform. When McGoo had filled out his request for backup at the Monster Chow factory, the entire UQPD had mobilized to respond. "A big mob is gathering in the parking lot. Like Mardi Gras ... only angrier."

"How did the mobs know anything about what's going on here?" I asked.

"Someone rallied them," said the minotaur meter maid. "A vampire woman started a telephone chain to sound the alarm. She's very organized, working with big hairy activists. Bigfoots I think."

"They prefer to be called Bigfeet," I corrected. Suddenly it all fell into place. After Robin had explained about her husband's bony condition, Regina Skelton had not sat idly by. Though Ronald seemed like a mousy sort, he'd certainly shown his exposed spine as well.

Now the large TV screens around the factory flickered, and the encouraging platitudes vanished. *Remember, There's No "I" in Team* was replaced by a burst of static, and then an image of Cyrus Redfarb's familiar face. "Welcome neighbors!" he said, and I was impressed with Ronald's imitation of the man's syrupy voice. "I have bad news for you all, a truly shocking revelation. Monster Chow Industries deceived you. Yes, they provide delicious and nutritious food for all unnaturals, but the secret ingredient is a terrible secret."

With rising energy and horror, he described how innocent unnatural victims were being whisked away, then thrown into the vats to be grown as tasty kibble dough, blaming the scheme on Ma Hemoglobin as well as the demonic chickens. He left out no details, exposing the whole gruesome story, even though at that hour TV programming was supposed to be family oriented and appropriate for all ages.

When he was finished, Ronald added a typical horror movie surprise scene, which he seemed to relish. "I'm not really Cyrus Redfarb. There was no Cyrus Redfarb." He reached up with his clumsy, rubbery meat-suit hands and fumbled with the stitches at the back of his neck. "At first this was just a discarded meat puppet filled with demonic feral chickens, but now—" He peeled open the back of his suit, unwrapped the flesh, and folded it down over his skull and vertebrae. He revealed his bony shoulders, his rib cage, and stripped entirely out of the suit. "It's me! Mild-mannered Ronald Skelton."

In the video studio, the skeleton stood from his chair and waved a bony hand. "Hi, Regina! I told you I'd be on TV."

All the UQPD cops watched the presentation on the big screens, shaking their heads and grumbling in disgust. They scanned the factory floor, saw the production lines, the ovens still roasting, the vats still churning, all unattended. McGoo and I left the remaining cops to mop up inside the factory, although they had never volunteered for janitorial duty.

We went outside to find a scene of total chaos. Hundreds of unnaturals had flooded the premises, breaking open the distribution warehouses, crowding the parking lot. They were agitated, many of them with smartphones and news alert feeds. The monsters had gathered around to watch Ronald Skelton's horrific revelations, and I could tell they were ready for violence.

"We still need to find the supply of Simply Irresistible," I said. "Dr. Zonda needs it for analysis so she can make an antidote for Alvina."

"If they were going to add it to all the Monster Chow, the chemical must be in one of the warehouses. There's got to be a lot of it," McGoo said. "We have to find it, Shamble—for our little girl."

Moving among the crowd, I saw tall hairy figures, the familiar yetis and Bigfeet I had encountered in the Quarter, even though it had slipped my mind until now. I was surprised to see so many of the furry brutes, at least twenty, but I kept losing count. They ambled through the unruly monster mob and started a chant in their deep-throated, growling voices, bellowing and pumping their furry fists in the air. "Fix the chow! Fix the chow!"

Oddly, nobody else picked up the chant.

The mob was in a furor after hearing the news. One frantic, unraveling mummy scrambled about, nearly tripping on his bandages, wailing to anyone who would hear. "Monster Chow is people! Monster Chow is people!"

The hunchbacked president of the Chamber of Commerce, who was normally a sociable guy, now seemed utterly terrified. He ran through the crowd, holding up a printed catalog of Monster Chow varieties, titled *To Serve Unnaturals*. "It's a cookbook!" he screamed. "It's a cookbook!"

With a rattle of bones, a skeleton emerged from the factory front doors to join us. Having left his uncomfortable meat suit behind, Ronald shook his head. "I don't know how anyone could wear that, even feral chickens. It's hot, and it stinks."

"And you don't even have nostrils," McGoo pointed out.

"That was great, Ronald." I carefully clapped him on the scapula. "Everyone's proud of you."

The monster crowd spotted him and cheered, calling out Ronald's name, applauding with hands and paws and flippers. With a squeal, Regina Skelton ran toward us. "You were wonderful. You're my hero!" She hugged him so hard she nearly cracked his vulnerable ribs, forgetting for a moment that he was a skeleton rather than a vampire. "Look what they've done to you. It's awful!"

"You told me I should lose a little weight," he said, then kissed her with his naked teeth against her lips. She found it awkward, but let him do it anyway. They hugged each other again, and Regina swung him around almost enough to displace his femurs from his sacroiliac joint.

The mob had begun pounding on the doors of the factory, rolling up the receiving-bay doors of the Chow warehouses. Just inside the Vampire Chow and Blood Shake warehouse, I saw that the redneck Suck Dynasty brothers/cousins had broken in. They had already rolled a keg, popped it open, and now sat around in lawn chairs, drinking from red Solo cups filled with carbonated blood product.

"Yep, it's a party," said Ernie, raising his Solo cup. He scratched his bushy beard until more cockroaches fell out.

McGoo and I saw them at the same time, the special tag on the fresh keg that had just been placed in the warehouse, the vampire brothers/cousins guzzling the potent drink. "I think that might be the spiked stuff," I said, "the new shipment Ma Hemoglobin was about to send out."

"If anyone deserves a little tainted blood, it's those boys," McGoo said. But we began to run anyway.

On our way to the Vampire Chow warehouse and the impromptu Suck Dynasty kegger party, I spotted the remaining two Hemoglobin boys, Dewey and Charlton, scuttling through the crowd of monsters, heads down and nervous, but their flannel shirts were a dead giveaway. Sticking to the shadows and the fringes, they hadn't yet been noticed. Ma Hemoglobin was the famous celebrity with her face all over the Wanted posters; the rest of her boys were nondescript and unattractive, not warranting a second glance. Dewey and Charlton wanted to take shelter in one of the warehouses, hoping to hide among the blood kegs and skids of packaged arterial shakes.

The Suck Dynasty boys gulped from their Solo cups and refilled them at the confiscated keg, but after guzzling the second round, I saw them began to shake and jitter. Ernie puffed up, burped, and drew a deep breath, expanding his chest until the buttons popped from his faded plaid shirt.

"This feels funny," he said. He twisted the trucker cap around on his head.

Dewey ran forward, arms outstretched. "You've got to help us! Our brothers are vampires, and we can get you all the blood you want."

"We have a stockpile for you," Charlton said. "Plenty of different types and flavors. Right now, we really need a new gang, though."

The Suck Dynasty leader gulped more from his plastic cup and belched. "Got all the blood we want right here, except ..." He growled and coughed, and then his eyes began to blaze red. Next to him his brothers, or cousins, each drained their drinks and in a demonstration of their brutish physical strength, crushed the red plastic cups against their foreheads and tossed them with a hollow rattle on the concrete floor of the warehouse. The group rose slowly from their lawn chairs, anger surging, power building inside their bodies as the Simply Irresistible took hold. Together, the bearded vamps roared, and their fangs elongated into large, sharp points.

"Yeah, Shamble," McGoo said. "I'd say that's one of the spiked kegs."

Belatedly, Dewey and Charlton realized their error and began to back away from the open warehouse. "Maybe we'll take our chances with the mob."

But the Suck Dynasty had fixed their gaze on two tender victims. They prowled forward. "Even blood fresh from the keg ain't as good as blood we tap ourselves from a nice ... human container."

The bearded vampires bounded forward. McGoo and I were too far away to stop them, not that we could. I had wrestled a berserk vampire a few days ago and it had nearly done me in. Now there were three of them.

The Suck Dynasty brothers/cousins fell upon the two Hemoglobin boys. Dewey and Charlton screamed as the vampires tackled them to the ground and sank overlarge fangs into their necks, their shoulders, anyplace with easy access to an artery. The contaminated blood had driven them wild.

Dewey and Charlton struggled weakly as the three redneck vampires drained them dry like a Big Gulp with too much ice. The berserk vamps gorged themselves.

Swaying after their heavy meal, the Suck Dynasty boys stood back and came to their senses. Apparently, all that fresh human blood was potent enough to burn away the contamination, and they were returning to normal. I wished the numerous transfusions had worked to cure Alvina like that. Another damned disadvantage of puberty!

Ernie and his two companions shook their heads. Their trucker caps were all askew, and when they looked down at the two chalk-white Hemoglobin corpses, they stared in dismay. "We killed 'em!" said Ernie, sounding horrified.

"Ooops," said one of his brothers, or cousins.

"Drained 'em dry," said the other.

We arrived just in time to correct them. "The proper term is *exsanguinated,*" I said.

The three Suck Dynasty boys looked at me. "Really?" Ernie said. "Huh, you learn something new every day."

They all looked deeply embarrassed, brushing blood specks from their old shirts. "Man, I didn't know those two were so flimsy. I wouldn't have killed them otherwise."

"We ain't never killed anything before," said one of the others.

McGoo was surprised. "You kept encouraging other vampires to feast on real human blood. Isn't that what you wanted?"

"Aww, that's just a lot of talk," said Ernie.

"Don't you go out hunting? Get yourself some varmints for dinner?" I asked.

"Never been hunting," said one of the others. "None of us is a good enough shot to hit a squirrel. Never been a killer before." He frowned. "Now I'm really sad."

I was confused. "But your ... your caps, your beards."

"It's just a costume. We're actually nice people," Ernie said.

All three of the Suck Dynasty boys heaved a deep sigh, raised their shoulders, and dropped them. "Well, on the bright side, we did drain 'em dry, so they'll turn. Yep, they'll come back as vampires, so nothing to worry about."

Murder was quite different after the Big Uneasy. The actual crime committed here would depend on whether Dewey and Charlton Hemoglobin filed a complaint once they resurrected.

We weren't concerned with the two fresh victims, though, any more than we had grieved for the other two Hemoglobin boys who had become fresh ingredients for the monster mash in the vats. Thinking about Alvina in the hospital, neither of us had any sympathy left. We needed to take care of the kid in intensive care.

"There, Shamble!" McGoo pointed to large metal canisters stacked in the corner next to the blood kegs ready for shipment. They were marked *Simply Irresistible*. "Just what we need."

"Let's get this to the witch doctor right away," I said. "We'll save Alvina."

Chapter Thirty-Four

While we let the restless unnaturals digest the new situation at the Monster Chow factory, McGoo flashed his badge and commandeered one of the parked patrol cars. "We've got to get to the hospital—fast!"

We loaded the Simply Irresistible sample tank into the back seat, using the seatbelt and handcuffs to hold it in place. I knew what kind of driver McGoo was, and I didn't want the jostled tank to crack open if he sped over a speed bump. Even though we didn't have to worry about cannibalistic demon-possessed feral chickens anymore, we didn't dare spill the insidious fluid all over us. We were irresistible enough.

After racing across town, McGoo screeched the patrol car into the emergency room parking circle, and momentum threw the secured tank against its rattling handcuffs. As he brought the car to a stop, he nearly smashed into a parked ambulance, where two emergency mortician techs were sitting at the open end, dangling their feet over the back bumper and smoking cigarettes. They didn't even flinch, no doubt assured by the fact that medical care was close by if they were injured. Watching us with sleepy eyes, they took long drags on their coffin nails and waited for the next emergency call.

We tried to uncuff the suspect tank, only to discover that McGoo had lost his keys. Fortunately, my lockpick kit was in my jacket pocket, and I soon freed the offending chemical substance. Lifting the tank, we placed it in a lonely empty wheelchair and rolled it into the hospital, running to the reception desk.

"Page Dr. Zonda Nefarious!" I said. "We have a special delivery for her."

Within minutes, the witch doctor emerged, straightening her crumpled black pointy hat. She shook her head. "That poor little girl is still in a coma. No change. Your other friends have been watching her closely."

"And we've been solving the case," McGoo said. "We exposed massive corruption at the Monster Chow factory, killed a demon and a gangster lady."

"My, you've been busy," said Zonda.

"And we found this." I rapped the metal side of the Simply Irresistible tank. "The contaminant chemical that was in the bad blood. Alvina drank some of it—that's what put her into a coma."

Flushed, McGoo wiped a hand across his forehead. "You can analyze it and make an antidote, right Doc?"

Dr. Zonda bent closer to the tank, looking skeptical. "I hope you realize that creating an antidote isn't so easy. I can't just reverse-engineer this substance and whip up a cure with a snap of my fingers."

"It wasn't easy to take down the Monster Chow factory either, but we did it," I pointed out.

McGoo was deeply concerned. "Yeah, we know how difficult the problem is, Doc. How long do you think it'll take?"

"It's a very complex case," Zonda said, considering. "At least an hour or two."

She buzzed on her walkie-talkie, calling for a lab technician. Instantly, capering members of the Igor Guild—widely recognized as the best scientific assistants—bounded out of the laboratory chambers in the back of the medical center. They swept forward to grab the sealed tank propped in the wheelchair.

"Don't spill any of that," I warned. "It's potent stuff. It made even Ma Hemoglobin attractive."

"To feral chickens at least," McGoo said.

The Igors rapidly donned full containment suits. At first glance, I thought they were hunchbacks, but they merely wore large backpacks under their lab coats. When the Igors were suited up in respirators and thick black welder's gloves, they wrapped the Simply Irresistible tank in plastic and added cushioned bubble-wrap around it on the wheelchair. Only then did they steer their dangerous cargo back into the rear chamber, where they had a bubbling pharmaceutical laboratory, hand-me-down organs preserved in jars, electrical experiments, collectible scraps from failed plastic-surgery attempts, and home beauty products.

"We should have a cure for you soon, if you'd like to wait," said Dr. Zonda. "We have a wide selection of old and uninteresting magazines in the lobby."

"We'll wait in Alvina's room," I said. We raced for the elevator.

Sheyenne hovered beside the kid's bed, and Robin sat in the guest chair, reviewing self-written notes on her magic legal pad. On the television, reruns of the afternoon talk shows had been replaced with the breaking news story and video of Ronald Skelton in Redfarb's meat-puppet suit revealing the horrors at the Monster Chow factory.

Lying unconscious, Alvina looked sweet and pale—both of which were normal—and deep in her coma. Her enlarged fangs still gave her a prominent overbite. The contamination continued to mess with her puberty blood chemistry. I felt so angry I wanted to set another flock of demon-possessed chickens on Ma Hemoglobin.

Robin and Sheyenne were both proud of what we'd done. Sheyenne drifted over to give me an unfelt embrace.

Normally, I would feel more satisfied at ending a case. "That takes care of the missing unnaturals, the tainted blood supply, the demonic chickens, and the dastardly plot to addict the unnatural population. Now if only we can help Alvina."

"Dr. Nefarious has her best Igors on it," McGoo said. "It shouldn't be long now."

"She might even solve world hunger while she's at it," I added, "but it could take an hour."

We waited at Alvina's bedside, worried and tense. Even though I'm a private investigator with many successful cases under my belt, I couldn't figure out how to solve my feelings toward this maybe-daughter I'd never known about before.

Some guys would shirk their parental responsibility, some would argue and demand paternity tests, although those weren't possible because of Alvina's vampire transformation. Some guys would have gone hunting for her mother, demanding that she take the girl back, dragging the matter through family court, and making everybody hate each other. I knew McGoo and I were of the same mind, that Alvina would not be better off if we reunited her with Rhonda. We were rescuing our little girl from a fate worse than ... worse than Rhonda.

Alvina belonged in the Unnatural Quarter, where she wouldn't be a misfit. I knew it would be awkward enough for a little girl—young woman?—stuck in puberty. But we had a team here, and we could take care of her.

If she ever woke up from her damned coma.

The witch doctor and the Igor lab technicians took only fifty minutes. Zonda bustled into the hospital room with a grin on her warty face, clipboard tucked under one arm, and holding a long syringe. "That was the most difficult thing I've done all day, but we had a lucky break."

"I told you she was the best witch doctor in the business," I said, greatly relieved. "She studied the chemical analysis and made an amazing intuitive leap."

The witch doctor scratched the wart on her chin, then the larger one on her hooked nose. "Actually, one of the Igors spilled coffee into a test sample, and the resulting mixture worked. It was quite a convenient coincidence."

McGoo rubbed his hands together. "A cure is a cure."

Robin was more skeptical. "And has it been thoroughly tested? Have there been control groups, test subjects, and a full set of administrative approvals to get the new drug ready for market?"

The witch doctor turned to her, indignant. "What do you think I've been doing for the past ten minutes?"

"If you're sure, Doc," I said. "Let's treat her and get our Alvina back."

Zonda Nefarious stepped up to the child-sized hospital coffin bed, bent over Alvina's motionless form, and injected the antidote. "This might take a while. Remember, it's unproven. We'll have to wait and—"

Alvina opened her mouth wide in an extravagant yawn such as I'd only seen on cats. Her long, curved fangs retracted into tiny, pointy baby teeth and she blinked her large eyes. "Where am I? That was a weird nightmare."

Then we were all cheering and laughing, delighted to have our little vampire back with us. I bent stiffly over the bed to give her an enthusiastic hug, but McGoo shouldered me aside, until we worked out a way to share the daddy-hugging duties. Sheyenne also did her intangible best, and Robin took her turn as well.

McGoo and I rushed to congratulate Dr. Zonda by patting her on the back, but she was a formal Harvard-certified witch doctor and simply nodded to acknowledge our gratitude. "I'm sure she'll make a full recovery. Now, do you have insurance?"

Alvina stretched, let out another huge yawn, and looked at us with that innocent expression that could melt any recently reunited father's heart. "I'm thirsty. Can I have something to drink?"

Both McGoo and I tripped over each other to agree.

"Anything you want, little girl!"

"Of course."

She grinned, showing her newly restored fangs. "I want a unicorn blood frappé."

CHAPTER THIRTY-FIVE

Due in part to her vampire blood, Alvina recovered quickly. Before we knew it, the witch doctor announced that our girl was ready to be discharged. From past experience with Travis Spade, however, I knew there would be nothing quick about the hospital discharge process, so I resigned myself to wait. The paperwork would surely take longer than the entire development, testing, and distribution of the cure.

After several hours, I went to the hospital gift shop and picked up some balloons and a cute, fuzzy stuffed bat for Alvina. Other options available were a traditional cute teddy bear and a more extreme squeezable doll with an embedded voice chip that would scream bloody murder when cuddled too aggressively. I think Alvina would have been happy to receive just about any heartwarming gift; Rhonda wasn't the sort of mother to buy the girl cuddly stuffed anythings.

McGoo joined me in the gift shop, also feeling delayed parental guilt. He picked up the traditional teddy bear. "Think she'll like this, Shamble?"

"It was definitely my second choice," I said, holding onto my stuffed bat.

"I don't want to be the second choice."

I wiggled the fuzzy bat. "Why don't we buy both and give them to her collectively? No competition."

McGoo considered. "No competition means no testosterone."

"There's already enough of that to go around."

"Hey Shamble, did you hear about the invisible man who walked into the emergency room?"

I foolishly thought he was talking about an actual case. "No, what happened?"

"The doctor said, 'I can't see you right now.'"

I sighed. "It's best you don't tell jokes like that around the patients. You might hinder their recovery."

When we headed back to the ward with our warm fuzzies, we passed a familiar skeleton and his familiar vampire wife in the treatment room next door to Alvina's. "Ronald and Regina!" I said, worried that one of them might have a serious medical issue. "Is everything all right?"

Ronald Skelton held up his bony hands. "Is everything all right? Look at me. I'm still not the man I once was."

"I told you it will take some time," said Dr. Zonda, who pressed her stethoscope, to no purpose, against his sternum.

The animated skeleton looked a little more orange than yellow and ivory; around his joints I saw traces of sinew and tendons just beginning to grow, like little sprouts.

"You seem to have a little more meat on your bones today," I pointed out.

"I suppose. For now, I'll just bask in my fame. People recognize me like this after my big TV debut. I'll look a lot different after my face grows back."

McGoo scratched the side of his nose. "You could wear Redfarb's meat suit in the meantime, while you recover. Nobody else is using it."

The skeleton lowered his skull. "It's not very comfortable, but I said I would do that if it would make Regina more comfortable. At least I'd have ... proper parts."

"It's not *you*," Regina said. "And I don't want to be reminded of that nasty man in our house. It would feel like I'm having an affair, and we're monogamous!"

Seeing her distress, he patted her arm with his bony hand. "I know. And I'm glad you're willing to wait for me."

Regina gazed adoringly at her husband. "You're my TV star, Ronald! You have a big future in broadcasting. You did so well in a stressful situation, and off the cuff! Imagine how great you'll be with a teleprompter."

McGoo considered. "Once Monster Chow Industries reopens the factory using its original recipes, and without any Simply Irresistible added, they're going to need a new spokesperson."

"Their customers will take a lot of convincing," I said.

Ronald shook his skull. "Not me." He turned toward us and grinned (at least I think it was a grin). "However, they will need new accounting and bookkeeping services. That's where the real glory is." He puffed up his ribcage.

The witch doctor tapped Ronald's naked patella with a rubber hammer, and his leg swung up so quickly that he nearly kicked her in the stomach. "Good reflexes, Mr. Skelton, considering you don't have nerves or muscles. You're recovering nicely."

Ronald reached out with his digital phalanges to lovingly caress his wife's arm. "Due to the extreme trauma I suffered, I'll heal slowly, but eventually I'll be back to the man she loves."

"*Right now* you're the man I love," Regina said.

McGoo snickered. He has a habit of knowing when to be inappropriate. "At least you won't have trouble getting a boner."

I flashed him a rude glance. "Comments like that are what got you transferred to the Quarter in the first place, and look how well that turned out."

Zonda Nefarious reached into the pocket of her white physician's smock. "Speaking of that, my Igors have developed a new formulation to help your ... little problem. It's a new prescription-only type of boner pill."

McGoo blinked, looking vindicated. "Really? I was just joking. Are skeletons too embarrassed to ask for them?"

"There's nothing humorous about the situation, Officer McGoohan." The witch doctor was stern. "Many skeletons need to regrow their flesh, and these boner pills assist in muscle and tendon regeneration, then a complete circulatory system, and eventually skin."

"That's not what I thought you meant," McGoo said.

She turned to Ronald, who sat on the paper-covered treatment table. "Vampire flesh has the ability to regenerate, but these pills will speed up the process." She tried to wrestle open the pill bottle, grunted, and finally succeeded in overcoming the child safety cap. She poured two large white pills into her hand.

Ronald held out his own palm, which was like a Venetian blind made of bones. "How fast will it work?"

"You should begin to feel the effects as soon as you digest the medication."

Without hesitating, Ronald swung open his jawbone and tossed the pills inside. They rattled around his dry teeth before he swallowed. The pills tumbled along his neck vertebrae, then fell through the empty chest cavity all the way down to his waist, where they bounced off the pelvic bone and rattled onto the hospital floor. "Oops."

"Hmm, I seem to have forgotten one detail." Zonda retrieved the pills and dropped them back into the bottle. "The treatment is premature in your case. You'll have to wait until your digestive system grows back so you can actually swallow the pill."

Regina hovered close. "I'll take care of you in the meantime. Don't you worry."

I wanted to give them privacy. Seeing that mushy stuff made me think about Sheyenne, and she was just down the hall. Returning to Alvina's room, we discovered another bona fide miracle; Her discharge paperwork had been processed, and she was ready to be released!

I waved the fuzzy stuffed bat and McGoo had his teddy bear. Both of us held our balloons. "It's time for a celebration."

"Stuffed animals!" Alvina said. "My favorites."

McGoo and I grinned at each other, pleased with our prowess. The kid snatched both stuffed critters and cuddled them against her chest, then cuddled each of us against her.

Robin reviewed the discharge paperwork and marked a few changes, just because lawyers always need to make changes, while Sheyenne helped Alvina pack her few things in the pink backpack.

"Are you ready to get out of here, kid?" McGoo asked.

"Want to head back to the offices?" I suggested.

McGoo and I still hadn't worked out whose turn it was. The little vampire nodded. "I'm ready to go *home*."

CHAPTER THIRTY-SIX

Now fully recovered, settled in, and eager to be part of the business, Alvina quickly set up her laptop on the conference room table. Sheyenne and Robin were delighted the girl could help them finish sorting the archive files at last. They were looking forward to the letter F, and I had fond memories of some of our cases that started with the letter F.

"I want to read them all," the kid said. "And I'm going to get the novels, too."

"The novels aren't very realistic," I said, embarrassed. "In fact, they're a little silly." I didn't want to admit to myself that I was pleased she took such an interest.

"I'm going to learn how to be a detective, too," she said, then glanced at Robin. "And a lawyer. And a policeman." She grinned at Sheyenne, showing her fangs. "And can you teach me how to sing, Sheyenne?"

"Whatever you want, honey."

"Then I can help you solve cases." She was completely serious. I found her just too adorable.

Alvina was still shocked at how long she'd been in a coma. As soon as we got back to the offices from the hospital, I had tried to soothe her. "Don't worry. We took care of you, and we took care of the bad guys."

"That's not what I'm upset about. All that time offline! This sucks. I can't imagine how far behind I am in my social media. And I missed a blog." She groaned. "I haven't missed posting a new 'I Was a Teenage Vampire' since I started."

"You have a good excuse," Robin said.

"My followers don't want excuses. If there isn't constant new content, they simply leave. How can I compete with all the cute puppy videos?"

But she had gotten right to work, posting furiously. She impressed me more each day as I watched her dedication.

Now I placed a hand on her small shoulder, growing serious. "You underestimate yourself, Alvina. Your blog has a lot of followers because you have a lot of things to say, and now you have something even more important to talk about. You've developed your Alvin persona, but you can still talk about what happened to you and the contaminated blood. All sorts of teenage vampires go through chemical imbalances."

"You're right," Alvina said. "I can also use it to warn about the dangers of drinking too many expensive high-sugar drinks. I'll be a role model. I'll confess everything in a fictionalized way. I'll make a real impact."

Sheyenne drifted in, carrying another bankers' box which she set next to the others on the table, segregating the sorted files from the messy ones.

"The letters E and F can wait a few more hours, Sheyenne," I said. "This little girl has important work to do."

Alvina nodded and hunched closer to the screen of her laptop. "Sometimes monsters just need a kid's perspective."

O   O   O

Even with a hole in the middle of my forehead, which I've decided to display proudly rather than fill with the nuisance of flesh-colored putty, I am an optimist.

As the chaotic repercussions of the Monster Chow scandal rippled through the entire Unnatural Quarter, I started to see silver linings. When I pulled open the door to the Ghoul's Diner and heard the familiar jingle of the bell, I sensed the difference inside.

What had been a ghost town a few nights ago, without even ghosts for customers, was now a thriving operation. Every stool at the counter was occupied and the booths were crowded. The buzz of conversation rose and fell as gremlins chattered and laughed, wizards used arcane spells to make their food more palatable, werewolves complained about finding hair in their salads, mummies banged their cups on ceramic saucers demanding coffee refills, while Esther scuttled around, yelling at customers with her harpy charm. Hissing and sizzling sounds came from the grill, and a clatter of dishes moved directly from the bus tray to the stew pot. Albert ladled protoplasmic sauces and lumpy entrees onto plates.

"Business is booming," I said to Esther.

"Stop complaining," she said. "Go somewhere else if you can't find a place to sit."

"I'm just leaving," said a lawn gnome who tottered on one of the high stools at the counter. I was afraid he might fall off and break, so I helped him gently to the floor. When I eased into the seat, I saw that he had left money for his meal but neglected to tip the waitress. Esther was so busy he managed to get out the door before she came back to pick up the check. When she swooped by, she glared at the money on the counter, then rounded on me. "You stole my tip! He would have left me five dollars."

I thought of possible responses to the accusation, the rewards versus the risks, and decided that five dollars out of my own wallet was a worthwhile investment. I fished it out. "Just holding it for you, Esther. There are some shady looking people in here."

"There are always shady looking people in here. That's our clientele."

Indeed, I was happy to see a number of shady-looking unnaturals happily eating their food. Albert was busy cooking up orders, setting plates on the countertop so Esther could serve them, though he paid little attention to what was actually written on the order slips and Esther paid just as little attention to who received which plate.

Seeing me, Albert wiped his hands on a dirty dishtowel, then smeared it across his face to remove perspiration and mucus, which he then wrung out into the large cauldron that contained that day's soup.

"Good business today, Mr. Shamble," he said as he shuffled up behind the counter. He grabbed one of the random plates under the heat lamps and placed it in front of me. "Here's your order." I hadn't even placed an order yet, but it didn't really matter to me or to any of the other customers. Besides, this saved me the pleasure of actual conversation with my waitress.

Albert seemed much more personable now. "Since the Monster Chow factory shut down, people understand the value of a good home-cooked meal and good service."

Behind me, the harpy shrieked at a dissatisfied customer until the poor man finally admitted that his meal was probably just fine after all.

"I hear they'll be reopening the Monster Chow factory soon," I said. "Under new management and with new recipes, all chemical free, unnaturally sourced with both basic and gourmet alternatives."

"Yeah, good recipes," Albert said. "It'll be more tasty than ever. No need for that special additive."

I thought he might be disheartened, afraid that this business boom would dwindle as soon as cheap and convenient Monster Chow became available again. Even with what Obadeus and Ma Hemoglobin had done, I knew that unnaturals needed to have nutritious and readily available meals so they didn't fall off the wagon and eat people. But I didn't want to put the Ghoul's Diner out of business, either.

When Albert grinned, I was amazed at how many twisted, brown, and rotten teeth could fit into one set of gums. "They've hired me as a consultant. I'm giving them some of my best recipes." He chuckled. "My face will be on some of the packages … and I get a royalty."

I felt relieved. "Then you'll be just fine, Albert." I heard Esther shriek again, this time because the large group of gremlins had finished their meal and requested separate checks. "And you can't beat the service."

He snorted a mucousy laugh, then shuffled back into the kitchen where he got back to cooking, or whatever he called it.

The door opened once more, and Fletcher's ghost entered as Harry Talbot held the door for him. Both were smiling, even though Talbot seemed reticent. "You sure about this place, Fletcher?"

"We can't go to our own blood bars every single meal," the ghost said. "Try their coffee. I hear it's good." Albert's coffee was actually vile, but I'd let Harry Talbot decide that for himself.

Fletcher waved when he saw me. "Mr. Chambeaux, you're looking good."

"I'm a zombie, but I take care of myself." I glanced from him to Talbot. "And you two have resolved your issues?"

The men beamed at each other; they had clearly settled their argument. "I won't be needing Ms. Deyer anymore. I am now reinstated as a Board member for the Talbot & Knowles blood bars."

Talbot broke in, "And we're going to keep the name exactly as it is, Talbot & Knowles. Just because my partner is dead doesn't mean he gets removed from the sign."

"All the legal paperwork is being redone," Fletcher said. "We share everything, just like best friends should." The ghost clapped his friend on the back, but his arm passed harmlessly through. "Sorry, Harry. Still getting used to that."

Two reptiles beside me had slid off their stools and slithered away after paying their bills. Harry Talbot and Fletcher's ghost took the vacant seats. When Esther came by and glared at them, Talbot ordered a cup of coffee, but the harpy waitress accused him into ordering a full meal, which I warned Talbot not to eat. "I hear the peanut butter and jelly sandwich is good," I suggested, and Esther flounced off in outrage.

"We're very wealthy men, both of us," Talbot said to me. "I could certainly pay for the peanut butter and jelly sandwich."

Fletcher said, "In fact, let's pick up Mr. Chambeaux's tab."

"Fine with me," I said. "Just don't forget to tip."

Harry Talbot received his cup of bitter, angry coffee, slurped it, winced, then rolled the flavor over on his tongue. "I've had worse," he said. I didn't want to ask for details.

"So what are you going to do with all this newfound wealth?" I asked, and I could tell they had been scheming.

"I'm going to buy back the Basilisk Nightclub," Fletcher said.

"We'll make them an offer they can't refuse," Talbot added. "And we'll set up a blood bar right inside the nightclub. It opens new opportunities for us. Satellite stores, souvenir shops. We'll be able to put blood bars in grocery stores, gas stations, doctors' offices, funeral parlors."

"Good luck with that," I said, finishing my meal. I settled my fedora back on my head and headed out into the streets.

The Unnatural Quarter was changing, that was certain. But the more it changed, the more it stayed the same. I don't think I'd have it any other way.

Acknowledgments

The fans of Dan Shamble are many and outspoken. Whenever I read a new Shamble story at a convention, I have a great crowd, and for years the readers have demanded to know when they could read the next case.

Tastes Like Chicken came about with the generous assistance of Rebecca Moesta and Diane Jones, the production juggling of Michelle Corsillo, the proofing team, Jonathan Miller, Aysha Rehm, Shane Garside, Pat Smythe, Holly Smith, Mia Kleeve and Jim Lehane, the great cover art from Jeff Herndon, and the layout and design from Quincy J. Allen.

Road Kill

As a special treat, enjoy Dan Shamble's first encounter with the Hemoglobin gang, which was originally collected with other Dan Shamble stories in *Working Stiff*!

Road Kill

A Dan Shamble, Zombie P.I. Adventure

1

It's never a good thing to wake up in a coffin, unless you're a vampire—and I'm definitely not a vampire. I'm an entirely different sort of undead.

Now, vampires *belong* in coffins; they actually find them comfortable. Vamps go there regularly to get their sleep. I've even known several who kept everyday coffins and vacation coffins (fitted with tropical interior décor). Some are just stripped-down pine boxes, while others are luxury models rigged with stereo systems for music or audiobooks. Some coffins even have tingly massage fingers on the bottom.

The coffin I woke up in wasn't one of those types, and I sure as hell didn't belong here.

I'm a zombie, and zombies aren't so picky about where they rest. Sure, coffins will do just fine, but once we've clawed our way out of the grave, we don't need to sleep often, and when we do, we're okay with sleeping on a sofa, or even just propped up in a corner somewhere. It doesn't really matter.

But I knew I hadn't taken a nap here on purpose.

I'm not just any zombie: I'm a zombie *detective*, and it's my job to figure out mysteries. I'm good at my job—though I try to avoid being part of the mystery itself.

The coffin was dark and cramped, with very little elbow room. I squirmed, thumped the sides of the box with my arms, managed to roll myself over onto my stomach—which did me no good at all—then had to exert twice as much effort to roll myself onto my back again.

I pounded the wooden lid with my fists. Yes, it's a cliché: I had become one of those things that go bump in the night.

I felt the entire coffin vibrating beneath me, accompanied by a low pleasant thrumming. No wonder I had dozed off for so long! But this wasn't a timed "Magic Massage Fingers" sensation. I realized the sound was road noise, the vibration of wheels.

I was in the back of a vehicle somewhere.

Worse, I was in a coffin in the back of a vehicle going somewhere.

I hammered on the lid of the coffin, felt around the edge. No safety latch there. That was a code violation, and I was starting to feel testy.

Coffins are supposed to have quick-release latches, otherwise it's a safety hazard. Ever since the Big Uneasy, laws had changed to protect the unnaturals. My partner Robin had hung out her attorney-for-hire shingle on behalf of the vampires, zombies, werewolves, ghosts, and other assorted "beings" that needed legal representation in the changing world. One of her early legal victories was to institute safety systems in coffins and crypts so that, in the event that a dead body came back to life, he or she could re-emerge without discomfort or inconvenience.

I got my hands in front of my chest, flattened my palms, and pushed up against the coffin lid. The planks creaked but remained fastened. Nailed shut. This was getting more annoying by the minute.

I tried to remember where I'd been and how I'd gotten there, but it was all a big blank. I'm better-preserved than most zombies, many of whom eat brains because they have a deficiency in that department (kind of like a vitamin deficiency). Me, I've always loved a good cheeseburger, but these days I rarely bother to eat except out of habit, or sociability. I don't have much appetite, and my taste buds aren't what they used to be.

My mind, though, is sharp as a tack … usually. Otherwise, I wouldn't be much of a detective. At present, I felt as blank and stupid as one of those shamblers who can only remember long strings of vowels without any consonants.

Moving in the cramped box now, I patted myself down and realized that I still wore my usual sport jacket with the lumpy threads where the bullet holes had been crudely stitched up. I managed to get my fingers up to my face, felt the cold skin, ran them up around my forehead and skull, felt a crater there—a bullet hole, entry wound in the back of my head, exit wound in my forehead.

Yes, everything seemed normal.

For many years, I'd been a detective in the Unnatural Quarter, a human detective at first, working on cases where unnaturals ran afoul of the law, or stumbled into curses, or just lost things from their original lives. I made a decent living at it, especially after I partnered with Robin, and the cases we dealt with were more interesting than typical adultery spying for divorce cases.

On the downside, I had ended up getting shot in the back of the head while investigating the poisoning death of my girlfriend. That would have been the end of any regular Sam Spade or Philip Marlowe, but the cases don't solve themselves, so when I came back from the dead … I went right back to work.

I pressed hard against the lid of the coffin again, heard the boards creak, listened to the nails groan a little bit. That was some progress, at least. I kept pushing.

Even though zombies have the advantage of being able to sleep wherever they like, vampires are generally more limber. I was accustomed to stiff muscles and sore joints, however, so I kept pushing. I put my back into it. (What, was I going to get a bruise?) With steady pressure, I managed to coax the nails farther out. The boards splintered, and the lid finally came loose.

I nudged the top of the coffin aside by a few inches and let in some cool air. But I was still trapped.

A thick silver chain and a padlock had been wrapped around the coffin. Great. Silver chains and a nailed-down coffin—exactly what would be required to contain a vampire. Okay, B+ for effort, but somebody really needed to go back to the field guides and do a better job at identifying their unnaturals.

How could anyone have confused me for a vampire?

Then one or two of the pieces fell into place with a big thud. I wasn't supposed to be here—this should have been someone else! I'd been duped, or switched.

Finally, I remembered about the witness protection program.

At Chambeaux & Deyer investigations, we take all sorts of cases—from a monster in trouble who lumbers through our doors, to humans having trouble with monsters, to monsters having trouble with one another. There's never a dull moment.

Occasionally, we get cases punted to us from the police, usually because Officer Toby McGoohan, my best human friend, brings them to us. McGoo appreciated the extra help on his backlog, and we appreciated the business.

McGoo and I were old friends well before I got shot—a down-on-his-luck private detective and a politically incorrect, often rude, beat cop with no prospects for promotion, even in the Unnatural Quarter. Some friendships survive even death. If I could put up with McGoo's lousy jokes, he could put up with my cadaverous infirmities.

He showed up in our offices wearing his full patrolman uniform and blue cap, leading a man in a ridiculous disguise: a trench coat, a wide-brimmed hat, and a curly wig that Harpo Marx would have found too extreme.

"Hey, Shamble," McGoo said. I had long since stopped objecting to his nickname for me, a deliberate mispronunciation of my last name.

When he didn't introduce his companion, I nodded to the stranger. "Correct me if I'm wrong, McGoo, but a disguise isn't supposed to *draw* attention."

The man in the goofy wig muttered, "I didn't want anyone to recognize me." He looked around, then muttered to McGoo, "Are we safe here?"

"Safe enough. These people are going to help get you into the witness protection program."

The man took off the hat, silly wig, and trench coat, to reveal he was a slight-framed blond man, as scrawny and skittish as if he had stepped right off the "before" side of a muscle supplement ad. He was a vampire.

"Let me introduce Sebastian Bund," McGoo said, "former blood barista at one of the Talbot & Knowles blood bars. He's also a key witness in an important case involving the illicit blood market."

Scrawny Sebastian slicked back his blond hair, which had been mussed by the wig. "Thank you for your help … as soon as you help."

Our receptionist at Chambeaux & Deyer is my girlfriend—and former client—Sheyenne. She's a ghost now, and I had been investigating her murder when I got killed, but we're still a couple. Many spirits linger because they have unfinished business, but even after I solved Sheyenne's murder, she remained, and she works for us now. Apparently her "unfinished business" now involved typing and filing in our offices. Chambeaux & Deyer couldn't have functioned without her.

"Could I get you some coffee or tea, or blood, Mr. Bund?" she asked, as she dropped the intake paperwork on her desk.

"Do you have any B positive?" Bund asked.

"I think we just keep O in stock for the clients."

Bund shook his head. "Never mind. I can't stand the generic stuff. I'm fine."

McGoo pushed the papers aside. "There can't be any record of this. Everything off-book."

Sheyenne frowned. "Then how do we send our bill?"

"I'll take care of it, don't worry. I'll find a way to get it out of petty cash."

"If it's only petty cash," she countered, "then maybe the case isn't worth our time."

"We have a big petty cash fund."

Robin came out to meet the new client as well, looking friendly now, but when she sinks her teeth into a case, she's as hard to shake as a zombie with lockjaw. We went into the conference room together, so McGoo could explain the case to us.

Sebastian Bund had been caught up in under-the-counter blood sales, watering down the product, selling the extra out a back alley and using a seemingly legitimate blood bank to move his supplies. He would swap out rare and expensive types for more generic flavors. No one had noticed ... until one of the mislabeled packets was actually used in surgery rather than for unnatural consumption, and the patient nearly died.

The plot unraveled, arrests were made, and the operation was pinned on an ambitious gangster family led by Ma Hemoglobin. (Her real last name was Hamanubin, but nobody referred to her by that.) She had six sons, two of whom were vampires. Ma Hemoglobin and her boys ran blood-smuggling operations throughout the Quarter.

The District Attorney had vowed to bring them down. The owners of the Talbot & Knowles blood-bar chain (former clients of mine, I'm pleased to say) were eager to press charges.

"Unfortunately, each witness who would have testified against Ma Hemoglobin suffered an unfortunate demise," McGoo said.

"Is there such thing as a fortunate demise?" I asked. McGoo ignored the interruption; I think he was annoyed that he hadn't thought of the joke himself.

Several vampire witnesses had "accidentally" been locked in sunlit cells, and their ashes weren't in any shape to testify. Some of the human witnesses were assigned to vampires-only holding cells, and after the prisoner meals were "accidentally delayed" by several hours, the human witnesses were too drained to be of any use and "accidentally" contaminated with holy water during the resuscitation efforts so they couldn't even be turned into vamps themselves (thus, doubly prevented from taking the stand against Ma Hemoglobin). Another particularly important witness had vanished from a locked bathroom, and the only evidence was a brownish-green slime all around the toilet. There were rumors of sewer-dweller hit men who came up through the porcelain access to strike their target.

"Sebastian is the only witness left," McGoo said. "And obviously our traditional police protection methods haven't worked."

"Sounds like you need a zombie detective," I said.

"We need someone competent. Sebastian has to go into witness protection until the case comes up for trial."

Robin just nibbled on her pencil, deep in thought. "So you need our help to make sure he's moved without being seen."

McGoo nodded. "We've already got an operation under contract. He'll be taken cross-country in a coffin in the back of an eighteen-wheeler. We'll disguise the truck, make it look like it's hauling pre-packaged school lunches."

I cringed, and Robin shuddered, both of us remembering our own experiences with school lunches. "No one's going to mess with that cargo."

So, McGoo already had the general plan and his connections to the police force. We just had to work out the details.

Obviously, as the ominous voice always says in movie trailers, *something went wrong*. I wasn't the one who was supposed to be riding in the coffin. Somebody had set me up.

Once I pushed the loosened coffin lid to one side, I began to work on the silver chains and padlock. Fortunately, silver has no effect on me—that's an advantage to being a zombie, and I try to look at the glass as half full.

As a detective, I'm quite proficient, or at least marginally adequate, with lockpick tools that I keep in a handy travel pack in my pants pocket. My fingers were clumsy, but no more than usual. I worked with the tools until I sprung the padlock, removed the hasp, and shoved the chains to the floor.

Just as I sat up, the semi truck hit a bump in the road, which made the coffin thump against the trailer bed. My teeth clacked together, and then the hum of the road became smooth again. I knocked the lid to the floor and lurched up out of the coffin.

This was actually easier than when I had clawed my way up through the packed graveyard soil back when I first rose from the dead—not to mention a lot less dirty, too.

The truck rumbled along, and I stepped out of the coffin, flexing my stiff knees, stretching, brushing the wrinkles in my sport jacket. I looked around the coffin, but saw no sign of my fedora. I hoped it wasn't lost.

Even though my leaky brain had recaptured the basic story of Sebastian Bund going into witness protection, there were still many gaps. Once again, I felt around my head, but discovered no lumps. It's difficult to knock a zombie unconscious by bonking him on the head, anyway. There must have been something else, maybe a sleeping potion. I felt groggy, rubbed my eyes, still trying to get awake.

"Coffin" and "coffee" both derive from the root word "caffeine," I think—and I could have used a strong cup right now to help wake the dead. I needed to be alert, to judge whether I might be in danger.

Inside the trailer, other crates were stacked high all around where the coffin had been stashed. The crates were all filled with prepackaged school lunches; from the "Use By" dates stamped on the sides, they would not expire for more than a century.

I worked my way toward the front of the trailer, hoping I could find some way to signal the cab. The driver up there needed to know he had the wrong cargo. If someone had knocked me out and switched me with Sebastian Bund, then the star witness might be in danger.

The engine noise was loud, but I leaned against the wall and started pounding as hard as I could. (For a trucker hauling coffins filled with the undead, that would probably be unnerving.) If he had the window open, maybe he'd be able to hear me back here. I pounded harder and then, to reassure him, hammered out "Shave and a Haircut."

Faintly, from the cab, I heard him pound back on the door, "Two Bits."

I pounded harder, more desperately. He pounded back, and I heard his muffled voice. "Quiet back there!"

So much for raising the alarm. I guess I would have to wait until he stopped for a potty break—I hoped he had a small bladder.

I sat back down on the edge of the coffin, slipped my hands into the jacket pockets—and felt immediately stupid when I found my phone. That would have been a good thing to remember from the start. I didn't like all these lapses in my memory. Could a zombie get a concussion?

Since I had no idea where the truck was, possibly out in the middle of nowhere, I hoped that I'd get a signal. I was pleased to see at least one-and-a-half bars; that should be good enough.

I kept McGoo's number on speed-dial, and he picked up on the second ring. He must have seen the Caller ID. "Shamble! What are you doing awake already?"

"Trying to figure out where the hell I am." He didn't sound surprised to hear from me. "You sound like you know more about this than I do."

McGoo snorted. "I know more about most things than you do."

"I'd argue with that, but today I'll give you a free pass if you can tell me why I woke up in a nailed-shut coffin surrounded by silver chains in the back of a semi truck."

"Silver chains? There weren't supposed to be any silver chains."

I stared at the phone, then put it back to my ear.

"*That's* the part you find unusual? Why am I here in the first place?"

"It was your idea, Shamble, but if you don't remember your own brilliant solution, I'll take credit for it. The narcomancer said you might suffer some temporary memory loss as a side effect. It was a powerful spell."

"Narcomancer?" The word meant nothing to me, and I couldn't call any image to mind. "Don't you mean 'necromancer'?"

"*Narco*—narcomancer," McGoo said. "I suppose you've forgotten you owe me a hundred bucks, too?"

"I don't owe you a hundred bucks. But narcomancer … like in narcotics?"

"No, like narcolepsy. His name was Rufus. He's a wizard who worked a spell to put you to sleep—and putting a zombie to sleep is no easy task."

"Rufus?" The name still didn't ring a bell.

And suddenly, it did.

I recalled the man whose matted mouse-brown hair seemed to have a moral disagreement with combs. His wispy beard looked as if someone had been experimenting with spirit gum and theatrical makeup but had given up halfway through the job. His watery blue eyes were extremely bloodshot, and he seemed jittery. Although he specialized in putting people to sleep, he seemed to be an insomniac himself.

I remember him rubbing his hands together, repeating his name and grinning. "Yes, Rufus ... are you ready for my special *roofie*? You'll snooze away the journey."

He began to speak an incantation—then everything went blank.

"It's all going down as planned," McGoo said on the phone. "We made all the arrangements for Sebastian to be whisked away in the truck to his new home, but we put you in the coffin instead, under a sleep spell—it was *supposed* to last for the entire drive— while Sebastian went by a roundabout route. A brilliant idea, actually. I suggested it."

"No, you didn't," I said. "That was my idea."

"I thought you didn't remember."

"But why would we *do* that?"

McGoo said, "Just to be safe. You were triggered to wake up if anyone tampered with the coffin. You were worried something bad might go down."

At that moment, an explosion hit the truck, blowing out the side of the trailer, scattering packaged school lunches everywhere, and hurling me out into the pitch-black night.

2

The squeal of the truck's air brakes would have made a banshee envious. The semi jack-knifed, its wheels smearing rubber along the highway like black finger paint. The truck groaned to a halt with a cough and gasp, and debris rained down everywhere.

After being thrown from the truck, I landed in a ditch—a mud-filled ditch, of course. I got to my feet, dripping; stagnant slime oozed out of my hair. It seems the harder I work to keep myself well-preserved, the faster karma comes back and smacks me.

The door to the truck cab popped open, and a stocky man with a black jawline beard swung out. His eyes burned like coals, and even from a distance I could tell he was hopping mad. He wore a trucker's cap, a red checked flannel shirt open to show his white undershirt, and jeans. He didn't seem injured, just furious as he stepped away from the wheezing and gurgling diesel engine that fought to keep running.

He stared at the ruined trailer, where a blackened crater and splintered wood surrounded the remnants of a slogan: "The Finest in Processed Lunches—Tolerated by Children for over Twenty Years!" On the image, a group of gaunt boys and girls looked dubiously toward the picture of their meal, which had been obliterated by the blast.

"They blew up my rig!" The trucker stalked back and forth, twisted his cap around backward, then, dissatisfied, twisted it back around front. "Out here on an empty stretch of highway? *They blew up my rig!*" He kicked gravel with his steel-toed boots, then looked up and saw me shambling toward him. "Did you see that?" Then he glowered, giving me a second look. "Where did you come from?"

"I was inside your truck," I said. "I'm Dan Chambeaux, private investigator."

The trucker blinked, still suspicious. "And I'm Earl—Earl Joe Bob, owner and operator of Earl Joe Bob Trucking." He scratched his beard. "Say, what were you doing in that coffin? You weren't supposed to be in there."

"Ever hear those stories about babies being switched in the nursery?"

"Yeah," he said.

"I guess it happens with coffins, too."

Earl Joe Bob put his hands on his hips and swung his head from side to side, looking in dismay at his mortally wounded rig. Under the bright running lights, which could have given a Christmas tree on the Las Vegas Strip a run for its money, I saw "Earl Joe Bob Trucking" and a phone number, as well as government license number on the driver's door. He sighed. "At least the cab and engine are still intact. But damn—I'm liable for all this! And, hey, you weren't supposed to be in that coffin!" He shook his head again, stuck his thumbs into the waistband of his jeans. "What a mess."

At least the trailer hadn't caught fire, though some of the shards of wood still smoldered. "I think we were hit with a rocket launcher."

"It happens," said Earl Joe Bob. He went back to the cab, got some flares and reflective hazard triangles.

I realized that out here on this open and silent stretch of highway, under the stars and with no city lights in sight, we were much too vulnerable. This truck hadn't run into a random migratory rocket. I patted my pockets, looked around—I had lost my phone during the explosion.

"We have to call for help. Can we use your CB? Or a cell phone?"

Earl Joe Bob shook his head. "No, wouldn't be wise to use it."

I was exasperated. "Why not?"

The trucker narrowed his eyes at me. "Just can't."

I couldn't argue with that logic. I walked around the other side of the truck again, working my way back to the ditch, where I hunted around for my phone. The weeds were tall, and I splashed through the standing water. Mosquitoes fled from me—another advantage of being a zombie. I would have to write all the advantages down one day, just as a reminder.

Fortunately, the phone's screen light was still on, though my call with McGoo had been disconnected in the explosion. I smeared it against my muddy shirt, making a marginally clean patch, and was dismayed to see that my *Angry Vultures* scores had been wiped out. That was a problem I would have to deal with later.

I phoned McGoo, who answered right away. "Where are you, Shamble? What happened?"

"I'm on a road somewhere," I said, glancing around. "And I don't see one of those You Are Here X's." I told McGoo about the explosion, and that we were stranded. He promised to call in reinforcements right away.

"I'll see if we can track your signal through the cell towers," he said. "Maybe the truck has a GPS in the cab."

I ended the call and began making my way along the back of the rig, when I froze, hearing voices. I saw two figures approach the wounded truck. It was a starlit night, clear skies, a quarter moon.

Zombie night vision is generally good, but I didn't need any supernatural powers to pick out the two young men. They wore camouflage jumpsuits—but light-colored desert camo, so they stood out plainly. They carried long rifles.

Since the side of the truck had been blasted open with a rocket launcher, and since these two men were approaching heavily armed, I decided it wouldn't be a good idea to wave my arms and hail them for help.

Earl Joe Bob spotted them as well, and bunched his meaty arms as he stalked toward them. "This wasn't the deal I had with Ma Hemoglobin! Which two of her boys are you—Moron and Imbecile?"

"No," said one of the young men. "I'm Huey, and that's Louis."

"Well, you're still Moron and Imbecile to me. You wrecked my rig! We were supposed to meet up at the Rest in Peace area down the road and make the transfer!" He spluttered, waving his hand at the crater in the side of his truck. "What kind of stupid—"

The two boys raised their rifles. Huey said, "Ma thought you might double-cross us, so we took matters into our own hands."

"You must be two of her human boys," Earl Joe Bob said. "A vampire wouldn't be that stupid."

"We'll show you stupid!" said Louis. He opened fire with his high-powered rifle. Not to be left behind, Huey shot Earl Joe Bob as well. The bullets slammed into the trucker's red flannel shirt, and he dropped to the ground.

I silently reaffirmed my wisdom in not waving my arms and calling attention to myself.

Now, as a detective, I solve cases, and I'm the hero in my own story. But sometimes heroes stick around longer if they aren't always … heroic.

I didn't know how I was going to get out of here, or how long it would take McGoo to bring in reinforcements. If this truck was on a cross-country trip to deliver a decoy into witness protection, McGoo could be miles away, even if he had been shadowing me.

With a jolt, I got a few more of my memories back: I did remember the idea of taking Sebastian's place in the coffin aboard the truck. Meanwhile, Robin would take our nondescript and rusty old Ford Maverick, lovingly named the Pro Bono Mobile, with the scrawny blond vampire dressed in my fedora and a similar sport jacket, sunshades down, traveling across the state line to where he would be hidden in his new life. My ghost girlfriend Sheyenne was going to ride shotgun. Nobody would be looking for them. They would be safe. It would be a lark. I was the one under a narcolepsy spell in the back of a semi truck, a decoy. It should have been a long sleep for me.

Now, Ma Hemoglobin's two boys climbed through the blasted crater in the side of the trailer. My best bet was probably to climb back into the ditch and hide in the mud, but McGoo would never let me forget it.

Instead, I crept along the opposite side of the trailer. If I could make it to the cab, open the passenger side door, and climb into the cab, I was sure to find some kind of firearm, baseball bat, or tire iron that Earl Joe Bob kept there.

I heard Huey and Louis rummaging around inside the trailer, shining flashlights; I saw the gleam through splintered cracks in the opposite wall. They tossed aside a clutter of prepackaged school lunches. "The coffin's empty! He's not here!"

The other voice said, "I hate it when coffins turn up empty! But was it empty in the first place, or were we tricked?"

I made it to the front of the rig, yanked open the cab door—and of course the hinges screeched and groaned loudly enough to make any haunted house proud. The two Hemoglobin boys clambered out of the blasted trailer, brandishing their rifles, looking around.

"There he is!" yelled Louis.

"I see him," said Huey. They began sprinting toward me, running past the body of Earl Joe Bob, who lay sprawled at the side of the truck.

Earl groaned and sat up, shaking his head. "Dammit! You wrecked my rig *and* you shot me?" He sprang to his feet and flashed a set of ivory fangs.

I should have recognized earlier that he was a vampire. Many truckers who specialize in all-night hauls are vampires; they have no trouble staying awake, though they had to park in Rest in Peace areas and pull down the shades by dawn.

248

The two Hemoglobin boys turned white and spun around, raising their rifles again. Each managed to fire one more shot. This time, Earl Joe Bob merely flinched before lunging forward again.

"I thought you loaded the rifles with silver bullets!" Huey shouted.

"I thought *you* loaded the rifles with silver bullets!"

Earl Joe Bob was pissed.

Moving with vampire speed (earlier, I did mention that vamps can be quite swift and agile), he lunged forward and grabbed the young men by their necks, one in each hand. His grip was powerful, and he squeezed hard. I heard the loud double crack as their necks snapped; it sounded like popcorn in a microwave bag. He tossed the two dead bodies on the ground—truly dead, because Huey and Louis had been two of Ma Hemoglobin's four human sons. (These days one or the other could still come back as an unnatural, but it wouldn't be anytime soon.)

Earl Joe Bob made a disgusted sound, brushed at his flannel shirt, looked down at the bullet holes healing in his chest. "I'm as much a mess as my rig is." He saw me hanging onto the door and flashed his fangs. "And where do you think you're going?"

The vampire trucker moved toward me. I held up my cell phone as if inviting him to play a game of *Curses with Friends*. "I already called in for help. The police are coming."

Earl Joe Bob scowled. "That doesn't give me much time, then. It wasn't supposed to go down this way." He straightened his cap, which sat askew from when he'd been gunned down. He sneered at the two Hemoglobin boys, who lay in their light camouflage on the ground, necks bent at improbable angles. "I hate dealing with amateurs. I've dealt with witness protection cases plenty of times, and I'm always available for additional 'enhanced disappearing' for a substantial fee. When I make people disappear, I really make them disappear."

I tried to move along the side of the truck; in a race, I could never outrun the vampire. "Isn't that a conflict of interest?"

"I don't lose any sleep over it," Earl Joe Bob said. "Pay is good, and I gotta earn a living."

I knew that he was going to have to get rid of me. I was the only one who could explain the mess around me, but Earl Joe Bob would make up some story of his own.

"We can be reasonable about this," I offered.

"Good idea." He lunged. I lurched—it was a much less fluid movement than his, but I did manage to evade the first pass. Earl Joe Bob slammed into the side of the trailer, shattering more wood.

"Careful about the splinters." My mind was racing. I could get one of the jagged spears and thrust it through the vampire's heart. In my imagination, it all worked out just fine, but in practice I wasn't quite the nimble athlete that I'd need to be for the scheme to work.

I did break off the long wooden splinter, lifted it—and Earl Joe Bob slapped it out of my hands. At least he got a splinter in his palm, and he paused to pluck it out. That brief respite gave me the chance to scramble through the blasted crater in the side of the trailer.

"Now I've got you cornered," the trucker said. While I shuffled and slipped among the debris of packaged school lunches, I saw his sturdy muscular form silhouetted against the starlit sky as he pulled himself through the hole. "Where are you going to hide?"

I hurled a package of Salisbury steak, which struck him in the center of the chest. Unfortunately, it wasn't quite the stake through the heart I required. The vamp trucker's eyes were glowing in the shadows. I could see him coming toward me. I nearly tripped backward over the coffin that had held me during my cross-country trip.

Police sirens howled down the highway, coming closer. Ironic, I thought: the cavalry was going to arrive much too late.

"At least we've already got a coffin to store you in," said Earl Joe Bob.

"Been there, done that," I answered.

He came closer, fangs bared, eyes glowing, hands outstretched. Earl Joe Bob was a burly guy, powerful enough to change one of his eighteen tires simply by lifting the rig and undoing the lug nuts with his fingertips. He could probably rip me limb from limb, stomp on any pieces still twitching, and then claim I'd been mangled in the explosion. McGoo already knew better than that.

"You haven't thought this through," I said.

The trucker laughed. "I could say the same to you—a vampire versus a zombie? The vamp will win, every time." He reached toward me.

That's when I pulled up the loose silver chains that lay draped over the coffin. I threw them onto Earl Joe Bob.

"Not every time," I said.

It was like Superman and kryptonite—a real sight to see. Within seconds, the vamp trucker went from being a scary, overpowering opponent to a whimpering and helpless guy in a flannel shirt who squirmed under the chains.

"Awww crap!" Earl Joe whined. "That's not fair!"

Now the sirens were louder, and I could see the flashing lights through the hole in the side of the truck. Squad cars raced along the highway, followed by the state patrol. I was still undead and kicking, but I no longer needed them to rescue me. Still, I'd be happy to let McGoo handle the wrap-up paperwork.

As soon as the police climbed into the trailer, I waved McGoo over. He looked flushed and worried. "Shamble, you all right?"

There were shouts outside as other officers found the two bodies of Ma Hemoglobin's boys.

"Better than they are. And better than he is." I nodded to where Earl Joe Bob squirmed on the floor under the silver chains.

His cap had fallen off in the struggle, and I reached down and plucked it up. It wasn't my style—I much preferred the fedora, but that was gone for now, apparently on the head of a disguised Sebastian Bund. Since I felt naked without a hat, I settled the trucker cap in place.

I started rattling off the full story as an officer handcuffed Earl Joe Bob with silver-plated handcuffs. The vamp trucker spluttered and groaned at the way I described a few things, but he didn't deny any of the details.

"I'll cut a deal," he said. "Ma Hemoglobin is scary, and she's got four boys left. I'll turn State's witness. Put me into witness protection, otherwise I'll never survive until the trial." His eyes flashed, and he struggled against the silver handcuffs. "I know where all the bodies are buried—some of them more than once."

3

Back in the offices, Robin and Sheyenne were both in very good moods, having delivered Sebastian Bund to his official new undisclosed location.

"He was delightful company." Robin flashed a smile at me. "Did you know he used to be a singing barista?"

"Broadway show tunes," Sheyenne said. "That's all we talked about. He's a fan of musicals. Why don't you ever see musicals with me?"

"Because I don't like musicals," I said.

She gave me a spectral raspberry. "When you go out on a date, you're supposed to do something you don't like. That's how you show a girl you care for her."

"I'll keep that in mind next time we go out on a date." Our cases almost always interfered with our love life—and so did the fact that, as a ghost, she couldn't physically touch me, which made the intimate aspect of our relationship much more problematic. "Did we at least get paid for the case?"

"We got paid in satisfaction," Robin said. "That's our purpose here, to know that justice is done."

"Right." I turned to Sheyenne, repeating the question. "Did we at least get paid?"

She showed me a Chambeaux & Deyer invoice, on which she had merely written in capital letters: SERVICES RENDERED, no other details. "Officer McGoohan was true to his word." She pulled out a stack of other pending cases and floated ahead to place the files on my desk. "One more step in making the world safe for naturals and unnaturals everywhere."

"It's a start." I looked down at all the folders Sheyenne had gotten out, and I knew exactly what they were. Job security.

About the Author

Kevin J. Anderson has published 140 books, 54 of which have been national or international bestsellers. He has written numerous novels in the Star Wars, X-Files, Dune, and DC Comics universes, as well as unique steampunk fantasy novels *Clockwork Angels* and *Clockwork Lives*, written with legendary rock drummer Neil Peart, based on the concept album by the band Rush. His original works include the Saga of Seven Suns series, the Terra Incognita fantasy trilogy, the Saga of Shadows trilogy, and his humorous horror series featuring Dan Shamble, Zombie P.I. He has edited numerous anthologies, written comics and games, and the lyrics to two rock CDs. Anderson and his wife Rebecca Moesta are the publishers of WordFire Press.

IF YOU LIKED ...

If you liked *Tastes Like Chicken*, you might also enjoy:

Death Warmed Over
Kevin J. Anderson

Working Stiff
Kevin J. Anderson

Monsterland
Michael Okon

Bad Blood
Luicenne Diver

THE DAN SHAMBLE, ZOMBIE P.I. SERIES
BY KEVIN J. ANDERSON

*Death Warmed Over**

*Unnatural Acts**

Hair Raising

Slimy Underbelly

*Working Stiff**

*Tastes Like Chicken**

Zomnibus
(includes *Death Warmed Over* and *Working Stiff*)*

* Available from WordFire Press

Join the Kevin J. Anderson Readers Group and get free books, sneak previews, updates on new projects, and other giveaways. Sign up for free at wordfire.com.

CPSIA information can be obtained
at www.ICGtesting.com
Printed in the USA
LVOW08*2310310118

564859LV00002B/33/P